ALL

THE

ANIMALS

ON

EARTH

ALSO BY MARK SAMPSON

FICTION
Off Book
Sad Peninsula
The Secrets Men Keep
The Slip

POETRY
Weathervane

ALL THE ANIMALS ON EARTH

A Novel

A BUCKRIDER BOOK

MARK SAMPSON

Buckrider Books is an imprint of Wolsak and Wynn Publishers.

Cover design: Michel Vrana
Interior design: Jennifer Rawlinson
Cover image: CSA-Printstock
Author photograph: Emily Lockhart
Typeset in Cambria and Hoosier Daddy
Printed by Rapido Books, Montreal, Canada

10 9 8 7 6 5 4 3 2 1

The publisher gratefully acknowledges the support of the Toronto Arts Council, the Ontario Arts Council, the Canada Council for the Arts and the Government of Canada.

Buckrider Books
280 James Street North
Hamilton, ON
Canada L8R 2L3

Library and Archives Canada Cataloguing in Publication

Title: All the animals on earth : a novel / by Mark Sampson.
Names: Sampson, Mark, 1975- author.
Identifiers: Canadiana 20200172360 | ISBN 9781989496107 (softcover)
Classification: LCC PS8637.A53853 A64 2020 | DDC C813/.6—dc23

for Rebecca

PART 1:
THE
ACCIDENT

CHAPTER 1

The accident was alarming in its brevity. The concise screech of tires. The crackling smash of metal on metal. My Corolla's twelve-foot lurch into the (thankfully) unoccupied intersection despite my foot planted firmly on the brake. It was a frigid January evening, and I'd been stopped at a red light on the corner of Sherbourne and Highway 2 when this butterscotch-coloured pickup truck hit a rind of black ice and sailed right into my bumper. The next thing I knew, my neck was twanging with whiplash and I had the wind knocked out of me after slamming sternum first into my deploying airbag.

Because I work for an insurance company, I knew, even in those first fretful moments, just how ordinary this accident was. Fender-benders happened all the time in our city, especially during winter when the streets and roads were unpredictably slick. The guy who hit me, despite having a pair of rubber testicles dangling from his hitch and a small, discreet Confederate flag decal on his back window, was incredibly apologetic and kind in the moments after our accident.

"Ah jeez, mister, I'm sorry . . . I'm so sorry . . ." he kept saying as he waited for the good folks at nine-one-one to come on the line of his cellphone. I waved off his concerns with several *Don't worry about it* sways of my hand, even as pain ricocheted round my neck and shock passed like voltage through my blood. Our collision had drawn notice from the homeless people who congregated under the single, sad overpass down here, the ones who often wandered up and down the light traffic paused at the stoplight, pleading for spare change. This part of the Lake Shore was one of the many impoverished neighbourhoods in our city, a place of drab, leaky concrete and empty, garbage-strewn lots, a strip of highway where a lone bus, the number seventy-five, passed through but once an hour. The resident vagrants approached us with curiosity and concern, but like I said, there was nothing unusual about our crash. The truck's driver seemed pleased when I told him I worked for Percussive Insurance, up on University Avenue, because that's where his own policy was (home and auto and life bundled together in our popular Assurance One package). Yes, this was going to be a straightforward transaction, a simple swapping of policy numbers. No headache at all.

I was really shaken up, though. The EMTs noticed it right away and, as a precaution, decided to give me a lift to the Sisters of St. Patrick, our city's lone Catholic hospital. I was in too much agony by then to protest. I did manage to call Morgana, my wife of thirteen years, to tell her what had happened and where I was headed. Her voice gave off a spritely pop of worry at first, but then quickly modulated into her schoolteacher calm as we discussed how to deal with our now towed-away and totalled Corolla, and how long it would take for her to come down on transit and meet me at St Pat's.

The hospital lounge was near empty – just one pimply teenager in a Burger King uniform cupping a shopping bag full of ice to his forearm, and a middle-aged woman whose "emergency" seemed entirely mental – and yet the wait felt unending. How many doctors would be staffing the ER at this hour? Two, maybe three? As I sat on my cheap vinyl seat and tried to keep my wrenched body still, as per the EMTs' instructions, my eyes gravitated toward a large poster hanging in front of me on the lounge wall. It was one of those posters you wanted to look away from the instant you glimpsed it but couldn't, thanks to its sheer audacity. It showed a young, pretty woman in her late twenties, radiantly Caucasian and infinitely smug, resting one light hand upon the shelf of her swollen stomach. With tilted head and downcast gaze, she stared at that massive bump with an under-stated smile as God's great light glowed like a sunrise cresting the horizon behind her. The message read:

HAVE

YOU

CONSIDERED

CONCEPTION?

Jesus Murphy, I thought. *Bloody Catholics.* Here we all were, in this dingy lounge with our whiplashed necks and scalded flesh and broken minds, and they were foisting *this* nonsense at us. Had the nuns no decency? I should have insisted the EMTs take me to the General instead, where my sensibilities would not be subjected to something so vulgar.

Morgana eventually arrived, still dressed for school in her smart, earth-coloured pantsuit. "Oh honey, honey, are you *okay?*" she asked as she sat down next to me. "I'm fine," I replied. "Just... you know, more rattled than anything." Her hug was gentle, but I still winced within its grasp. She laced her fingers into mine and got me to briefly recount the details of the accident. Then, to no doubt distract me from my pain, she began describing *her* day to me, in all its joys and convolutions. Morgana, being Morgana, had already started to get her grade four music class jonesed about the upcoming Spring Fling triple-threat recital. Today, she had even conscripted one of her fellow teachers to join her in a mock concert in front of the tiny class, showing how one could combine singing, acting and dancing into a performative extravaganza. I imagined the kiddies watching on with looks of amusement, bemusement or indifference as she and her co-worker minced and pranced around in front of them. There were just eight other teachers at the school where Morgana taught, but in the stories she told, she could make them sound like a cast of thousands. It was so important to my wife that this tiny coterie of colleagues also be some of her closest friends. They had garden club; they had movie night; they had drinks at Kelsey's once a month. Morgana could relay the most specific and even intimate aspects of their lives at will. I always felt bad that, even after a decade, I still struggled to keep their names straight, these people my wife worked so hard, with middling success, to be close to.

The interminable wait soon took the wind from my wife's sails, and we sat in silence for a while. The Burger King kid ordered himself a pop from the Pepsi machine in the corner, the can emerging from the wide slot on its own tiny drone and buzzing its way into his waiting hand mere seconds after he hit SEND. Meanwhile, a nurse in teal scrubs – the lone attendant for this floor, it seemed – shuffled by wordlessly. Before long, Morgana's eyes strayed up to the poster on the wall. She too gave a shudder of revulsion, and she *works* with children all day.

After what felt like an epoch, the nurse summoned me to follow her. "Your wife can come too, if you like." So Morgana accompanied me into the little office and helped me climb gingerly onto the examining table. The physician who arrived – after another lengthy wait, I might add – was positively geriatric. With his frizzy grey hair and brittle physique and gremlin face, he had to be ninety if he was a day. He went about the rote business of diagnosing me: acute whiplash and a bruised rib. He got the nurse to fetch me a neck brace and wrote a prescription for Tylenol 3. It all took less than five minutes.

"Yes, but what about the shock?" I asked.

"You're not in shock," he replied. "Shock has a very clinical definition."

"No, no, I mean . . ." I raised my hands and made the jittery gesture.

"That will pass," he told me.

Morgana helped me down off the table and we gathered up our stuff. The doc had turned to go, but then he turned back. "Oh sorry," he said, "but I'm obligated to give you *this* before you leave." From the clear plastic rack next to his blood pressure machine, he pulled out a pamphlet and handed it to me. My stomach lurched as I turned it toward my face. On its folded front cover read the words:

CONSIDER GIVING THE WORLD
THE GIFT OF LIFE

And beneath this was a picture of a fetus, coiled up like a veiny, translucent peanut on a vine, its out-of-proportion eyes all black and alien.

Oh, for mercy's sake! I thought.

Indeed, Morgana and I made a point of chucking the pamphlet into a trash bin the moment we stepped outside the ER's automated doors. That broad bucket, we noticed, was already overflowing with these brochures, a thousand unloved and rejected fetuses staring up at us. Then we grabbed an orange taxi to take us home to our spacious condo unit in the sky, an expansive gondola that overlooked this wide, hollow city.

❧

Morgana was sweet and efficient as I lay at home in a neck brace during my brief convalescence. She said not to worry about the car, or the days I was taking off work, or my share of the chores around our condo. She would look after everything while I healed. This proved to be an adjustment for us both. I'd never been seriously injured before, never been seriously *ill* before, and, I had to admit, didn't cope with feelings of helplessness all that well. This entertained more than annoyed my wife. Morgana's eyes would sparkle with amusement as she watched me struggle with simple tasks like putting on my own socks or reaching for a mixing bowl on its high shelf, grimacing as I did over the invasive strain on my still-whiplashed body. "You know, you don't have to do that yourself," she'd say with a smirk.

During my recovery, while she was at work, I spent most of the day flipping around the twenty-four-hour news channels – CBC Newsworld and CNN and BBC International. I was by no means a news junkie, but one could not help but get absorbed in the defining crisis of our time; one could not avert one's eyes from the Great Catastrophe as it unfolded. The decades-long global economic recession, these channels told me, had reached a breaking point. Nineteen of the world's twenty largest economies now had double-digit unemployment rates. The price of gold had just hit a massive new high – a bad sign. Economic powerhouses from years gone by – China and Brazil and Germany – had all but collapsed. There was no argument over the source of this entrenched malaise, what billions of people just like me and Morgana all around the world were doing – or, more specifically, *not* doing – to cause it. This was the new climate change; this was the new computer glitch that was going to cause airplanes to lit-erally fall out of the sky. Even those cultures traditionally reliable to "pad out the teams," so to speak, had embraced the world's most dominant and pervasive social trend. Imams and rabbis and the Pope stood shoulder to shoulder pleading with people to get with the program. Governments, by and large, felt powerless to stop it. What could they do, make sex mandatory and ban the pill? No. They couldn't *force* us into anything. All they could do was re-port the latest mind-boggling statistics: for the last two decades, thirty-nine out of forty couples worldwide aged twenty-two to forty-five chose to be childless, and that figure was on the rise. If this phenomenon continued . . . well . . .

I got squirrelly when the news reported that a consortium of scientists from around the world – via direct funding from the private sector – had developed a biochemical workaround to the crisis. They had the technology, the news told me, to alleviate the problem without compromising people's right to have as few children as they wanted. But the environmentalists were all over it. *Think of the ecological implications!* they screamed during the violent clashes with police that unfolded on my screen. *We'll destroy the planet for sure this time!* Various religious groups became their unlikely allies. *Your Proposal ≠ God's Will!* their own placards hollered. But no matter. The biological workaround was going to happen with or without the masses' consent. Governments would not stand in the way. That was when I had to turn the TV off. This kind of conflict was very much outside my comfort zone, and I longed to be back inside the cocoon of my job.

Before I knew it, the neck brace came off (its inner padding now reeked of old, rancid sweat) and my rib was as good as new. Morgana actually gave me a tiny round of applause on the morning I managed to pull off five toe-touches without blanching in pain. I returned to work. Percussive Insurance, with its two hundred employees, was one of the largest insurance companies in Canada, and I was its HR manager. Very little had changed in my absence. Someone had replaced, without my knowledge or consent, the perfectly serviceable coffee machine in the staff room with a newfangled espresso-dispensing device that looked like a droid from *Star Wars*. Meanwhile, a couple of supervisors had swapped offices and forgotten to submit a personnel update to me for the intranet. Otherwise, the place was as I had left it, and things began returning to normal.

Except the driving. Goddamnit, the *driving*. What was wrong with me? Morgana noticed it right away, how reluctant I was, even after my recovery, to get behind the wheel. (We had a new car now, thanks to Percussive Insurance – a Camry!) Typically, we'd split our driving fifty-fifty, but she found during these days that I would lunge for shotgun whenever we went down to our parking garage.

Part of the problem, I figured, was that we didn't actually use our car very much. We lived right downtown, and our small (some might call it mid-sized) city on a lake had a fairly decent transit system – an antiquated subway *and* streetcars *and* buses left over from more populous times. It was all very convenient and pleasant to get around; indeed, one could stand on a subway platform, even during rush hour, and not feel crowded or harried. It did feel unnatural, to be honest, to have all this legacy infrastructure at our disposal. Sometimes, there on the platform, I would stare into the dark, wet throat of the subway tunnel and see it not as a place of steel track and cement wall, but as a portal into another dimension, the entrance into a kind of Narnia. I swore I could almost hear the sweaty crowds living in that other world, their angry jostling for position, or their groans of annoyance as a distant PA system announced yet another delay. Me, I was able to *walk* to the offices of Percussive Insurance, and Morgana had just a short subway ride out to the east end to her most obscure of professions – an elementary school music teacher who taught to classes of hardly more than ten children each. We really only used our car for cumbersome chores (I had been buying a new shelving unit from Walmart the night of the crash) or for longer-haul trips down south to wine country or up north for antiquing or visiting our rural friends, Alanna and Mitch. Yes, driving was not a big part of my day-to-day existence, and post-accident, I was a jangle of nerves at the thought of it.

Morgana put up with it for a while, but *three months* was not something she could abide. My physical injuries had healed in good time but this psychological damage, this nettlesome trauma, refused to dissipate. "You can't *not* drive," she told me, trying to keep her frustration couched in a kind of jokey insouciance. "You need to be a big boy, Hector, and get over yourself."

Fine. I would get over myself. I would get myself back behind the wheel.

☙

My first solo excursion that April was to the book club I belonged to, hosted deep in the city's west end by my friend Rick. I didn't actually require a car to get out there – a subway and then a bus would have done it – but I figured this was a safe, familiar journey that wouldn't rattle me too much. I had been a member of this book club for more than seven years now, but I hadn't attended a meeting since my accident. The type of books we read varied, but we tried to stick to a solid "no trash" rule. My recommendations hewed toward military histories and political biographies. Rick, an accountant, liked true crime. Elizabeth, an oft out-of-work librarian and archivist, usually picked the latest award-winning work of literary fiction or even a book of poetry. Rachel, a social worker, chose humour or the occasional well-written celebrity screed.

Yet the selection for this month was a kind of dystopian science fiction novel: *The Children of Men*, by P.D. James. Everyone in the group got a turn picking a book and everyone had a veto, but this choice seemed to be a direct result of my absence, since I often made it clear that I loathed science fiction, and so somebody (Rick didn't say who) managed to squeak it into the queue when I wasn't around. Thankfully, my concerns were unfounded: *The Children of Men* proved a surprisingly smart and gripping read. In the bleak future that James described, mankind was doomed by the simple fact that women could no longer bear children, and this caused the world to slip into chaos and totalitarianism as the population plunged. I found myself struck by the deep moral dilemmas raised when you removed the very concept of posterity, of a future generation for your species, from the equation. *How apt*, I thought, *that a book from so long ago could raise such questions for* our *generation.*

Indeed, I very much had *The Children of Men* on the brain as I navigated our new Camry through the city's centre and out to the west end. It was just coming on dusk of a Saturday in spring, and the tall, glassy office towers above me were mottled with window light, the blackened vacancies so dominant against the few glowing specks of yellow. The sidewalks I passed were nearly deserted. A traffic light ahead flashed a sorrowful red, over and over, warning of a four-way stop. When I braked at it, my knuckles squelched into a tense white on the wheel as I braced myself, irrationally, for another abrupt BANG! at my rear end. Just as I was about to pull ahead, a kid on a skateboard came racing down off the curb and through the empty intersection, the scraping sound of his wheels filling the dome of my car. He was maybe fourteen, thin and gangly and with a head of thick, unkempt hair. As I watched him pass, I thought that in *The Children of Men*, he would be too young to even be an Omega, the last generation on Earth to be born and the one that would have to face the human race's extinction head on. *Wouldn't it be terrifying*, I thought, *to watch as the world's population just dwindled and dwindled until you* knew *your cohort was the very last one?* But of course, that was not quite *our* world. This kid would almost certainly be capable of procreation, just like the rest of us. But the question was, would he one day *choose* to procreate, to add to the world's population? That was the real dilemma, and one that – if you were to believe the news – the politicians and scientists and Wall Street money men were on the verge of solving through their great and unholy collaboration. All those hours of daytime television had made me hyperaware that a new age, a great demarcation in history, was about to unfold. They were very close to unveiling the great workaround, the one that had been brewing for years in large, industrialized labs in the Mojave Desert and the abandoned industrial parks of Beijing and Rio de Janeiro. The tycoons of Wall Street, due to their substantial investments in this technology, wanted it unveiled in a giant spectacle in their own backyard, and for us all to watch live on our TVs – watch as capitalism once again came to the rescue of the world; watch as the financiers' sad, lonely city glimmered once more with hope.

A horn blared behind me at the intersection.

"You can *go*, moron!" The shout came through an open car window.

Yes, I could go. So I went.

෬

Rick and Rachel and Liz didn't really want to talk about the more intellectual aspects of the novel. Over our cheeseboard and wine (*Just a half glass for me, guys. Yep, that's right – I'm driving again*), all they could do was go on about both the large and minute differences between *The Children of Men* and the film version that had been made from it. I tried to steer the conversation toward the text itself, but Hollywood's allure was just too strong. *We really need some fresh blood in this club*, I thought. *We're all just phoning it in, and have been for a while.* Truth was, we only kept this hobby up because none of us (even Liz) read very much on our own, and we felt guilty about that.

As usual, the discussion of the book was just a brief interlude between two larger chats about things that were not the book. The guys asked how I was feeling, and I said, "Oh fine. Physically, just fine. I'm still a bit skittish behind the wheel, but, you know . . ." and they assured me that this was perfectly natural. We asked Liz about her job at the legal library, but she glumly informed us that her hours had once again been cut and she was uncertain how she'd make her mortgage payments over the coming months. We asked Rachel about her clinical work, but there wasn't much to tell. The people who needed her help were few and far between. I wanted to tie all this back to *The Children of Men,* our own current predicament, and what was most certainly looming to resolve it. There was an obvious confluence, wasn't there? Had we, the childless masses across the globe, given up on the point of posterity and grown blithely willing to sacrifice history for our own selfish desires? And had we all become so disengaged that we were willing to allow a secretive consortium of scientists and distant government officials to decide the fate of the world for us? Had we as a species *given up hope* – just like the society described in the novel? Had we? But these questions appeared all too heavy for Rick, Rachel and Liz. They couldn't bring themselves to follow these thoughts to their logical end. They just wanted to sip wine, have a light, brisk chat about the book, get caught up with each other and then return to their own solitary lives. What was wrong with that?

~

Afterwards, I faced the drive home. The city seemed darker, more ominous, as I passed through the core of its concrete thorough-fares. I arrived back at our high-rise condo building and parked with jittery precision in our assigned space in the underground lot. Then I rode our elevator, a sleek and silent room of mirrors, up to our ninth-floor unit. Unlocking the door with my Google Watch, I stepped inside our huge, spacious domain. To the left of our front entry was our master bedroom, spare bedroom, bath-room. To the right, our den and the alcove for our washer-dryer. In front of me, our sunken living room, and beyond it, our large kitchen next to our dining area overlooking glass doors leading to our balcony, which in turn overlooked the dull, grim skyline of our city and the lake beyond it, now hidden by the night.

Morgana was sitting on the couch in the living room watching TV, her face in profile to me. The jumping light from the screen cast silvery shimmers across her dark, kinky hair. She had a hand cupped to her mouth.

"I *did* it," I said with exuberance. "I drove the car! Things got a bit dicey at a four-way flash at Dufferin, but I perserv–"

She turned to me then, and I could see that her eyes were full of horror.

"Morgana, what is it?"

She extended her hand in a gesture that said, *Come sit next to me.* Which I did. We turned and faced the TV together.

She was watching CNN. Above the frantic scroll of the news channel's chyrons, we could see images of what was clearly New York City, its ragged bank of skyscrapers looming large, the sky above them huge and high. On the left side of the screen, the

Statue of Liberty made its perpetual, torch-clutching salute to the world. The ships in the harbour beyond it seemed to have stopped still.

Something wasn't right. I stared at Manhattan's dark sky as the news cameras flicked from angle to angle and couldn't quite grasp what I was seeing.

"There was an accident," Morgana said. "At least they *think* it was an accident. No one's quite sure. Oh God, Hector, it's just . . . it's just *terrible*."

What the hell was I looking at? It was not quite a mist, not quite a blob, not quite a funnel cloud. It was some combination of the three, spiralling upward from the city and into the vast ozone above it. The thing, whatever it was, was the ghastliest, most unnatural shade of green – a neon green, a Mountain Dew green. It rose radioactively from a point that couldn't have been more than a couple of city blocks and stretched up like a giant Y over lower Manhattan and into the heavens.

"What the . . . ?" I gasped.

"They say it's going right into the atmosphere," she told me. "It could cover the whole Earth in just a few –"

"Shh-shh," I said. "Listen."

The camera had switched to street level, and the journalists there were speaking in manic tones. The view panned upward. Tiny, dark shapes, barely perceptible, began plummeting out of trees and off buildings. As they did, they seemed to grow, to swell, to take on a new and foreign shape. What were they? Pigeons? Crows? Sparrows? Yes . . . yes – all of the above. Only, by the time they hit ground, they were something else entirely. Their feathers retracted into their skin, and that skin turned a shade of beige or brown or red. Wings became arms, and arms sprouted hands. The camera lingered over a pigeon's face, there on the sidewalk, and it was – it was *horrific* what was happening to its eyes and beak as that face contorted and ballooned.

"What the . . ." I said. "What the . . . *hell* am I even looking at?"

"Oh my gosh," Morgana exclaimed.

The camera swished. A squirrel had climbed down from a streetside tree and ran up to where the pigeon writhed on the sidewalk as if to offer it help or comfort. Only, something was happening to the squirrel as well. Like the pigeon, it was doubling in size every few seconds, and its fur withdrew back into its skin, as if someone had filmed a blooming flower and then played it in reverse. Within another second – a *second* – the squirrel had . . . it had . . . sprouted *human ears.*

"Pullulation," one of the TV commentators in the CNN studio was saying. "Obviously, this is not how the consortium wanted today's experiment to go."

"That's right, Phil," concurred a journalist on the ground. "The scientists had warned it was too dangerous to bring those canisters into New York, and to do it by rail no less. But the financiers insisted. They wanted to put on a show for people tomorrow, but boy howdy are they getting one tonight. Nobody could have *imagined* that a train derailment could cause –"

"Phil? Sarah? Sorry to cut you off. Sorry. Can you hear me? Yeah, yeah. Listen. We're getting reports now out of multiple cities in Connecticut, New Jersey and New York State. Okay? Okay. Hang on. Yeah, and satellite images are showing that this . . . this *thing* has moved as far north as Ontario and as far south as Georgia. We have someone at the State Department who . . . hang on . . . they're saying now that the entire globe could be – I don't know the proper term, Phil. Infected? The entire globe could be infected with pullulation by as early as . . ."

Morgana and I looked at each other.

"This is going to change everything," she said.

"Oh *man*," I replied, feeling dread roil through me like thunder.

CHAPTER 2

Still, you couldn't allow something like this to spoil your plans. That was Morgana's attitude. Not that anything like *this* had ever happened before – the TV and newspapers and Internet now provided 24-7 coverage of a phenomenon that seemed straight out of the science fiction novels I'd held such a distaste for – but my wife insisted we continue living our lives. For example: Alanna and Mitch, our rural friends, had invited us up north to their home in Hope Mountain for brunch on a Saturday not long after the New York accident, and, goddamnit, Morgana said, we were going. I tried to talk her out of it. Until we could get a handle on exactly what this pullulation thing entailed, I was happier to just stick close to home. But my wife would have none of it. We nearly had a fight, and I was once again reminded of how obsessive she could be when it came to her social network – and not the online stuff either, the parade of comments from near strangers that showed up in our Whackr and JooJoo feeds. At a time like this, we need to be around friends, she argued. We are *going* to Hope Mountain.

So I did the driving, determined to quash the last of my vehicular anxieties. Getting out of the city was, despite the government vehicles and army checkpoints stationed every few blocks, a relatively easy endeavour. We hit Highway 407 in good time and were soon sailing up beyond our city's outer suburbs. Morgana managed to find a radio station that was playing music rather than news reports, and the FM dial's Top 40 blandness soothed my edgy self as I clutched the wheel at ten and two and kept my eyes straight ahead. Once up on the empty road, we began to speculate as to why Alanna might have invited us to this lunch. There seemed a hint of, well, *ulteriority* to the email she had sent. Was there something wrong? Had she gotten ill? Did Mitch lose his job again and they were looking to borrow money from us?

Morgana, Alanna and I had met fifteen years ago in teachers' college. As professional training went, it was not as bizarre a choice as one might think: society considered it perfectly natural, and far less morbid, to want to educate children rather than bear and raise them. I think the reason the three of us grew so close in those days, and stayed so close, was because we all arrived at teachers' college at similar points in our lives: we were in our early twenties, with freshly acquired undergraduate degrees and huge ambitions for ourselves – none of which worked out. Me, I had wanted nothing more than to become a high school teacher after finishing my B.A. in political science.

Unsurprisingly, I didn't make the cut for even the supply-teacher list and drifted into a career in HR instead. Morgana, meanwhile, had done her undergrad in classics, but treated the acquisition of her B.Ed. as a mere backup plan until she could launch the *real* career she wanted – one in musical theatre. Indeed, this aspiration played a big role in why I was attracted to her in the first place: I had done quite a bit of acting as a child, and I found Morgana's passion for the stage deeply alluring. The theatre thing didn't pan out either, but she did – unlike nearly everyone else in our cohort – land a scarce full-time teaching gig, and had proven herself a delightfully adept elementary school music instructor.

Meanwhile, Alanna, after doing a commerce degree, decided that the business world was not for her and thought she'd try education instead. But once she had come to befriend and trust Morgana and me, she revealed her true and slightly uncouth desire. Yes, Alanna was the rarest of rare souls: what she *really* wanted was to move home to Hope Mountain immediately after graduation and make lots and lots of babies with her then boyfriend, soon-to-be husband, Mitch (whom she'd been dating seemingly since elementary school), and become a full-time mom. This did not work out either. Due to unmentioned issues with her womanly plumbing, Alanna managed to have just one child with Mitch, their son Isaac, who was now ten, and they'd struggled to get pregnant a second time ever since.

It was probably just as well: Mitch worked as a welder and suffered from long stretches of unemployment, and they were always strapped for cash. He had done time in the oil fields out west, like so many men in the rural communities that surrounded our city, but he just couldn't hack the three-months-on-one-month-off commute. So, much to her irritation, Alanna had to take a job in Hope Mountain's local post office after Isaac started school. Her days were long and dull, the tasks monotonous. We often said to them, *Look, you guys really should move into town. Seriously. There aren't that many opportunities, but certainly more than what you'll find out in the sticks.* But this would not fly. Alanna and Mitch were rural folk, through and through. Mitch drove a pickup truck, not unlike the one that rear-ended me back in January. Alanna dragged him and Isaac to church every Sunday. Despite their relative poverty, their bungalow sat on nearly two acres of land, which Mitch had inherited from his parents. He kept hunting beagles in that large backyard – yapping, snapping beasts in eight-foot cages.

So there we were, beating it along at a good clip. Highway 407 became Highway 17, and Highway 17 became Concession Road 10. Up here, the houses were few and far between, the vast farm fields making their decades-old claim across the land. With no traffic for miles around, I felt myself relax behind the wheel, my shoulders easing up, my left hand slipping down to six o'clock while my right fell away entirely. Morgana rested her head against my side and propped her feet on the dash, as she often did on long car rides.

Ahead of us, where the road tipped into a brief valley, I could see someone walking along the shoulder toward us. No, not some*one* – a group of people, marching in twos and threes along the edge of the asphalt. There were no sidewalks out here on Concession Road 10, and I grew uneasy at the idea that some of these individuals might wander thoughtlessly into our path. I slowed the Camry.

Morgana sat up. "Oh wow," she said. "Just, just veer a bit to the left, Hector. Give them a wide berth."

I did what she said. And then we noticed two things simultaneously: one, that there were even more people on the other side of the road, walking in the same direction as those on the right – that is, back toward the city whence we came; and two, that they were all, every last one of them, stark naked.

It was them – *them!* The progenies of pullulation. For the first time, we were seeing them in the, well, *flesh.*

Now Morgana really sat up in her seat. "Oh my *gosh*," she said, cupping a hand over her mouth and blushing. Her big eyes gawked and her neck twisted around. I too took a brief gander as we passed this human caravan. A medley of body parts raced across my view. I glimpsed a set of vacant but determined eyes, a bouncing breast, pronounced brows, a swing of shoulder, a big, swaying dick.

"Watch the *road*," Morgana chided me with a frantic whacking at my arm. "And slow down, would you. You're going to hit somebody."

So I faced straight ahead to concentrate on my driving while she watched the lumbering masses go by. Their numbers were soon thinning out, but then I spotted something in my peripheral vision on the other side of the highway. A group of four or five people were on their hands and knees and appeared to be grappling with each other there in the deep ditch. No, not grappling. They were . . . they were . . .

"Holy shit, Hector – those people are *fucking*."

"Morgana, sit down!"

Her face was flush, excited, as she settled back into the confines of her seat belt. My eyes peered ahead, my lips pressed tight.

"Wow," she said slowly. "The news reports didn't warn us about *that*."

❧

We pulled into Alanna and Mitch's driveway to find Mitch sitting on their cement stoop in a plastic chair with a twenty-two rifle laid across his thighs. As I killed the Camry's engine and we climbed out, he rose to his feet and greeted us with, "I'm gonna seriously fuck up any of them there guys that come here. I am seriously gonna fuck them up."

"Mitch, put the gun away," we heard Alanna call through the front door screen as we approached. "For Pete's sake, would you just calm down."

He stood the twenty-two up in the stoop's corner and shook my hand as we climbed the blunt concrete steps. Below his Pittsburgh Penguins baseball cap, I could see Mitch's eyes were manic and twitchy and teeming with fear, with the need to hurt someone or something. They were eyes that could not be reasoned with.

"We brought cantaloupe!" Morgana exclaimed. Through the screen door, she could see Alanna moving dishes from her kitchen counter to their small table in their small dining room. "Oh, sweetie, let me help you," she said, and pushed her way into the house, the screen door squealing on its spring.

I gave Mitch's shoulder a manly slap. "Everything's going to be okay," I told him. But he flinched, seizing up like someone who didn't want to be touched.

Soon we were eating brunch – passing plates of bacon and pancakes, a cast-iron skillet of hash browns and our bowl of cantaloupe. Isaac had joined us, sidling into the seat next to his mother. Whenever she got up to fetch us more food or coffee from the kitchen, Alanna would tousle the boy's hair or tell him to tell us about some vaguely interesting thing that had happened at school. Beyond the dining area, in their living room, a large flat-screen TV hanging on the wall blared Fox News bombastically even though nobody was watching it. The drone of reports coming in from New York and Mumbai, from Paris and Cape Town, from Seoul and Mexico City, was like the hum of white noise behind our conversation. Another racket soon joined the bluster, sailing in through the open dining room window that faced the backyard: the sound of Mitch's hunting beagles, barking and yipping and snarling inside their cages.

"What I want to know," Alanna said when our talk shifted, as it inevitably would, to the topic of pullulation, "is what are they all eating? I mean, there's thousands of them, right? And they all have to eat. What are they *eating*?"

"Well, you should see the centres they've set up for them in the city," I told her. "Banquet halls, hotel conference rooms, school gyms – the government has commandeered everything. And it's not just food they're giving out. It's clothing, too, and sleeping bags. There's even talk of giving them books."

"*Books*?" Mitch made a face. "But how can they –"

"Well," Morgana said with a flourish, "I heard from a colleague at school that you can teach one of them to read in about twenty minutes. It's amazing."

"But how do they know to go to the cities?" Alanna asked. "I mean, that's one thing the news won't say. How are they drawn to cities in the first place?"

"Well, it looks like it's instinctual," I replied, "at least for the ones who used to be birds. They're no strangers to mass migration, I suppose. The rest – the gophers and foxes and bears – just follow the pack."

"The cities won't be able to contain them for long," Morgana said, salting her hash browns. "If their numbers keep growing, they'll have to expand the city out to the suburbs and beyond to accommodate them. You guys might even lose your country life out here."

"The *fuck* with that," Mitch said, steering a triangle of pancake into his mouth.

"Mitch, the *language*," Alanna chided, and made to cover Isaac's little ears.

"May I be excused?" the boy asked, squirming away from his mother's grasp. "I wanna go play army men on the deck."

"That's fine," Alanna said. "But if you get hungry, just come back in and grab some more, okay?"

Meanwhile, Mitch's beagles, through the open window, barked on.

After Alanna poured us all more orange juice, she took Mitch's reluctant hand atop the table and gave it an assured squeeze. "So I have to admit – we had a bit of an underhanded motive for inviting you guys out here."

Morgana and I flipped a brief, suppressed smile at each other, a look I was sure our hosts didn't catch. *Told you*, my eyes said to her. *You called it*, her eyes said back to me.

"So, we're pregnant again," Alanna announced, right there as we ate. My fork paused, hovered briefly at my mouth, and I looked over to see the valves of Morgana's throat do a spastic little dance before turning back to Alanna. *Whoa now*, I thought. *Come on. Surely it's still bad form to bring up procreation while people ate? It's like toilet talk.* Not according to Alanna. In that moment, she could have stood in for the woman in that poster I saw in the waiting lounge at St. Pat's.

"Hey, wow," I replied, trying to smile through my revulsion.

"Oh *sweetie*," Morgana sang, and rose her rump off her seat to give Alanna a hug across the table. I offered Mitch my hand to shake, which he took even as he cast his eyes down.

"This has been a long time coming," Alanna went on. "You both know . . . I mean, I think we told you . . . that, well, I've had three miscarriages since Isaac was born . . ."

"Yeah, we knew that," I said.

"Anyway, so . . ." She shrugged, smiled and turned her palms to the ceiling. "It looks like this one took."

"Oh, Alanna, congratulations," I stammered. "You guys, you guys must be just *tickled*."

"Yep," Mitch replied. He seemed about to say more but then a raft of snarling and yowling from the dogs cut him off.

"Anyway," Alanna went on, raising her voice above them, "so we did want to ask you. And seriously . . ."

"Feel free to say no," Mitch piped up.

"Yes, feel free to say no. We'd totally understand. But. Well." They looked at each other, then back at us. "Are you interested in being little fetus's godparents?"

A bolt of lightning moved up my spine. Morgana and I exchanged another glance, one I hoped was as inscrutable as the last – a flicker of surprise, of doubt, of *Well, we'd need to talk about this.*

Alanna, no slouch in the empathy department, caught it immediately. "You don't have to answer right away," she said in a hurry. "You'd need time to discuss it . . . between yourselves. It's a big decision."

"A *huge* decision," Mitch concurred.

"But we just think . . . God forbid anything happened to us, you guys would make excellent guardians for little baby."

What on Earth gave you that *impression?* I wanted to say but maintained a neutral veneer. I conjured then the first and only exchange Morgana and I ever had about this sort of thing, back when we were a year, maybe fifteen months into our relationship. *Look, this probably goes without saying*, she said one evening while we were out for a stroll, *but I'm really against having kids.* Her words were tinged with awkwardness and hesitancy, since, even then, she had no idea if I was one of these weirdos, these whack jobs, who actually wanted to procreate. *That's so great to hear – me too!* I replied with sincerity, and I could tell Morgana was relieved. There lingered, however, an uneasiness between us, an uncertainty about the future of this relationship that had, up until then, been going very well, very smoothly. So I followed up with a quick, *But I'm still going to marry the ass off you. You know that, right?* And she laughed, loud and generously, before taking my hand and pressing herself to my side, a gesture that said, *Yep, you're the one.*

I licked my lips and looked at Alanna and Mitch. "Wow, guys, this is ... umm ..." *What? A huge imposition? The most ridiculous request asked of us by anyone who wasn't family?* The dogs' barking through the window had taken on an almost incantatory quality, and I raised my voice to speak above them. "... very flattering. We're just ..." and I looked at Morgana. "... just so touched ..."

"Yes, touched that you'd even ask," Morgana finished. The barking grew throaty, guttural, as if one of the beasts were choking to death. "But we'd have to think about this, right? I mean, we're total city slickers. If, God forbid, something *did* happen to you both, would you really want your kid growing up downt–"

"Dad! Dad!" Isaac was yelling from the deck's screen door. "Come quick!"

Mitch rose off his seat and flew to the window overlooking the backyard. As he pulled back the frilly curtain that hung there, his voice lowered to a deep timbre, almost tuba-like. "What ... the ... *fuck*."

He darted to the front door. We heard it peel open on its spring and then, a second later, slam shut. He came racing through the house with the twenty-two and toward the back deck.

"*Mitch?*" Alanna got up and went to the window. Looking out, her face suddenly crumbled, filling with a slack, baggy horror. Then she too bolted and followed her husband toward the yard.

Morgana and I got up and raced after them. The May sun was bright in our eyes as we hurried out onto the deck and descended to the grass. Ahead of us, we could see that Mitch had the gun raised and pointed at the beagles' cages. Isaac had tried to run to him, but Alanna now clutched the boy around the shoulders and held him tight against her.

There, in one of the enclosures, among the kibble bowls and water dishes and polyps of dog turd, sat a man. Naked and huge, he was huddled in one corner while the dogs in the cage barked and snapped at him. From where we stood, I could see the man's face. It was broad and fleshy, his brow a big bulging protuberance over his eyes. When he snarled back at the dogs, he revealed massive gums, monstrously wide inside his mouth.

"Get the fuck out!" Mitch screamed, the rifle's butt tight against his shoulder. "Get out now!"

The man scurried crabwise along the cage and toward the door as Mitch approached. One of his large, meaty feet sprung outward then and kicked the door open, shattering its bolt lock and knocking Mitch to the ground. We watched as the man sprung from the cage and zoomed around it in fear. He darted off to a copse of trees on the edge of the property. Before Mitch could even get to his feet, point the rifle and squeeze off a shot, the guy had vanished into the forest beyond.

We all stood there in the sun, panting in terror. Above us, a small string of cloud blemished the sky, its underbelly sporting a strange filament of green.

"Wait," Mitch said, looking the cages over and over. "I'm missing a dog. Where's Sammy? I'm missing Sammy."

Alanna, forever cursed with that queer and unknowable nature of hers, those maternal instincts, came up behind him and placed a gentle hand in the centre of his back. Yes, indeed. She was a mother, through and through – even to her husband. And she knew then what we knew, what Mitch was being a bit slow in realizing.

"Honey, dear," Alanna said, her voice quavering.

"Sweetie, I think . . . I think that *was* Sammy."

CHAPTER 3

A nickname has emerged for these new members of the human race: blomers. The pundits had whittled down this sobriquet over several weeks from two previous and unworkable options. Someone had suggested they be called *boomers*, since their appearance in the wake of the New York accident had been like a bomb going off in the world's population. But then another pundit pointed out that there had been a whole generation of people, from years ago, called *boomers*, and so we all eschewed the term to avoid confusion. Then it was suggested they be labelled *bloomers*, since their presence seemed to bloom through society with such potent abruptness. But then the British kicked up a stink because, of course, over there *bloomers* meant something else entirely. So a compromise was struck, and the word *blomer* eased its way into our vernacular in no time at all.

What was to be done with blomers? They came staggering out of barns and forests and national parks, looking bleary-eyed and lost, as if they had just awoken from a centuries-old sleep. They lined our roads and highways, causing traffic to snarl on exit ramps and turnpikes. They flowed into the cities and clogged the streets. All over the world, government officials ushered them into countless help centres, providing food and clothing and medical aid. Psychologists and linguists and educators were summoned. They learned that blomers were capable of language acquisition almost instantly and (as Morgana had heard through the teacher grapevine) could learn to read in about twenty minutes. What other aptitudes did they possess? If the government officials knew, they weren't saying yet. And as for the blomers' penchant for group sex? Well . . . the hope was that societal norms would kick in eventually.

Lord knows I certainly got an eyeful on my walks to work. I typically varied my commute – sometimes cutting along Carlton Park, sometimes strolling through the gay village, sometimes swinging through ritzy Isabella with its sprawling, turret-peaked homes. But now, it was as if each of these routes were hosting a raucous block party, every single day, all the time. The sidewalks teemed with lineups of nude or semi-nude blomers looking to get served at a help centre. Police and volunteers would move through the crowds, handing out donated food and bottles of water from large plastic tubs. Fights would sometimes break out. The less gracious people who lived along these streets would scream from windows for quiet. At one point, a blomer dressed in a mélange of borrowed and ill-fitting denim touched me on the forearm as I passed. "Excuse, excuse me, sir, can you, can you, can you help?" And I said, "Um, sure, I can try." And she said, "I want to go to, um, ug ug ton?" And I replied, "Ug ug ton? Oh, do you mean *Ossington*? Ossington Station?" And she replied, "Yes, Ossington Station. That's it. If you could tell me how to get there, I would greatly appreciate it." And as I explained how to reach Line 2 of the subway from where we stood, I was blown away by how the sparrow had perfected her grammar and vocabulary in that one brief interaction, right before my eyes.

As for the blomers' public acts of sex? Well! I could hardly describe what I saw, the sidewalk threesomes and foursomes and moresomes. I thought: *I can't fucking take this. It's like the end of the world – only with orgies!* And I wasn't the only one bothered, either. People would pause and look on in revulsion or shock as the blomers twisted themselves into the most elaborate, most creative sexual positions I'd ever seen. Some people, possibly Christian or Christianesque – religious types anyway – would step forward and make a half-hearted attempt to break these congresses up, only to be shooed away with slaps or shoves or barking. Others just stood there, as I did, with their mouths hanging open. One guy, a total stranger, nudged me with his elbow as he passed me by. "May see if the wife's into *that* when I get home tonight," he said, and nodded at the extravagant contortion happening not five feet from where I stood. No, we were powerless to stop these open-air debauches, these streetside gangbangs. It felt like something fundamental was changing. It felt like the end of the world. We had all just assumed that Armageddon would mean a massive *reduction* in the world's population due to a superbug or environmental disaster, like something out of a Stephen King or J.G. Ballard novel. (James's *The Children of Men*, I had to confess, had whetted my appetite for these kinds of stories.) But the opposite proved true. There was something about the overnight doubling, or tripling, or quadrupling – no government official would say for sure – of the world's population that carried a distinct air of apocalypse.

◅

Morgana and I, despite these tumultuous times, had a more pressing problem.

"I still can't believe they asked us," she said with a shake of her head. It was a Saturday night, and we sat in a booth at Milestones, sipping Bellinis. It had been like a game of hopscotch across the sidewalk out front to get into this restaurant, due to a massive construction project next door. Somebody was throwing up a new condominium tower, seemingly overnight. "I mean, we're not even family."

"I know. But who has *family* anymore?" I shrugged, fiddling with the little plastic toy that came with my drink. "Neither of them has siblings or cousins. We're all they've got."

"I know, but still."

"Look, it's a token gesture," I assured her. "I mean, what are the odds they're both going to die at the same time? Being godparents mostly means giving . . ." And here, I released another shudder of distaste. ". . . the *kid* a gift on its birthday and at Christmas. It's no big whoop."

"So you want to tell them yes?"

I thought it over. Truth was, I felt a certain loyalty toward Alanna. She was a good friend. Our personalities had really clicked, from the earliest days of teachers' college – to the point where I might have considered asking *her* out instead of Morgana before I learned she'd been dating Mitch since the earth was still cooling – and we'd maintained a platonic closeness ever since. She always looked out for me, and I discovered that this was her jam: she tended to mother everybody she cared about. Indeed, after graduation, when it became clear I wasn't going to make even the supply-teacher list, it was Alanna who suggested I adapt my new skills to the, Lord love me, *exciting* world of human resource management. Which got me a job, at least. I felt like I owed her a lot.

"I think I do," I said to Morgana.

I thought my wife might protest some more, but then she raised herself up and over the table to kiss me and smile, her frizzy halo of hair blocking out the lamplight above our heads. "Fine," she sang as she sat back down. "But if those two are killed in a plane crash and fetus comes to live with us, *you're* changing its diapers."

"Deal," I smiled back.

❧

During those first two months after pullulation, my job at Percussive Insurance provided a much-needed sanctuary for my unease. With the outside world erupting in change, I longed to lose myself in all the white-collar regimens that had given my life shape for the last decade and a half. Every day I would come in and promptly close my office door against the gossip and chattering that ricocheted down halls; I would do a couple hours of busy-work, approving performance evaluations or reviewing copy for a new job ad going out; and then my best friend, Otis, a fraud investigator, and I would engage in our daily routine. We took turns stopping by the other person's office at ten thirty every morning with coffees we'd pick up from the Second Cup coffee shop in the lobby. He was a black-with-one-sugar guy; I was a single shot of milk. We always had this time blocked off in our Outlook calendars, and we never seemed to lose track of whose turn it was to buy the coffees. In these post-pullulation days, we usually got our snarking about the state of the world out of the way first. He'd say something like, "How was your walk in this morning?" and I would answer, "Oh, you know, medium scandalizing. How's the subway these days?" And he'd say, "Oh fuck, you don't even want to know. I mean, can you explain to me how someone who was living as a bear in the woods a month ago needs to ride the train now, let alone at rush hour? The one I saw today brought a cello on board. A fucking *cello*. It was in its case, but still." Eventually, we moved on to work matters. Otis loved his job. Fraud investigation, in these straightened economic times, was a truly genteel profession. Sure, more people were wont to commit fraud during a recession, but when they got caught – and Otis always caught them; he was extremely good at his work – they would confess right away and be very contrite in the hopes of cutting a deal. And he would treat them so reasonably, so kindly, these people who were trying to rip us off. He would sometimes even develop a personal rapport with the ones who were in really bad straits. I admired that about him. I admired that he, like me, was very prim and proper, very into hierarchy and procedure. He tended to dress up a bit for work, even on casual Fridays, securing a well-cut vest and jacket over his string-bean physique. I liked, however, that he also kept a bit of length to his sandy blond locks, a tribute to his former life as an aspiring but failed rock musician. Yes, like me, like Morgana, like Alanna, Otis carried a thwarted ambition in his past, one that he had decided, in a very grown-up way a dozen years ago, to move beyond. Music had been everything to him once, and then one day, it wasn't.

As I said, I had come to look forward to, even long for, this ten thirty ritual of ours – to see Otis sauntering up the hallway toward my office at exactly the prescribed time, carrying the two coffees from Second Cup on their tray. For him and me, this mid-morning gabfest had a normalizing, stabilizing quality to it, a way of creating continuity from one day to the next, and to nurture this work-born friendship that had become so important to us both as we cascaded toward middle age. So imagine my dismay when, at ten twenty-seven this morning, I saw not Otis's skinny presence stepping out of that elevator down the hall, but rather the bulky, greasy-haired waddle of Brennan Prate instead. He stepped from the elevator and headed like a liner ship toward my door. Brennan was a supervisor in our IT department and had a propensity to drop by uninvited rather than book a proper meeting in Outlook whenever he wanted to talk to you. He always carried himself with an air of immediacy and aggression. In appearance, Brennan was the very cliché of a helpdesk drudge: sneakers that barely passed for business casual squeezed onto his wide feet; wrinkle-free khaki dress slacks from Dockers; lanyard with security badge that dangled, permanently it seemed, from around his neck; and a cheap golf shirt that cupped his cauldronous gut like a hammock.

He came into my office then, sat uninvited in one of the guest chairs in front of my desk and said, quite cryptically, "Pigeons."

"Pigeons?" I asked, perking with surprise. I must confess now that I don't like Brennan Prate, and here's why. Brennan is a shit disturber. He disturbs shit. You take a shit, and he disturbs it. We HR people don't like our shit disturbed. We like to take our shit in a solitude of impunity and then send it off to a watery oblivion with one rote and well-calibrated flush. But Brennan will not allow this. He will not allow a shit to go undisturbed. "Brennan, what are you gibbering about?" I asked.

"We need to hire ourselves some pigeons," he said. "Right? Am I right?" When I displayed no understanding one way or the other, he pressed on. "It's going to get intense, Hector. Believe you me. There are thousands – no, *millions* – of blomers now living in this city, or soon to be. Things may seem chaotic now, but you wait. The government is teaching these folks to read and write and do math and hold down jobs. They're going to build homes for them and cars for them and integrate them fully into society. It's already beginning, Hector. And so what are all these blomers going to need?"

My head bobbled with incomprehension.

"Insurance!" he barked, his jowls parting up like curtains around the word. Despite his astonishing girth, Brennan spoke with a high-pitched voice, like the sound a balloon made when you slowly let some air out. "*Insurance*, Hector. We are in a growth industry now, thanks to pullulation. *Every* industry is going to be a growth industry before long. You wait. The economy's going to take off like a rocket, and everyone is going to need what we're selling. And do you honestly think that two hundred staff are going to cut it when this new world order comes? Do you think these people," and he motioned to the world beyond my office, "most of whom sleepwalk through their jobs anyway, are going to handle the inevitable workload when it comes?"

Just then, Otis arrived at my door with the coffees. My eyes gave him a halting look, and he tossed me a smirk when he saw who I was with. He sidestepped to the little waiting area to the left of where my admin assistant sat at her desk.

"Okay," I said slowly, turning back to Brennan. "But why pigeons?"

"What, don't you *read* anything? The scientists are already starting to figure out the different talents that blomers have. They all got aptitudes. The ones who used to be pigeons are supposed to be logistically minded. Like, *intensely* logistically minded. They would make excellent project managers. There was a whole feature on them in *Newsweek*. Didn't you see it?"

"No, I must have missed that piece," I told him.

"Now, I don't mean to be a shit disturber," he said with the tenor of a man right on the cusp of disturbing some shit. "And I certainly don't want to tell you how to do your job. But you're the HR manager, Hector. This is your bailiwick. Imagine a Percussive Insurance that won't employ two hundred people by this time next year. It'll employ two thousand people, or five thousand, or more. Think about it. We'll need pigeons to come in, when they're ready, to set up whole new systems, to implement whole new processes, to head up whole new departments. It's going to be *crazypants*. But we have to get in on the ground level of this, before other companies figure out the same thing and scoop up all the pigeons."

"Oh, I don't know, Brennan," I replied. "Nobody's sure how any of this is going to play out. I think we should take a more cautious approach before we go hiring blomers willy-nilly. Don't you agree?"

"No!" he snapped. "I don't agree at all. What is it with this place and its 'cautious approaches'? I swear to Christ, it's like we work in a bloody museum. Why do I feel like the only one who shows any initiative or pushes the envelope around here?" That was one way of putting it. Brennan did possess a certain scheming, ladder-climbing demeanour. He saw himself as far more than just a workaday code monkey and always seemed to have grander, more ascendant plans for his career. Me, I found his entrepreneurial gumption rather distasteful.

"Well, I'll take it under advisement," I told him. "We can do some exploratory research. Launch a needs assessment for the sales department. Get a sense of the employment landscape out there if we need more bodies."

"Yeah, yeah," he said, and rose with great effort back to his feet. The guest chair seemed to gasp with relief. "You take it under advisement. You do your needs assessment. But I'll warn you now, Hector. The future is coming. The future is *here*. We'll all have to show a lot more resourcefulness, and fast. The blomers, once they come online with the rest of society, will change the game. You mark my words."

And with that, he left. But before he could reach the hallway, my admin called him over to help her with something on her computer. He made a face as she described the problem to him, and then he said, "Can I drive?" before clasping her mouse in his beefy mitt and leaning over her screen. I could hear him lording his IT knowledge over her in that way that only IT people can.

Otis, meanwhile, slinked into my office with that smirk still on his face, and I made the quack-quack-quacking gesture with my hand as he passed me my coffee.

"What was that all about?" he said, sitting down.

"Oh, you know – the future."

It was funny, then, how Otis and I got on the same page almost immediately, deciding to talk loudly about something unrelated to work *or* pullulation so that Brennan, just outside my door, would hear. We chose as our subject a particularly inane, old-timey sitcom that was enjoying a real resurgence on TV – one set in a suburban American family where the dad's an idiot and the mom's a shrew.

By the time Brennan wrapped up with my admin, Otis and I had really worked ourselves into a lather. Brennan's chubby face loomed just beyond my door and we turned to stare at him. He made sure to toss us a big, dramatic roll of his eyes – he'd always found our work friendship highly inappropriate – and we in turn tossed him a synchronized wave that no doubt boiled his blood. We watched him sway himself back down the hall to the elevator and press the button. As he stepped inside and turned to face us once more, I gave him a theatrical wink, which only seemed to baffle him. In response, his lips pulled away from his teeth in a kind of sneer, and just as the elevator doors closed in front of his face, he mouthed a single, silent word at us: *pigeons.*

❧

Summer came and Morgana was done teaching for the year. Her two months' vacation stretched out before her like a river of relief, as stress had been brewing at the school board in the wake of pullulation and had begun bleeding into the classroom. Teaching had always been a sweet gig for my wife, enrollments being what they were. With only eight to ten kids per class, she could grow close to each and every one of them, remembering their names for years to come, recalling which instruments they had played and which of the kids had loved music and which ones had really struggled with it. But now, ministries of education all over the world were raising difficult questions about how to go about the mass instruction of blomers. With great haste, Morgana's own school board had set up huge teaching farms throughout the city – old, abandoned warehouses converted into giant classrooms – and they hired any unemployed person with a university degree (there were lots of them) to come in and teach. Because blomers were such quick studies, they managed to move through the system fast, as if on a conveyor belt, but there were always more to take their place. Talk now involved mobilizing the entire teaching profession come September to deal with the overflow. Morgana and her colleagues were given the choice of working during their vacations in these farms, but she promptly turned it down. Come next summer, she told me, it may not even be optional. Better to enjoy this year's summer break in case it might be her last.

On the first day of her vacation, I came home from work to find her bouncing off the walls. At first, I thought it was due to all the construction noise coming from the condo unit next to ours. The neighbours had begun what sounded like a rather complicated renovation, and the days (and even some evenings) had been full of drilling and banging and grinding and crashing. But no. It wasn't that. "I've got it!" Morgana said, skipping through the living room toward me and throwing herself into my arms as I set my briefcase down. "Oh Hector, I've got it!"

"Got what?" I asked with a smile, throwing my keys onto their little table by the door as Morgana dangled and swayed off my shoulders. Her kinky brown hair looked damp, and her long, creamy neck carried the faint scent of chlorine.

"What I want my main activity to be this summer," she replied. "Come see."

She led me by the wrist to the couch, where her computer rested open on the far cushion. We sat and she placed the machine on her lap to show me the website she'd been looking at.

Morgana, I learned, had fled all the noise coming from next door and spent a good portion of the day at the community centre near our condo building. A cheerful, brightly lit touchpoint for the mixed-income citizens of our neighbourhood, the centre was one of my wife's absolute favourite places. It contained an Olympic-sized swimming pool, a large library branch, a gymnasium and a lovely sculpture-strewn courtyard with picnic tables where you could eat your lunch on sunny days. Morgana had gone there to return some library books and browse around, then took a long, leisurely swim in the pool. As she was leaving the community centre, she passed the bulletin boards on the wall near the Ping-Pong tables and saw a large, garish flyer tacked to the cork. It featured a web address that offered more information.

She showed that website to me now. "I called the number. They're auditioning for lots of parts, including music assistant. I think it would be ideal for me."

"Oh, I agree," I said, channelling some enthusiasm.

The web page read:

COMMUNITY THEATRE 647

NEEDS VOLUNTEERS FOR

HARPIES: THE MUSICAL!

COME BE A PART OF THIS

FRESH, RAUNCHY RETELLING

OF *LYSISTRATA*.

Raunchy? I thought. *Oh dear.*

"I spoke to the director," Morgana said, "and do you know what she told me? She said this play won't be so much a retelling of *Lysistrata* as an 'inverse' of the story. Which, as you know, would suit me right down to the ground."

I did know this. As mentioned, Morgana had done her undergraduate degree in classics, and there was a time in her life when ancient Greek theatre had been the be-all and end-all of culture for her. Of the ancient Greek playwrights, the greatest of these, as far as she was concerned, was Aristophanes. And of his eleven surviving plays, the greatest of *these*, as far as she was concerned, was *Lysistrata*. A cheeky little number, it told the story of a group of women from the warring city states of Athens and Sparta who conspire together to withhold sex from their menfolk to get them to stop fighting and negotiate a peace. Morgana wrote her honours thesis on the play; and while she loved *Lysistrata* with all her heart, she did argue therein that a flaw marred the play's core premise. All that pent-up aggravation and sexual energy, she claimed, would make the men want to fight with each other *more*, not less. Morgana's thesis posited that Aristophanes should have taken the exact opposite approach with his play, turning it into a kind of proto-porn movie, where Lysistrata and the gals overwhelm their men, sexually exhaust their men, to get them to stop fighting.

This, it turned out, was more or less the concept behind *Harpies: The Musical!* I tried not to blanch as my wife described it to me. The whole show was to be a series of orgies set to show tunes. *Good gravy,* I thought. *They may have to change the name from* Harpies: The Musical! *to* Herpes: The Musical!

"I couldn't believe the coincidence of it," Morgana informed me. "It's like this director is going to bring my thesis to life, right there on the stage."

"That's, uhh, great," I said. "So . . . you'll, um, *audition* . . . for the role of . . . ?"

"Music assistant," she restated. "Apparently, if I play my cards right, I might even get to do a bit of composing. Oh Hector, isn't that *grand*?"

"Well, I'm excited," I said, feeling a rinse of relief. "It sounds like a wonderful summer project for you." I took a moment, then, to linger on my own days in the theatre as a child actor. This sometimes happened to me, when Morgana announced she had managed to put together some musical or show at school, and I would feel the warmth of my own memories on the stage, long before I became a doyen of HR. "But . . . wait," I went on, and gestured to the words on her screen. "Doesn't *harpy* mean, like . . . a harridan? You know, a coarse and disagreeable woman?"

"Oh, they'll be coarse and disagreeable all right," she said. "These ladies are going to wield sex like a stick in this play. I suspect the director wants to take back the term *harpy* for women – you know, the way fat people have with *wide-o*."

"That's fascinating," I said. I was about to say more, but we were interrupted then by the most thunderous, most hellacious explosion from the other side of our front entry's wall. "Jesus Murphy!" I shouted as we both flinched on the couch. It sounded like a large monster had just vomited rubble into the hallway beyond our door. Morgana and I got up to investigate.

Out in the hall we saw that, sure enough, the floor was strewn with broken plaster, and a couple of sledgehammers, brandished by two burly construction dudes in hard hats, were retreating into a gigantic hole in the wall they had made not far from our neighbours' door.

That door opened then and our neighbours, Terry and his wife, Agnes, a retired couple who had lived in the building for more than forty years, came out to greet us.

"Oh, hey, folks," Terry said. "Sorry about all the noise."

"No problem," I lied. "You, you guys seem to be undergoing quite a renovation in there."

"Oh, it's more than a renovation," Agnes said. "Terry, should I tell them?"

They looked at each other conspiratorially. "I don't see the harm," he replied.

"Tell us what?" Morgana asked.

"Well, a man came by the other week," Agnes said, "a real estate guy. And do you know what he did? He offered us one-three-fifty for our spare bedroom. He's converting it into a bachelor unit."

"*Really*?" I said. My first thought was *how the* hell *did the condo board allow that?* My second thought was *nobody offered us one-three-fifty for* our *spare bedroom.*

"You've got to take advantage of these opportunities when they come," Terry said.

"Oh, I . . . I know," I replied distantly.

"So, when does the new person move in?" Morgana asked.

"*People*," Terry answered. "*People* moving in. He's hoping to fit five, maybe even six blomers in there."

A silence, a boggy simmering dread, dangled between us for a moment.

"Well," Morgana said, her word curling upward into a kind of cheekiness. "Sounds like the thumping and banging may become a permanent fixture."

And, by golly, didn't Agnes blush.

CHAPTER 4

It turned out that Brennan Prate was right. Pigeons, with their flairs for logistical thinking, made excellent project managers. The scientists, or government officials, or whoever was in charge of figuring out such things, had in fact discovered aptitudes among all the animals who had transmogrified into human form. It amazed me how fast this knowledge bled into the culture that was rapidly changing around us; it soon felt as if we had always known which blomers were good at what, from the very first day of pullulation. Gophers, for example, had a propensity for courage and a sense of duty and thus were conscripted into the military. Dogs, we learned, possessed great physical stamina and strength, and soon went to work on a million construction projects launched in a thousand cities around the world. Blue jays, meanwhile, displayed an artistic temperament and went about becoming graphic designers and painters. Cows had photographic memories and near-perfect recall. Foxes were mathematically inclined. Eagles found jobs as nurses and social workers due to their nurturing natures. Sparrows, predisposed toward science, donned white lab coats and learned how microscopes worked. Crows soon starred in their own sitcoms, in their own Broadway and off-Broadway shows, due to their acting acumen. Cats showed a talent for reading comprehension and thus became book editors and literary critics. Bears, as Otis had glimpsed that day on the subway, were musically inclined. And hawks, determined to rule us all one day, showed an unsettling penchant for capitalism, for business cunning.

It was easy to explain how one could identify a blomer, but it was entirely more difficult to say how you knew which animal it had been. What did blomers look like, generally? How did one tell them apart from us? (*Us* nicknamed *vips* now, short for "those born of viviparous means" – in other words, carried in our mother's wombs rather than spawned through the pullulation process.) Physically, blomers took on several features of the disease known as acromegaly – *gigantism* to the layman. This meant larger than normal hands, feet and face. It meant something called *frontal bossing* – that is, distinctly pronounced brow ridges. It meant dental malocclusion: gums that seemed too large for the mouth, teeth that seemed too small. Blomers were often taller than us vips, but not always. The myth was that, due to their fleshy features, they were physically stronger than us, but this was only the case in dogs. At any rate, blomers stood out – even when standing next to a vip who actually suffered from acromegaly.

But how did you know a cat from a crow? How could you tell former foxes, gophers and hawks apart? This was harder to explain, as blomers did not retain many features of their animal antecedents. No feather, no fur, no fangs. At best, you might see something in the bone structure of the face, beneath that dense canopy of brow, that hinted at it. Otherwise, it was all mannerisms. A certain squint of the eye said, *That had been a bear*. A slinky, sexy saunter to their walk screamed *cat*. Pigeons nodded their heads three times when they agreed with you; sparrows, only twice. We all picked it up, as if through osmosis. In no time at all, we took these distinctions for granted.

Indeed, on my morning jaunts to work, as the eastern sun played its ragged games of peekaboo around the homes and buildings of downtown, smearing glass towers in gold, making

thatches of sidewalk weed seem almost lush, almost esculent, I
played observation games with the blomers I passed. *Cat, bear,
hawk, bear,* I sang inside my head. *Gopher, crow, crow, fox.* I was
getting good at this. Such mental exercises helped distract me
from what I saw and heard on these strolls. It wasn't just the
public orgies I had to step around or glimpsed in the back alleys.
The blomers' wont of stripping down and having sex with one
another wherever and whenever the feeling moved them had yet
to become visual white noise, but I managed to keep my shock
and revulsion in check. Which was more than I could say for other people. The right-wing nutjobs, so offended by these sidewalk
shenanigans, had organized themselves. The religious leaders
and conservative parent groups had begun staging small, sombre
protests hither and yon around downtown: hand-holding prayer
vigils and elaborate bristol board placards that featured massive
photographs of traditional nuclear families, the parents of which,
presumably, had their sex behind closed doors and with the lights
off. These groups would hold their rallies mere feet from where
a gaggle of blomers – three or five or sometimes fifteen – would
wail away at each other in the most pornographic of positions.
The protesters would sometimes look to the rest of us to join
them in these hate-ins and were baffled when the vast majority
of us moved on, hustling toward our increasingly busy jobs.

No, no. It wasn't that – or *just* that. It was the relentless construction that I now encountered, a new disruptive project on
each city block, instituted daily it seemed, that really spoiled my
commute. Every park, every knoll, every green space between
home and work was now a gaping hole or nascent condo skel-
eton rising with haste out of the ground. The very air of the city
was now choked with both physical and aural pollution: dust and
grit and the shrill yodelling of jackhammers. Even our building
had not been spared. The huge, pleasant courtyard on the south
side had been commandeered for yet another condo tower, its
assembly running twenty-four hours a day directly outside our

bedroom window. Yes, this was a new city ordinance – similar to ones enacted all over the world – that allowed shifts of dogs, in their hard hats and blazing orange safety vests, to work round the clock to get living spaces up quickly for their fellow blomers. From our bedroom window on the ninth floor, these workers looked small and oblivious to our presence, unaware of how their construction noises were ruining our sleep, sex lives, sanity.

As bad as the construction was outside, I found no relief from it at work. The offices of Percussive Insurance were undergoing a physical (not to mention cultural) revolution. Brennan Prate had proved right: we did need to hire pigeons – lots of them – to develop processes to handle all the new business coming in. We also needed cows (to help with investigations), cats (to work in Contracts & Deeds) and hawks (to spot new market opportunities as they arose and pounce on them). My days grew long as I began the tedious chore of shepherding blomers into our company – blomers who had no resumes, no formal qualifications beyond what they learned in the education farms, no experience, but only the keen and unambiguous aptitudes that had arisen in them from pullulation itself. Management had given me a whole slew of new admin assistants – chickens and goats, all of them – to help. Chickens and goats made excellent admins, I learned – pliant and obedient and phenomenal notetakers – and they provided tremendous support as we added scores of blomers to our company's head count. Consequently, the office itself underwent an eruption of change. Walls were coming down. Workstations, offices and meeting rooms reconfigured themselves. Construction was relentless. Every day, it seemed, I came in to discover an octopus of fibre optic wires dangling from an open ceiling panel or rows of desks lined up in a hallway somewhere, ready to be put to use.

Today, I arrived at work to learn that the offices along the entire west wall of our floor were to be torn out and replaced by cubicles. Cubicles! Now *this* was going to be a big blow to morale at Percussive Insurance. Prior to pullulation, we had been just two hundred souls divided among six floors, and everyone (with the exception of admin assistants) got their own spacious office. Now, somebody had made the executive decision that everyone ranked supervisor and below would need to sit in a cubicle. Naturally, as the HR manager, I would have to deal with the emotional fallout from the affected employees. I needed to gather the evicted and speak to them in soothing but clear-cut tones. *Change is hard, people, but this is for the best,* I'd say. *Spacing issues are an ongoing concern, and your co-operation today will help ensure the long-term sustainability of the firm.* And I would have to withstand their silent stares that said, *Well, that's easy for you to say, Hector, you got to keep* your *office.* It was discussions like these that made me feel officious and phony, like a mouth organ for upper management, a ventriloquist's dummy sitting on the lap of senior leadership. If there was one thing worse than speaking bullshit, it was speaking bullshit that someone else had put in your mouth. What's more, I hated how these after-effects of pullulation just hijacked my day, hijacked my routines and put unpleasant duties on my desk that I preferred not to do.

Speaking of disagreeable tasks, I had one on my plate this morning before confronting the now-officeless folks at the other end of the floor. It was Friday, and I had booked a meeting with one of the girls down in Accounts Payable, a vip named Annie, whom we'd been having trouble with for quite a while. Annie's problem involved her blanket inability to recognize the boundaries and parameters of casual Friday. Whereas the rest of us came to work on the last day of the week dressed in decent jeans and respectable tops, Annie arrived looking like she was in the middle of doing her laundry. Her standard Friday ensemble included a parched and faded Winnie-the-Pooh T-shirt that looked like it had been part of her wardrobe since middle school, as well as unflattering pink sweatpants and sneakers with attention-grabbing neon green laces. She had been warned, lightly at first by her supervisor and then more sternly by her department's manager, about these dress code violations. Now she had to come see me. These awkward conversations were the very worst aspect of being an HR manager.

The little peanut arrived at my office at exactly 9:00 a.m., and I beckoned her to sit in one of the chairs in front of my desk. Yes, indeed – there it was, the aged Winnie-the-Pooh icon, his smile a gaping idiot-child's as he sat on his plump duff and buried his paw up to the wrist in a pot of honey. "Annie, my dear, thank you for taking this meeting with me," I began.

"No problem," she said, eyes downcast. She was not old – probably just a few years out of school – but surely old enough to know that such wardrobe choices could not stand in an environment such as ours.

"Do you know why I've called you in here today?" I asked.

"I think so," she replied, not looking up. Her long, dark hair was utterly styleless and flecked with dandruff on either side of its part, and her glasses, wine-coloured and far too large for her face, slid down her nose.

"Now, you've been warned several times about this," I said in the po-faced tones of the high school teacher I never got to be. "Am I right?"

"You're right," she conceded. "No, you're right. It's, it's just that . . ." Her eyes shifted to one side.

"Just what?" I asked. When she dawdled with her answer, I pressed on. "Now, Annie, you know how important it is that we all remain professional here – not just for our clients, but for ourselves." God, I hated how my voice sounded in these moments. Frankly, I didn't give a hot black shit how little Annie decided to dress on casual Fridays, considering that she worked alone in the hobbit hole of her office on the first floor, cutting cheques and receiving invoices, with hardly any contact with the outside world. Who was this buttoned-down prick sitting behind my desk who feigned otherwise for the sake of corporate appearances? How did I *become* him? "And I know the company prides itself on a fun, relaxed atmosphere," I went on, "but we have to ensure we don't take advantage of its generosity, now don't we?"

"I guess I just don't see it as unprofessional," she said. There was a swelling confidence in her words that neither I nor anyone who worked alongside Annie, as far as I knew, had encountered from her. She glanced up at me then, her eyes blazing with a look I couldn't read. "And I guess I don't see it as the company's business, anyhow."

I huffed a little. "Well . . . well . . . Annie, you know as well as I d–"

"And I'm not the only one around the office doing it," she said. "Lots of girls are. And some of the guys, too."

"Wait, what? I . . . I have no idea what you're even talking about."

"Well, that's because you're squirrelled away up here on sixth, Hector, not paying attention to how much this place is changing. But I'll tell you what I told my supervisor *and* my manager: it would be no business of the company's if I were involved with a vip on staff, so what difference does it make if I'm involved with a blomer?"

"Oh . . . Annie, no, Annie, my dear, that's . . . that's not what we're here to talk about . . ."

"I mean, it's not like we're being indiscreet about things. We've only done it in my office a few times, and always after hours and with the door closed. My office, which – *by the way* – I'm losing next week for a cubicle anyhow."

I sat there, gawping at her like a fish. I had in no way come to this conversation prepared to talk about staff's romantic entanglements with blomers, or how those entanglements might spread to company property. *Easy does it*, I thought, feeling a new anxiety, a fresh concern, start to boil at the back of my throat. *Easy does it. One problem at a time.*

"Annie, we're here to talk about your work attire," I said.

She perked in the chair. "Oh? Oh! Oh *dear.*" Going flush, she brought a hand to her mouth and turned her head away from me. In that moment, an image flickered behind my eyes, a grotesque visual of this meek, mousy, poorly dressed little woman contorted into a pretzel and gleefully engaging with some fleshy-faced blomer in some activities I had witnessed on my walks to work, and in her *office* no less. Where did they do it? In her chair? On the desk? *Oh God*, I thought. *How revolting.*

"Sweatpants are not appropriate for work," I said, "even on casual Fridays. Now, Annie, I know the firm's dress code policy is a bit buried on the intranet, but you need to go find it and read it in detail."

"Okay . . . okay . . ."

"Blue jeans at a minimum," I went on. "And a nice blouse, or a dress shirt with a collar. Mr. Winnie-the-Pooh needs to stay at home, okay? If your supervisor and manager have pussyfooted around this point, please allow me to be clear. You cannot come to this office dressed as you are today. Okay?"

"Okay."

"Thank you. I know this has been difficult."

She stood to go, but I had one more thing on my mind. "And, Annie, please spread the word – and I can't believe this doesn't go without saying – but people, vips or blomers, should not be having sex at the office."

"Well," she replied, "you may want to write up a policy about that and put *it* on the intranet. A bit too late now, I'd say, to nip it in the bud." Then she gave me a shrug that asked why I, as the HR manager, didn't already know this.

❧

". . . and I realize these changes are hard," I wrapped up. "But please know that this is all to ensure the long-term health of the business. And we really appreciate your co-operation, okay. Any questions? Hmm? No? Okay. Thanks, everybody."

When I finished, the gathered crowd of evicted office dwellers began to disperse, murmuring under their breaths and heading back to the cubicles that had been freshly installed for them. Otis lingered at my side, and when the rest were gone, he turned and gave me a big shrug.

"I'm sorry, brother," I said. "It wasn't my decision."

"I know," he replied. "After all the new hires, I sort of figured this day was inevitable."

"And there are other changes coming. *Worse* changes."

"Yeah, I know."

He and I stared out together over the busy vista of cubicles that now spread across the entire length of this floor. Vips and blomers darted in and out and around the baffle walls, and the air seemed full of an unprecedented din – chatter and phone calls and the relentless clitter of computer keys. At one point, a pigeon came scurrying up to me with a huge stack of legal-length paper in her arms.

"Hector, hi," she said, head bobbing. "Yep, um, are you busy?"

Otis and I gave each other a surreptitious smile. "Not too bad," I replied, turning back to her. "What do you need?"

"Well, this here is a printout of the new process map for the One Life product."

She handed the printout to me, and I took it up in both hands. The bottom end unfurled a bit, and I discovered the pages were all attached, as if someone had composed the document on one giant scroll.

"You'll find next week's head count requests on pages six, eleven, twenty-eight, one thirty-four and two eighteen."

I began flipping. Jesus Murphy. The array of charts, graphs, notes, deadlines, milestones, dependencies and contingencies ranged out over the pages like Egyptian pictograms. Now *this* was a project plan. Who but a pigeon could have devised such a thing? Who but a pigeon could understand it?

"If I could get your feedback and any adjustments you suggest by close of business Monday, that would be ideal," the pigeon said.

"Um, okay," I replied, folding the pages back up.

She gave me three decisive nods, in her pigeon way, and then left, disappearing back into the jungle of cubicles.

"Well, I guess I know what *you're* doing this weekend," Otis smirked.

"God," I said, tucking the project plan under my arm and rolling my eyes.

"Listen, man, it's Friday night. Why don't you grab Morgana after work and join us down at the Cage? Ellen's shift ends at ten and we're going to stick around for drinks. There's a new band playing. Should be good."

By *Cage* he meant the Cajun Cage, a little New Orleans–style grotto up on Markham Street that had live music four or five nights of the week. Otis's wife, Ellen, worked there as a waitress. The two had met in the Cage, years ago, when Otis himself was still a struggling musician and taking gigs there. Now, as a man of insurance, he often went back to the Cage to greet his lady at the end of her workday. He would have a drink, take in a band, reminisce about the good old days.

"Nah, I can't," I said. "I just . . . I have to deal with *this*." And I gestured to the project plan under my arm. "I have to figure it out before the new head counts are due."

"Okay," he replied. "But you work too hard, you know that. This place isn't everything. We haven't seen you guys in a while. Ellen really misses Morgana."

And me too, right? I thought, but then quickly shoved that notion away. Or, if not shoved it away, attached a quick and proper caveat to it. *I mean, we come as a package, right? She misses us both.*

"Yeah, I know," I said with a sigh. "Next week, I promise. We'll come see you guys."

Just then, the elevator doors opened and Brennan Prate emerged into the hallway. I noticed almost immediately a different air about him, a lightness to his heavy step, a newfound confidence to his stare. He approached us and gave a nod. "You boys know where cubicle 6W-4453 is?" We blinked at him, not sure we should assist in whatever shit-disturbing mission he had set for himself. "Some idiot downloaded a virus off a porn site," he clarified, "and I have to unlock their machine so I can wipe the hard drive. Then I'll send them over to you, Hector, for a dressing down."

"The *W* stands for west," I told him, and pointed toward the west end of the floor. "Go four cubicles in, take a left, and it'll be the fifth row on the right."

"Yep," he said, forgetting to thank me as he turned to go.

"Oh, and Brennan," I called after him. "Sorry to hear about your office. We fought really hard for supervisors, but at the end of the day, we just needed the floor space."

"I'm not losing my office," he told me. "Didn't you hear? I've been promoted to manager. I get to keep my office."

My mouth fell open with an audible click. "Well, why would I hear about *that*?" I scoffed. "I'm only the HR manager around here."

He rolled his eyes as if to say, *Another ball you've dropped* and then headed off on his mission.

"Well, this will take some getting used to," I said to Otis. "I've never had to treat Brennan Prate as a peer."

❧

On my way home I stopped, as I often did on Friday nights, at a Pita Pit on Wellesley Street to pick up two chicken shawarma plates to go, our typical end-of-the-week treat. Due to my frequency here, the Middle Eastern woman who worked behind the brightly lit, sneeze-guarded counter, Fatima, knew our topping choices by heart (no rice and extra salad for Morgana – she was forever watching her figure; no onion or hot sauce for me) and didn't need to ask, save for a quick smile and a "The usual tonight, sir?" I suspected that this Pita Pit's busy time, at least prior to pullulation, belonged to the late hours, well after Morgana and I had retired to bed, when the bars and clubs of the gay village let out. Back in those days, I could arrive here after work at six or even six thirty on a Friday and find the joint relatively dead. This allowed me to get served quickly and chat with Fatima as she shaved meat off the glistening poultry on its spit.

No more. Now, even if I got to the Pita Pit by five thirty, the lineups were all the way back to the door, if not out onto the sidewalk. Tonight, I arrived to find the place packed with jostling blomers trying to get served. Over the skyline of their heads, I could see Fatima now orchestrating a team of four young people behind the counter as they dashed from stove to topping bar to cash register over and over, struggling to keep up with orders.

Just as I took my place at the back of the line, I felt my phone rumble in my pocket. I took it out to discover a text from Alanna.

Are you free to talk? Can I call you?

I hesitated, gawking at the line in front of me. *Well, I'm not getting served for a while anyway*, I thought.

Sure thing.

She rang just as I stepped back out into the early evening's still-blazing sun. I plunged a finger into one ear – there was another massive, noisy construction site across the street, the air vandalized with jackhammering and the *beeeeep beeeeep beeeeep* of dump trucks backing up – and brought my phone to the other. "Hey there," I called out.

"Hey, Hector," she replied, her voice deep, almost moist, inside my phone. "So sorry to call you, and on a Friday night." This was another way in which Alanna was old-fashioned: she still used her phone to *call* people, on occasion.

"No worries. I was just grabbing Morgana and me some take-out. What's up?"

She paused for quite a while, to the point where I thought the line had dropped. "Alanna?"

"We lost the baby," she told me.

I'd heard her perfectly well, and yet, in that rabbit punch of shock, acted like I didn't. "Come again?"

"Hector," she said, my name so heavy, so distant on her lips. "I just wanted to let you know that, unfortunately, Mitch and I lost the baby last week."

"Oh, Alanna," I replied, bringing my hand briefly to my mouth. "Oh, sweetie, I'm so sorry to hear that. Jesus."

How far along had she been? *Pretty far*, I thought. That brunch had been in May, it was now July, and they would've waited at least three months to tell us. Jesus. It must have been a particularly brutal miscarriage this time. A late second-trimester miscarriage.

"Yeah, thanks," she said, her voice like a plucked guitar string as she tried to keep it under control. "We thought we were far enough along to start telling people, but . . . I guess not."

"That's just terrible," I said, and meant it. As freakish and in-explicable as her desire to have children was, I had found myself empathizing with it, rooting for it, especially after she had asked for us to be godparents. I thought, *What would a child – a child – bring to a life like ours?* I was so staid, so safe, so *boring*; Morgana, in turn, was the ultimate social butterfly. Surely a child would have disrupted that equilibrium. A child was engineered to mess up what we, like hundreds of millions of other couples across the planet, had chosen to embrace – a life of pristine self-focus and predictability. But would I have loved it? Would I have loved that child despite all the disorder it brought to my life? Or maybe *because* of it? And I would look at it and think: *You came from Alanna. I love you because . . . because you came from Alanna.*

Whoa. *Whoa.* What the fuck? I tamped *those* thoughts down

before they had a chance to seep up to the surface.

"Hector, you still there?"

"I'm sorry," I said. "I'm sorry," I said again. "I, I know how much you guys were looking forward to having a second kid."

She kind of scoffed. "Yeah, we were – strange as it sounds in this day and age. It would've made us quite the weirdos, eh?"

"Alanna –"

"But at least you're off the hook now for being little fetus's godparents. I know you guys had waffled about that."

"We would've done it," I told her. "We considered it an honour that you even asked."

I could practically hear her shrug on the line. "Well, it doesn't matter," she said. "A moot point now."

"Alanna, I'm so incredibly sorry."

"Yeah, thanks." She took in a big inhale of breath. "Anyway. Look, I'm also calling to ask your advice about something."

"Oh?"

"Yep." She paused again. "So, a developer made an offer on our land," she began. "One-eight-seven for the whole parcel, including the house. It's roughly what he offered each of our neighbours for their places, which have already sold. The condo towers are going up as we speak."

"Really? Way out there? Wow. So, what are you going to do?"

"We're going to take him up on it, of course," she replied. "But we're also thinking about doing something else – something you've said we should've done ages ago. We're thinking about moving into the city."

"Oh? Oh, wow."

"Yep. Mitch has gotten all these offers for welding gigs in town, and I can transfer my post office job pretty easily, too." We discussed the particulars: one-eight-seven would only get them a mid-size unit in some midtown high-rise now, as housing prices in the city had exploded through the summer – all those blomers competing for a place to live.

"Surely Mitch could get a welding job out there?" I said. "Be cheaper to live, wouldn't it?"

"Of course it would. And as you well know, we've never considered moving into town before. We're both born and raised in Hope Mountain and always said we'd stay country folk come hell or high water. But now . . . with the loss of this baby, I think . . . I just think I need a change, you know? We need to shake things up. So, I wanted to ask you: Do you think it's a good idea?"

"I think it's a great idea," I replied, and meant *that* too. I found myself growing suddenly eager at the thought of having her – sorry, *them* – closer. Morgana had been right: It was vital, during these harrowing, transformational times, to have as many true friends around as possible. "This may be just what you need. There are jobs aplenty down here now, Alanna, and good schools for Isaac. Morgana and I will do whatever you need to help you adjust. This could be a very positive thing."

"We'd be city slickers," she mused. "Imagine that."

I gave a shrug. "The way the world is going, Alanna, *everybody*'s going to be a city slicker soon."

Not surprisingly, this offered her zero comfort.

CHAPTER 5

I sat at our dining room table, hunched over my work laptop, staring into a spreadsheet that seemed to go on forever. Scrolling through its cells felt almost hypnotic, as if I were being seduced by its lists and lists of names, hundreds of them, blomers who had joined the Percussive Insurance family over the last three months. I thought: *Who names a blomer? Have they explained that to us yet?* Probably it was some government official (most likely a blomer him- or herself, now) sitting behind a desk set up in a gymnasium somewhere, assigning monikers to scores of eagles, dogs, sparrows, cats and cows who came huddled, hungry and desperate, each looking for his or her own small slice in the new order that pullulation had spawned. We vips had created this accident, had caused it to happen through the widespread greed of our childlessness, and we owed it to these newcomers, these blomers that we had made, to welcome and integrate them into society. It was the least we could do. And besides, people were getting rich! Brennan Prate had nailed it. The blomers, by their sheer volume, were creating unprecedented demand. For the first time in decades, the economy was not in the toilet. Unemployment was down; new business opportunities unfurled practically overnight. The New York Stock Exchange, the Toronto Stock Exchange, the Nikkei – all through the roof!

I almost wanted to tell the Christians and the right-wing parent groups and other whack jobs: *This* is why more people aren't joining your protests against public orgies. As jarring as they seem to the vip sensibility, most people are willing to ignore them, to look the other way, because blomers are making everybody loaded! Money talks and your old-world morality walks, apparently.

As I worked, Morgana moved through the living room in long, dramatic strides, back and forth, back and forth. Her hands were on her hips and she kicked out her legs, tossing them into the air, one after the other. "And *tu* and *vous* and *moo* and *goo!*" she sang with each upward thrust of her foot.

Percussive Insurance had hired so many blomers. There had been an almost random approach to assigning them to departments and divisions of the company. It became my job to figure out a more logical, more strategic way of arranging them. My eyes began to hurt as I clicked on the dozens of tabs in the spreadsheet and moved blocks of names around via cut-and-paste, trying to devise an organizational chart that made sense.

"And *shoe* and *boo* and *stew* and *Jew!*"

"Um, Morgana, sweetie," I called over, "what are you doing?"

"Oh, sorry, Hector. Was I being annoying?"

"Well, no, but . . . well . . ."

She gave me a big, toothy smile, then Rockette-kicked her way over to me. "I'm. Getting. Ready," she said. "For. My. Audition."

"Audition?" I asked. "Wait, I thought you already had a role in that play. Weren't you going to be the music assistant?"

"Well, here's the thing about that," she replied, and plopped herself into the chair across from me. "I've wanted to talk to you about it for a while now, but you've been pulling such long hours at work, I haven't had a chance." This was true. My days at the office had begun spiralling out of control: some mornings I left before Morgana was even awake; some nights I came home too late to even eat dinner with her. "Anyway. Carolina told me this week that she thinks my talents are wasted as the music assistant.

She said I'm a really good actor and that I could hold my own with these super-talented crows who've been auditioning for parts in the play." Carolina was the intrepid, innovative director of *Harpies: The Musical!* and now, it seemed, Morgana's new best friend. While she had decided to retain the show's core premise, Carolina was expanding the cast, music and complexity of the production itself. Morgana returned from those early rehearsals to report that the play's dramatis personae had grown from fifteen to fifty, mostly due to the exceptional batch of blomers – specifically crows – who had lined up to get involved. This did not surprise us. Crows, as extraordinarily capable actors, had begun cropping up on the television now, appearing in sitcoms and police procedural dramas.

"That's, that's *great*," I said.

Morgana turned then to pluck a sucker out of the candy dish we kept on a shelf near the table. She fiddled with its cellophane wrapper but did not pull it off. "She wants me to audition for a new part she's created: Titania, who leads a group of harpies on an overnight raid of an Athenian platoon on the road to Sparta. There'll be a whole song-and-dance number where we convince the boys that fucking is way more fun than fighting." She twirled the sucker then, like a parasol.

"Wait . . . sorry . . . *what* kind of scene is this?" I asked.

"Oh, it's going to be great," Morgana exclaimed, and abruptly climbed back to her feet. "It's going to have kicks," and she kicked, her knee nearly reaching her forehead, "and shimmies," and she shimmied her rump at me, "and twirls, and a song with a rhyme scheme where the lines all end in the *ooo* sound." She strutted around in front of me. "'Come on, boys, don't be bluuue. Put down your spears. I wanna dooooo yooooou!'" And here, she ripped the cellophane off the top of the sucker.

I wondered, then, about the expression on my face, because whatever it conveyed had caused Morgana to stop in her tracks. As dull and awful as the Excel spreadsheet before me was, I had a sudden urge to disappear back into its tedium, to shield myself from the growing discomfort I felt. Morgana, of course, would have none of it. She wanted my eyes on her then; she wanted nothing less than the full measure of my attention. *She's such an exhibitionist*, I thought. *Everything is a performance for her, even the making of a basic domestic point.* I shouldn't have been surprised that she'd become so enamoured of a play like *Harpies: The Musical!* Did it not tap the deepest reservoirs of her personality, that unbridled extroversion? It was a proxy fantasy. The blomers had given her something to live vicariously through.

"Hector, don't *worry*," she said, and returned once more to her seat at the table. "I know what you're thinking. You're thinking this play is going to be silly, or even offensive to people. But it's not like that. Blomers are changing society's views on sex with all their openness. The show's supposed to be fun. It *is* going to be fun. And besides, it's quickly becoming everything I ever wanted to be a part of back in school."

"I, I understand that."

"I mean, you know me. I've always doubted whether I had the chops to be right in the thick of the action rather than working backstage or in the orchestra pit. This is my chance to live a little bit of the life I didn't get to have."

These words rang true to me. Yes, there *was* always something of the performer in Morgana. She loved to be watched. She loved to be the focus. I supposed that was why teaching had become a tolerable surrogate for the career she couldn't have. But those words also rang true because, of course, they were *my* truth as well. I found my thoughts once again turning to my past as a child actor and how much I had wanted to succeed in that. I thought of how Morgana's own theatrical ambitions had captivated me when we first met during our B.Ed. days. And I thought of my own desires back then, to become a teacher myself, to be given a chance, just a chance, to live that dream. It was important to take your chance if you got one. I knew that. I knew that.

"No, totally," I said. "And I want to support you. I do."

"Good," she replied. "Now. Should I start dinner? How much work do you have left to do?"

I turned back to the spreadsheet. God. I could feel my brain go numb at the prospect of dealing with all these cells, all these names, the salary calculations and org chart balances. It felt as if they could go on forever, spinning off into infinity and taking me with them.

"Give me an hour," I said with a sigh.

She leaned in to squeeze my shoulder and kiss my neck. "My man," she said, and then got up to head to the kitchen.

"One more thing, Morgana," I called after her, and she spun back to me on her heels. "About the musical. I meant to ask this before. These scenes Carolina is writing. We're, we're talking about *simulated* sex, right?"

But she only slid the sucker between her full, meaty lips and threw another of those smiles at me, her eyes sparkling.

❧

Despite this insane surge in my workload, I had somehow found the time to engage in an activity that I'd scarcely made room for in my life prior to pullulation. I was reading more. I was reading *a lot*. That night at book club back in April, the night of the catastrophe in New York, the night that I finally dragged myself back behind the wheel after my own accident, had triggered something in my mind. It felt counterintuitive, but during these crazy, harried days of summer, I felt myself drawn to reading novels whenever I had a chance. I found snippets of time for them in the late evening hours, when my workday was finally done but before Morgana came home from rehearsal. Or I found a few scant minutes at lunch while I quickly shovelled a takeout salad down my gullet with a plastic fork. Or I read voraciously in those early morning hours when troubled dreams stunned me awake before my alarm did and I could not return to sleep.

I was drawn not just to any novels but to postapocalyptic or dystopian tomes along the same vein as *The Children of Men*. I had inhaled the ethereal nightmares of *The Drowned World* and *Crash*. I had marathoned through *The Stand*. I had read *The Handmaid's Tale* for its political intrigue; I had just finished the spare terror that was *The Road*. And I was now beginning a bizarre novel about overpopulation called *The Wanting Seed*. These works, more than all the profiles of blomers in magazines and all the coverage on the twenty-four-hour news channels, helped shine a lantern down the convoluted corridors of that first summer after pullulation.

The blomers *were* changing our society, there was no doubt about that now. It wasn't just the way we had all normalized their (very) public acts of carnality. Nor was it the ubiquitous sight of their exaggerated features we'd spot on every street corner and in every subway car, the broad brows and bad teeth, the thick, fleshy hands that reached out for ours in rehearsed politeness. It wasn't just the hawks who had penetrated the upper echelons of the businesses that ran our lives, or the crows we watched every night on TV, or the dogs who filled our skylines (and, now, our suburbs and farm fields) with condo and office towers. No. Changes in *mentality* were everywhere, too. We vips could not escape them. We could not flee from their designs for us, the way they seemed to erupt out of the very ground we walked on. Every headline in the paper or on the web jolted us in shock. Every minute of CNN felt like it introduced a new fresh hell.

Example: A movement emerged a few weeks ago, a trend that the media had dubbed *meat shaming*. It was true that nearly two-thirds of the world's cows and chickens had been transmogrified into blomers during pullulation, and the rest had left their concomitant meats a scarce item on supermarket shelves and in restaurants. Now, if you wanted a steak or a chicken pot pie, or even a hamburger, it would cost you a pretty penny. But it would cost you in another way, too. If you ordered the meatloaf or poulet cordon bleu in a restaurant, you had best sit as far away from the windows as you could. Why? Because the sidewalk out front would no doubt hold a rabid band of protesters – cows off duty from their jobs as linguists or detectives; chickens off duty from their roles as admin assistants – pumping placards and chanting slogans against your act of cannibalism. So many vips, it seemed, had gone vegetarian now, for both economic and conscientious reasons, on a scale that environmentalists and animal rights activists couldn't have dreamed of a decade ago. The irony was that even this had strained the food supply, since so much of the world's farmland was now being urbanized. Pundits began labelling this development as neo-Malthusian – meaning pullulation had generated blomers far faster than we could figure out a way to feed them all.

Other issues loomed in the culture. In bed, Morgana and I watched the late news in horror as journalists reported a new idea developing in America's southern states – or, more accurately, a very old idea *re*developing. We couldn't believe the chyrons that flashed across the screen night after night: Blomer Slavery – Good Idea or Not? It was a concept seriously discussed in the state legislatures and town halls south of the Mason-Dixon Line, and on Fox News. Some argued that by letting the southern states scratch their human property itch, it might actually ease tensions with all the Blacks and Hispanics down there. "Well, if you've *got* to subjugate somebody," Morgana said with a sarcastic roll of her eyes. Meanwhile, much of Europe had gone in the opposite direction. Some blomers – mostly hawks, cows and cats – had begun running for public office over there, which, of course, created its own cultural stress.

But there was something else far more localized, something so horrific I could barely mention it inside my own thoughts. It was something borne but also hidden by the crowds that choked the streets on my walks to and from work, something that so many of us who clogged these sidewalks chose to ignore. Violent words, violent acts seemed to loom in the atmosphere, in the rangy spaces just beyond our peripheral vision. A scream, the thud of flesh striking flesh, a body slapping to the ground, skin breaking on asphalt. I'd turn my head but the carnage would already be over, already hidden, swallowed up by the scores of people, vips *and* blomers, hustling to their destinations, stooping to tie shoes, pausing to stare at the sky. I'd step over three eagles fucking on the sidewalk – two hunky guys spit-roasting some insatiable young woman there in the grit – and from the alley behind them, someone would scream out in terror. I'd turn. But again, the savagery would end before I could even glimpse it.

༄

When Otis came by today for our ten thirty coffee break, he had the strangest song on his lips. He belted it out over the hubbub of ringing phones and clicking computer keys as he approached my door. It had been a while since he'd reminded me what a lovely singing voice he had.

> *"Man oh man, there's a traffic jam*
> *from here to Louisiana.*
> *It stretches for klicks and traps all the chicks,*
> *including my girl, Pollyanna."*

The tune's melody bobbed and swung like a hypnotist's pendulum through this short snatch of lyric, and I felt myself drawn to it, to its queer insistence that there were other worlds than the one I lived in, worlds that churned below the surface of everything I knew. Otis sat in the chair in front of my desk and handed me my coffee. I raised the cup to my lips and sipped, the caffeine igniting behind my eyes. I'd already been at the office for nearly four hours.

Otis continued his carolling from the chair:

> *"Sing me a song about all that went wrong*
> *and I promise you I will come clean*

and confess my sins over the engine's din
long before we reach New Orleeeeeans."

I gave him a little applause, then asked, "What is that tune? I've never heard it before."

He smiled at me. "Well, that's because you and Morgana still haven't come down to the Cajun Cage yet – *like you promised."* He leaned back. "Dude, this song is huge. There's a blomer band that's been singing it for weeks down there. They're called Thursday Banana, and they're all the rage. Ellen is absolutely in love with them. You and Morgana really need to come check them out."

"I know, I know," I said, and sighed. "It's, it's just an issue of time and energy."

"Yeah, yeah," he said back with a smirk. "Time and energy."

I looked him over. "You seem in a particularly good mood today. I heard you finally nailed the Pro Forma Bandit. Is that what's put this spring in your step?"

He made a little farting noise with his mouth. "Oh, please. To call that guy a bandit is to insult *actual* bandits." He shifted in the chair and sipped his own coffee. "I mean, if you're going to commit insurance fraud on a series of overseas bank accounts, you may want to consider that the World Wide Web means the *World* Wide Web. Anyone with an Internet connection could have caught that asshole."

"Except not just anyone caught him. You did. Nice work."

"Thanks, brother," he said, pride brimming in his expression. "Anyway, I'm getting duly rewarded. As of next week, I'm a supervisor. *Finally."*

"Hey, that's great," I said. "Well deserved. Too bad it won't mean getting your own office again."

He shrugged and rolled his eyes. There was a brief but pregnant lull between us, and he may have caught the hint of sadness, of anxiety, that flickered across my face. "What about you?" he asked. "You've been putting in killer hours all summer. Where's *your* promotion?"

"I have no idea," I replied, and meant it. "I swear I've had my head down for so long I don't even know if people are paying attention to how hard I'm wor–"

Just as I said this, a meeting invitation from the company's director of operations landed in my inbox. I caught its arrival out of the corner of my eye and turned to glance at it. Its subject line read:

PROMOTION.

I snorted. "You're not going to believe this," I said, and swivelled the screen so Otis could see it.

Leaning in, he read the subject line and chuckled. "Well, look at that. Promotions for everyone!"

I moved the screen back and opened the invitation. Sure enough, it was summoning me to a meeting later that afternoon in the director's office, where we would discuss his proposed mid-year elevation of me to the role of associate director of human resources. As I silently read the accompanying note and accepted the meeting invitation, Otis began to hum the song he'd been singing when he arrived. By the time I turned my now-smiling face back to him, he was once again serenading me:

"Man oh man, there's a traffic jam
from here to Louisiana.
It stretches for klicks and traps all the chicks,
including my girl, Pollyanna."

When he finished, he said, "Now there's no excuse. Call your wife. Tell her you've gotten a promotion and you're joining Ellen and me down at the Cage tonight to celebrate. No discussion. No excuses. Deal?"

"Deal."

With that, he got up to go, the rest of the song sailing from his mouth as he headed back down the hall:

"Sing me a song about all that went wrong
and I promise you I will come clean

and confess my sins over the engine's din
long before we reach New Orleeeeeans."

❧

"So, sorry . . . how much of a raise?

I told her.

"Whoa," she said. "Just . . . whoa."

Having returned from the meeting with the director, I sat back in my office chair, my door closed in front of me. I moved the phone from one ear to the other. "So, Otis wants us to come down to the Cage tonight to celebrate," I said. "What do you think?"

While I waited for her to answer, I ruminated then on what this new money would mean. Like most vips, Morgana and I had experienced a breathtaking spike in our cost of living recently: our condo fees had tripled since pullulation; our grocery bill had doubled; gas, insurance, our phones, even our parking space had all gone through the roof. My new salary would, at least for the time being, help shelter us from the inflationary trauma that was unfolding everywhere.

"Well, I am kind of tired tonight," Morgana said. "These rehearsals are just kicking my ass. Carolina is really driving us hard." She had landed the role of Titania in *Harpies: The Musical!* and had begun putting in long hours at the theatre. She was, in fact, there right now.

"We won't stay long," I assured her.

"Well, okay. If we don't stay long. I'm supposed to be done here at seven, but you know how it is – things may go longer. If I'm late, will you save me a seat?"

"Of course," I said. "Thanks, Morgana. This'll be fun."

"Okay."

"Anyway, I love you."

"Ooh, ooh, they're calling my scene! I gotta go. Love you, too!"

And then she was gone.

❧

The lineup to get into the Cajun Cage stretched northward for half a block up Markham Street. Otis and I took our tense, anxious place in it, even as he conspired with Ellen via text messages to help us jump the queue. We had been standing there for about ten minutes when she finally confirmed that she'd have a table ready for us in another ten minutes. Meanwhile, I monitored my own phone to track Morgana's movements through the subway system as she came to meet us. The late summer evening loomed hot and muggy, the air feeling dense with pollution and distant construction noises. The line shuffled forward a couple of paces, and the people in it – vips and blomers – jostled a bit to maintain their place. Thursday Banana, Otis had informed me, was a kind of neo-calypso rock band that had developed a devout following in just a few short weeks. Lineups like this one were now a common occurrence outside the club, even on weeknights. The Cage was a kind of lounge/restaurant on the ground floor of a low-rise hotel; and now, four and a half months after pullulation, it had expanded to offer live music pretty much from noon to close – three or four bands playing three or four sets each over the course of the day – seven days a week. You couldn't buy a ticket to get into the Cage. You just had to line up and wait through the normal churn of the restaurant. Tonight, we had already missed the first of Thursday Banana's three sets.

I turned back to look at the line as it enlarged behind us, hoping once more to glimpse Morgana headed this way. Instead, I watched as a tall, hulking fox and a pretty, young sparrow asked their friends to hold their place, then stepped out of the line, moved over to a patch of grass beyond the bollards of the adjacent property, stripped off their clothes and contorted themselves into an elaborate sixty-nine on the ground. I sighed and looked away, moving my gaze up to the Cage's entrance, hoping that Ellen would grace this sidewalk with her presence sooner as opposed to later. Otis's head, meanwhile, was still bowed over his phone, presumably waiting for another missive from her.

I was just about to look at my watch for the tenth time when I felt an arm slip lovingly up under mine.

"Hey there!"

"Oh, hey, you made it."

We kissed. Morgana's curly hair, I noticed, was pulled into a bun away from her face and looked damp, as if she had recently climbed out of the shower.

No sooner had she and Otis greeted each other than Ellen came bounding up the sidewalk toward us. She was dressed in her typical Cajun Cage attire: black, form-fitting miniskirt that ended a third of the way down her thighs and the equally black, deep-plunging top that offered an ample gawk at her soft, tip-earning cleavage. Her honey-brown hair fell in two waves on either side of her tight yet gentle face, and where they met near her chin sat her lipsticked mouth like a lush, wet rose in half bloom. I thought now as I often did, even as a happily married man, that Ellen was the most attractive woman that any of us knew personally. In fact, I would never say this aloud to Morgana, lest I hurt her feelings, but if Ellen were any more striking, she would have to be on television. It was just that simple. Seeing her stand next to prim, lanky Otis, with his goofy face and goofier sense of humour, his big, horsey teeth, you would've never guessed, not in a million years, that the two of them were together. I mean, I loved the guy dearly, but every time I saw them, it made me think that he had won some kind of bizarro-world lottery by getting her to marry him. I think most men they socialized with felt the same way.

Indeed, Ellen offered Otis no kiss or touch when she arrived. Instead, she just made a commanding gesture with her hand and said, "Okay, guys, follow me. Quick-quick-quick."

The queue gave a grunt of disapproval as we cut ahead and darted toward the doors.

Inside, the Cajun Cage felt like a steamy, crowded oven. The sunken dining room in front of the stage was packed with revellers, but Ellen managed to park us at a small, round table for three at the rail overlooking it, near the bar. "Oh, sweetie, there's no room for *you*," Morgana said to her, but Ellen was already frantically placing menus in front of us before saying, "Okay, I gotta go. I'll try to catch up with you guys when I'm finished in an hour." And then she dashed away, sliding like a knife through the thickets of people waiting for Thursday Banana's second set to begin. Otis, I noticed, had raised his face to her, as if in hope that she would double back and kiss him, but then retracted it when she didn't.

Our own waitress eventually came to take our orders. We asked for a round of margaritas and a large plate of nachos to share. "They're vegetarian only," she told us. "No chicken or beef, obviously." Obviously. She jotted all this down in her little pad and then was off again. The tension in the room climbed. This break between sets, it seemed, was lasting longer than the band had promised. Otis was craning his neck over the crowd in half-interest as Morgana began detailing aspects of that day's rehearsal to me, the music she had to learn by next week and the talented group (murder?) of crows helping her to fully embody the role of Titania. As I listened, I caught sight of Ellen at the far side of the dining room, near the stage. She stood at a table of seven, though not really there, it appeared, to take their orders. She clasped her pencil and pad casually in one hand at her hip, her elbows out, her head tilted. Someone at the table must have cracked a joke because I watched then as Ellen threw her honeyed hair back between her shoulder blades and laughed uproariously. It wasn't a fake waitress laugh. It was a real laugh, a laugh brimming with familiarity. Soon after, someone at the table leaned in to ask everyone else a question. Heads nodded, one after the other. Then, the seven of them rose in unison and began to march single file toward the stairs that led up to the stage.

Ah, I thought. *Ellen is on a first-name basis with the band itself.*

Applause pealed through the room like ocean waves crashing. The cheers and hoots persisted, grew louder, as the members of Thursday Banana manoeuvred themselves into place and took up their instruments. Otis, having risen to his feet, hooked four fingers into his mouth and gave a shrill, modulating whistle. He sat back down and grinned at us. "This is going to be *great*," he said.

And, truth be told, it was great. Thursday Banana certainly knew what they were doing. One song in and I was hooked, hypnotized, grooving along and wondering how these seven blomers, living as bears in the woods beyond our city just a season ago, had become such masters of music. Morgana laced her fingers into mine and leaned her head on my shoulder. The music was so good that we barely noticed when our waitress dropped off our drinks and nachos. We noshed away absently as the songs swept us up – sweaty, blistering numbers that filled the room with a frenzied energy.

The band paused briefly to thank everyone for coming out before launching into the opening riff of their next song. It appeared as if everyone in the room knew it except me, as everyone was climbing to their feet and screaming maniacally. I narrowed my eyes, trying to find a level of acquaintance with the tune, and thought I sensed something in it, something I had in fact heard before. It was just dawning on me when the lead singer stepped up to the mic and thrummed out the opening lyrics:

"Man oh man, there's a traffic jam
from here to Louisiana.
It stretches for klicks and traps all the chicks,
including my girl, Pollyanna.

"Sing me a song about all that went wrong
and I promise you I will come clean
and confess my sins over the engine's din
long before we reach New Orleeeeeans."

The room boomed this out, a thrust of sound that seemed to coalesce in one direction, right to the core of the lead singer's microphone. He welcomed that energy, that solidarity, with nothing more than a happy contortion of his bear's face. He bobbed and weaved like a boxer around the microphone stand between verses, his fingers digging and dancing on the neck of his guitar. The two trombonists behind him blared out sharply, their slides swinging and swaying in unison. The audience became like a political rally as the tune down-geared into a lengthy call-and-response bridge. I didn't know the words, as we were now far beyond the smattering of lyrics that Otis had brought with a swagger into my office. But I seemed to be the only one who didn't. Everyone else chanted exactly the same thing in exactly the same way at the lead singer's bidding.

Including Morgana. I looked over at her. She was right there in the thick of it, belting out these lines as if she had been singing them since childhood. I blinked at her for a moment before nudging her shoulder.

"You know this song?" I yelled over the music as she reluctantly turned her attention away from the stage.

Her smile was huge – all bright-white teeth and broad lips stretched taut across her face. At some point, she had released her hair from its bun without me noticing, and it now sprang outward like a frizzy halo around her head.

"Of course!" she yelled back. "Hector, everyone knows this song. It's all Radio Two and Indie88 and the Edge are playing. Where have *you* been, under a rock?"

A flash of hurt must have crossed my face at that because she gave a little pout of faux contrition and then kissed me fully, wildly, lustily on the mouth, her cocoa eyes intent upon mine before returning her attention to the band. But this did not help. In fact, it made it worse. I suddenly felt very alone in that room, like a stranger. Where *had* I been? *Did* I live under a rock? How could a song so catchy and simple enter the collective consciousness without me noticing? The very thought soaked me in dismay.

The tune ended then to wild cheers, and Thursday Banana took its second break. Otis and Morgana returned their attention to the table, to their drinks, to me. It was like they were emerging out of some wonderful trance. It didn't take long, however, for Otis's look of longing to return, and he once more began scanning the room. His neck craned over the crowd; his shoulders tightened with a perceptible anxiousness.

And then we *all* glimpsed her, sidling with elegance through the dense throng of people, her delicate elbows up, her face tender yet determined as she navigated around the groups of oblivious bros who bumped and jostled her.

"Welcome back," I said when she finally arrived at our table.

"Thanks," she replied, and eyed our demolished plate of nachos and diminished margaritas. "Do you guys want anything else? I'm about to punch out but I can put in an ord–"

Before she could finish, Otis leaned forward on his stool and swept his arms around her, letting out a jovial, almost drunken "Heyyyy there!" as he made to pull her onto his knee. She resisted him at first – I saw it, plain as day – but then relented, finding her spot on his lap as if it were the most familiar place in the world. She draped her arms absently around his skinny shoulders, and he kissed her on the neck, just above her exposed collarbones.

"They were *wonderful*," he said, and nodded at the stage.

"Yes, just wonderful," Morgana concurred.

And Ellen turned then with her own glance of yearning – not to the now-empty platform where the band had played, but to the table nearby where they had resumed sitting and were now engaged in another animated discussion.

She turned back to us then, and her eyebrows did a little dance. "You're damn right," she said with an intimacy I could not peg.

PART 2:
HERMS

CHAPTER 6

"Forty-*five*," Morgana said, incensed.

"Forty-*five*?" I asked. "Jesus. Jesus Murphy."

Early September. My wife had just returned to work after the summer break, and we were discussing her new class size. Yes, forty-five students. It couldn't be helped. There was runoff from the education farms and every teacher in the province had to pitch in. The exigencies of pullulation had overridden all manner of pedagogical sense, not to mention union rules. This number would have been harrowing enough, shocking enough, except Morgana had an additional problem. *Harpies: The Musical!* had not yet been staged. Carolina kept delaying its debut as she added more and more scenes, more and more cast members. The production had grown by twelve blomers over the Labour Day weekend alone. With no end to the rehearsals in sight, Morgana dreaded the idea of balancing them with all the extra work she'd have to do with this now grotesquely oversized class.

Forty-five students, I thought. *Fucking Christ.*

"What are you going to do?" I asked her.

❧

Mid-September. Morgana was practically in tears. She hadn't anticipated what forty-five students in a class designed for twelve would actually mean. These blomers sat at desks that were more like bunk beds, stacked three high to the ceiling and with a little climbing rail on each to get to the top tiers. She suspected the students at the back couldn't even see her whiteboard, not that it really mattered. Her duties of teaching actual music to vips had been relegated to the last period of the day. For the rest of her time, Morgana churned out lessons on reading, writing, arithmetic and social mores to a new cohort of blomers who passed through her room every two or three days. The fact that they were all startlingly quick studies offered her no solace. This was assembly-line education, plain and simple. What's more, all the extracurricular activities that had made the job tenable – the recitals, the concerts, the triple-threat showcases – had been cancelled. Now, she had no creative outlet at all, at least at work. What's *more*, she barely saw her colleagues-cum-friends anymore: they were all working the same insane teaching schedule and had zero time to socialize. There was also an entire crew of new teachers at the school, and Morgana didn't know them at all. Which, Morgana being Morgana, she just couldn't abide.

～

Third week of September. My wife was not practically in tears now; she was *literally* in tears. She refused to quit *Harpies: The Musical!*, absolutely refused to, despite the fatigue that had swallowed her whole over the last fortnight. We hardly ever saw each other now: she rose at 4:00 a.m. to do all of her prep work and grading before dawn. Then it was nine full hours at the school (the teaching day had been extended) before coming home for a quick supper and then back out to Theatre 647's rehearsal space. During the weekends, Morgana could be back there for as many as twelve hours at a stretch. I was putting in long days, too – arriving at the office early, leaving late, working through lunch, taking part in evening conference calls from home while I folded laundry or did the dishes. We both knew that this was not sustainable.

"I just can't . . ." she wept one night in bed, late, well after both of us should've been asleep. "Hector, I just, I mean . . . I love the play so much. And I'm *good* at it. I can't . . . I mean, I just . . . I *can't.*"

I set aside my paperback – another harrowing postapocalyptic doorstopper – and turned to stroke her hair and kiss her brow, fighting against the gravity of my own exhaustion to provide the comfort she so desperately needed. "What do you want to do?" I asked with a supportive, dulcet lilt to my voice. "Morgana, sweetie, what do you want to do?"

❧

Early October. She floated her idea past me for the first time. I couldn't say I was surprised to hear it finally vocalized, the suggestion that had been brewing beneath the surface of our conversations for a while now.

"What if I . . ." she began after another intense crying jag, this one during a brief, harried dinner at home. "What if I just . . . quit?"

"The play, you mean?" I said, feigning ignorance as I spooled some linguine alfredo onto my fork. "But, sweetie, you love the play."

"No, not the play," she replied. And then she looked up at me with those eyes. Those eyes that said: *You know, I never really liked teaching that much anyway.*

❧

Mid-October. We did up a budget – something we had never done before in our marriage. The pay raise from my promotion had long kicked in and it was clear that, despite the cost of living increases that had come in the wake of pullation, we were still very much to the good. Plus, in an act of impeccable timing, an independent contractor had come by to offer us one-five-eight (take *that*, Terry and Agnes!) to convert our condo's spare bedroom – a chamber we used for exactly nothing – into a bachelor unit. This cinched the deal.

"Are you sure?" Morgana asked me when I agreed to what she proposed.

I nodded and squeezed her hand lovingly. "No, this will be good, this will be good," I assured her. "You deserve to live your dream. You do." And I believed it, believed it in my bones. I knew what it was like to have a dream. I'd been a child actor. I could well remember the allure of the stage. And I myself had dreamed of being a teacher, back when teaching was still a real profession, and knew what it felt like to have a desire, a sense of self, slip through your fingers. I wanted to spare my wife that feeling.

"Oh, thank you, Hector!" she exclaimed, throwing her arms around my neck. "And really, this may be only temporary. Carolina says with the way the play is growing, we may actually take it on the road after its run here and make some real money."

"For sure," I said. The cast of *Harpies: The Musical!* had grown by another ten people in the last month. It was, apparently, becoming quite the production.

"And even if we don't," she went on, "it may very well open doors for me toward a paying gig."

"That's true," I said. "You *are* very talented." Though, to be fair, I had yet to see her acting in action to know whether she had any chance of competing with all the crows and bears who were taking the showbiz world by storm. "This will be good," I continued. "This will be great."

And she hugged me again, cooing with satisfaction.

❧

After the hiring blitz had calmed down somewhat, Percussive Insurance announced that it wanted to throw a massive party to celebrate its growth and welcome new staff. I was not part of the social committee that organized the event, but several of my new underlings were, and I watched as they dashed off to near-daily planning meetings that occurred in one of the now-truncated meeting rooms on the fourth floor. What's more, I got wind that the chair of this committee was none other than Brennan Prate, which struck me as ludicrous considering he was as socially inept as I was. Whatever his merry band of minions was planning, it was huge. I would often run into Marni Jenkins, our director of finance, in the lunchroom, and she would allude to the parade of acquisition requests and expense forms from the committee that was constantly crossing her desk for signature. Whenever I asked for more detail, she just gave me a schoolmarmish roll of her eyes.

Truth be told, Morgana and I usually enjoyed the parties that the company threw. They always occurred during the lead-up to the holiday season and, back when Percussive Insurance had just two hundred staff, were hosted at the King Edward Hotel downtown. It was a tasteful evening, very classy, very much our speed. We would arrive in our semi-formal wear and join colleagues in the dark, well-heeled hotel bar for cocktails. Then, at the appropriate hour, we got shepherded into an elegantly decorated conference room adorned with round tables with white tablecloths and centrepieces that managed to be both elaborate and anodyne. The light was dim and warm. The music was usually classical or, if we were feeling rambunctious, jazz. Dinner was served by anonymous wait staff in white collared tops and black pants. The food was sumptuous and not too filling. Wine bottles – one white, one red – were brought to the table and discreetly replaced when empty. After the dessert course, there might be waltzing on the makeshift dance floor. Morgana and I stayed for this part of the evening for only a short time before taxi-chitting it home, curled up in the back seat and feeling grateful for having such a lovely night out.

But as information about this new, ad hoc, one-off soiree began trickling in, I knew something was afoot. First off, it would not be held inside the cozy old-world confines of the King Eddie, but rather down in the large, loud, gaudy, glass-and-steel eyesore of the corporate convention centre on the lake. (This, I conceded, made sense, considering our staff numbers had swelled so volu-minously since pullulation as to have outgrown our usual venue.) Second, the evening was going to have, the e-vite that eventually came around informed us, a theme. I grumbled at this. Why does a party need a theme? The "theme" for this party was Fire and Ice. I didn't know what that could possibly mean, but I nonetheless frowned at the thought of it. Third, the e-vite had designated the dress code for the evening as casual, and I shuddered to think how the gaggles of blomers now on staff (to say nothing of little Pooh-loving Annie down in Accounts Payable) would interpret such a directive. Indeed, one of my favourite aspects of the annual party was getting dolled up in semi-formal wear, since Morgana and I had so few opportunities to do so throughout the rest of the year. I felt scored by disappointment at the thought that we'd be reduced to blue jeans for this event.

And then, to make matters far, far worse, Brennan Prate stopped by my office to ask if I would like a role in the skit they were planning for the party.

"A skit?" I asked. "What do you mean by *skit*?"

"We're putting on a skit," he told me. "The blomers on the planning committee want to do it. A little play," he said, "to thank the C-suite for hiring them. It's going to be hilarious."

I gritted my teeth to keep my mouth shut, but the whole time I kept thinking, *Jesus Christ, Brennan, why can't you just let our staff sit and drink wine and talk amiably amongst themselves, like civilized people? Why put on what will no doubt be a cringe-inducing, sycophantic little burlesque and embarrass yourselves and everyone else? I mean, what kind of shit are you trying to disturb here?*

"We need someone to play a starchy, buttoned-down vip," he went on, "and I immediately thought of you."

"Flattered," I said sarcastically, though I did feel a momentary glint of intrigue at the idea, no doubt a residual allure from my acting days. "But I am not interested in taking part in," *or, frankly,* I thought, *watching,* "a skit that's going to make everybody uncomfortable."

"It's not going to make everybody uncomfortable," he replied. "It may make *you* uncomfortable, Hector, but that's because you're a party-pooper. The skit is meant to be fun, and a chance for the blomers on staff to show their appreciation to senior leadership."

If they want to show their appreciation, I thought, *they could stop spending a third of the day fucking each other in the storage rooms and bathroom stalls and actually knuckle down to their work. I'm tired of walking in on an orgy every time I need a box of paper clips or to take a dump.*

None of this I vocalized to Brennan. He just stared at me and then said, "C'mon, Hector, don't be a stick in the mud. What do you say? Will you help us out?"

"No," I said. "*No,*" I stressed when he hesitated to reply, as if I might change my mind. "I'm not an actor, Brennan," I told him, and thought, *At least not anymore.* "If my wife worked here, I'd recommend her. But she doesn't. I just want us to sit there and enjoy the party and have a sensible evening."

With slant of head and flare of eyebrows, he conveyed an expression that said, *Yeah, well, good luck with* that. Then he emitted a great grunt of disappointment and got up to leave.

❦

When the night of the party finally came, I tried, Lord love me, to get into the right frame of mind, but I just couldn't shake my sense of dread. Morgana, who always loved a soiree and insisted we not bail on this one, proved far more optimistic. Despite the casual dress code, she wore this black party dress that I loved, along with a shawl of deep royal purple, and she was all smiles as we stepped through the glass doors and inside the massive convention centre foyer. We followed the signs to the correct escalator, one that whisked us with elegance up to the level where the Percussive Insurance party was held. As we stepped off onto the richly tiled floor, I could already hear the *thumpa-thumpa-thumpa* of dance music coming from our destination. My stomach sank. We followed more signs to a tunnel-like hallway, where I spotted a mist of dry ice creeping through the air like a vaporous hand.

"Oh Jesus," I said, feeling the urge to turn back and go home.

"Now, Hector, try to keep an open mind," said Morgana, taking my arm.

I spotted colleagues I recognized and we followed them toward the source of the sound. Stepping into the passage, wide and white and incredibly throat-like, it became apparent where the Fire and Ice theme came in. Tiki torches lined the hallway on either side, leading up to the entrance to the party room and its registration desk. Behind this flickering avenue of torches lay large, elaborately stacked cubes of ice. No, not cubes. They were more like barges, or stages – two, three or, in some places, even four tiers high. On each icy level stood a female blomer in knee-high leather boots, hot pants and a shiny bra, go-go dancing to the music's thrum. It amazed me, then, how I needed to see go-go dancing up close to realize just how much I *hated* go-go dancing. Each of the strutting vixens (perched on a plywood slat embedded into the top of the ice) held a vacant, drugged-out stare, and they didn't seem to put any effort into synchronizing their movements to either the music or each other. The girls just sort of flailed and shimmied and stomped around on their boxy platform of ice. A few were making a listless, half-hearted attempt at dancing the monkey. I looked at these blomers as we passed – the guitar ears, the archipelago of brows, the misaligned teeth that peeped through grimaced lips – and I wondered why, and how much, the company was paying these performers to put on such a horrid, freakish welcome.

"Unbelievable," I muttered.

"Unbelievable!" Morgana exclaimed.

We made our way to the registration desk, where one of my underlings, a chicken named Betty, handed me an envelope with my name on it. Therein Morgana and I found our name tags, drink tickets, our table card and a taxi chit for later. "Please enjoy yourselves," Betty said with a smile, motioning to the large red-velvet curtain that hung like a vulva over the entrance to the party room.

We stepped through its lips and into an enormous conference space. More dance music bombarded us as we tried to orient ourselves. A series of spinning, hot-red laser lights went zapping and shimmering through the dark air, clearly meant to replicate the flickers of a fire. We craned our necks upward. Above us, dangling from the room's rafters, was a series of what looked like oversized birdcages, their bars decorated with sparkling white and grey glitter meant to simulate the appearance of ice. These cages were accessible via catwalks that ran along the perimeter of the ceiling, all of which held long lineups of blomers. There in the shadows, through drifting plumes of dry ice and the zapping laser show, we could see that each cage contained a mattress and its own small strobe light. The cages dipped and swung as three or four or even seven blomers went at each other in their abhorrent versions of lovemaking. When each group finished, they pulled their party clothes back on and gingerly exited these suspended sex prisons to give another cohort a turn.

"Oh *my*," Morgana said.

"Let's just find our seats," I grumbled, turning my face away in disgust.

Just as we were about to navigate through the rows of tables adorned in icy blue tablecloths and flaming orange centrepieces, Otis and Ellen appeared at our side, a sight for sore eyes. One could not have missed Otis: he had, as I suspected he would, completely ignored the evening's casual dress code. He wore, perhaps in tribute to his days as an ex-rocker, one of his more flamboyant leather suits, complete with tailored vest, pleated slacks and polished black shoes. Ellen, by contrast, resembled a normal human being. She wore a simple brown turtleneck and dark blue jeans, a small buckskin handbag hanging off her shoulder. Despite her informal wear, she seemed more elegant, more confident in her own skin than he did as the four of us exchanged warm greetings.

"Oh, wow, Otis," Morgana crooned. "That is quite the outfit."

"I know, eh?" he said with glee. "When I party, I like to par-tay."

I was staring at Ellen when he said this and watched as she gave off a wifely roll of her eyes. The words of the argument I imagined them having as they got ready for the party rang through my head. *I can't wear this if you're going to wear* that, she would have said. *Oh, c'mon, nobody's gonna care!* he would have replied.

"Where are you sitting?" Otis called over to me, and I turned my gaze to him.

"Uhh, table five," I said. "You?"

"Table twenty-seven."

"Fuck." I suspected that Brennan Prate, as chair of the planning committee, was behind this, that he had somehow made sure Otis and I got seated at different tables as punishment for my refusal to take part in his ridiculous skit.

Speak of the devil. Brennan drifted then into my peripheral vision, and the four of us turned to face him. He himself had dressed exactly as he did every day for work – those Dockers slacks, that unspeakable golf shirt. He took one look at Otis's eccentric outfit and released a guffaw of disgust. "Well, *you* guys seem to be enjoying the party," he burbled.

"We just got here," I informed him.

At the sound of my voice, he pivoted his face in my direction, and I could see it coming, see it like a meteorological phenomenon sliding across a great green radar – the shit disturbance. He grinned like a wolf at me. "Say, Hector, is this the first time that your wife-wife," and he nodded at Morgana, "has met your work-wife?" and he nodded at Otis.

The girls gasped but then snorted, and Otis kind of blanched.

"Brennan, *Jesus*," I said.

But he was already walking away. "Find your seats, folks," he called out, giving us a gruff wave from behind. "We're about to begin."

So, Morgana and I parted company with Otis and Ellen and found our way to table five, where, it became apparent, I knew exactly nobody. This did not faze my wife, and she smiled and chatted and made friends with the blomers around our table in about twenty seconds flat while I sat grimly playing with my napkin. Soon the proceedings commenced. Our new CEO, a willowy technocrat named Roger Bradbury, took to the podium at the front of the room. He began with "I know I'm what's standing between you and dinner, so I promise to keep my remarks brief," before duly breaking that promise and unleashing a long and rambling welcome speech laden with Percussive Insurance's own internal corporate jargon. I grimaced silently as he referenced two major projects, QPM and ISF, by their acronyms only without defining them for the spouses and guests in the room, and I shuddered when he used *placemat* as a verb – our way of describing how to get bundles of insurance products in front of clients at once. When he finally finished, Bradbury motioned to his left and said, "Now head on over here, folks, and help yourself to this sumptuous feast."

At that, convention centre staff opened a large partition to reveal rows upon rows of stainless steel buffet-style troughs. *Buffet?* I thought. *What, no table service?* Nope, no table service. So we rose from our seats and went to stand in the lines – one to acquire a plate and cutlery and a second to get at the food. It was, in a word, *chaos*. These weren't lines so much as a crush of people, vips and blomers moving like a slow, rowdy wave over and around the spreads of food. I craned my neck. Off in the distance, I caught a glimpse of Otis and Ellen – him in that outrageous leather, her with that sheen of hair the colour of fresh caramel. They were standing together and, yet, not really standing together. She had her back to Otis and was conversing with a hawk there in line next to them, tucking a strand of that hair behind her ear, nodding and smiling, touching his arm and laughing as the blomer talked and talked. Otis, by contrast, seemed alone as he stood there in the crowd. I was again struck with the impression that those two had had a spat before coming here, and perhaps one about something larger than just their mismatched wardrobe choices. *What did other couples fight about?* I often wondered. Otis had once intimated to me – very subtly, of course – that he and Ellen were not entirely on the same page about their own childlessness. Could this be true? Could one of them, as vile as the thought was, actually want to have kids – and if so, which one? I shuddered at the thought. But the thought caused something else to happen. In that moment, I once again sensed the presence of what felt like an alternate dimension of reality, a portal into another world. I felt that if I turned my head then to the broad bank of windows on the south side of this room, I would not see the dark expanse of Lake Ontario but instead get a glimpse inside another room, identical to this one, and we vips would all be there, except it wouldn't be us. Not really. It would be another version of us, doppelgängers who actually wanted to procreate and had had kids, lots of them, and all these blomers, with their chemically induced and highly prescribed aptitudes and their desire for sex cages that dangled from the ceiling, would have been completely unnecessary.

Perhaps to coincide with the "Fire" part of this evening's theme, the meal turned out to be an array of Indian food. As soon as we realized this, Morgana touched my wrist and asked, "Oh, Hector, are you going to be okay?" Spicy cuisine and I did not get along – whether we were talking about Indian, Mexican, Korean or whatever. As we approached the troughs of pork curry and lamb vindaloo, I couldn't help but think of the dreadful gas that would plague me for hours to come. Indeed, one plate of that stuff and it would be like my innards were performing "Ode to Joy" as arranged for the tuba. Still, what could I do? I was starved. "I think I'll be okay," I said. Examining the various troughs, I tried to locate dishes that looked like they wouldn't kill me. I took as small a sample of each as I could manage.

We returned to our table and ate. As usual, I was amazed at how easily Morgana could make conversation with people she didn't know. The blomers sitting to her left along this wide, round table were a couple of cats who worked in our Contracts & Deeds division. "That's so *interesting*," my wife said when they explained how their reading comprehension skills came to bear on the minute differences between home and auto insurance agreements. "Even the most meticulous vip might miss a detail," said a well-spoken cat named Jessica, "but not us. We're on it!" I, meanwhile, silently choked down an overspiced potato. Seeing me start to zone out, Morgana took my hand and told the cats about our evening at the Cajun Cage on Markham Street to watch Thursday Banana, that increasingly popular band, live and in person. The cats mewed with envy, and then Morgana accompanied them as they unmelodiously began singing a few bars of the group's most popular song. "*Man oh man, there's a traffic jam / from here to Louisiana . . .*" I did my best to smile but did not join in.

Not surprisingly, the first tremors of indigestion struck me just as I spotted Brennan Prate, seated several tables over from ours, rise hugely from his chair and begin making his way toward the front of the room. He gestured to several blomers at other tables as he passed, and they too climbed to their feet. I circled a piece of butter chicken through its neon orange sauce and then steered it into my mouth.

"Oooh, what is *this* going to be?" Morgana cooed, wrapping an arm around mine and snuggling into me.

"A skit," I said, making dramatic scare quotes in the air with my free hand.

And a skit it was. Brennan took to the mic and began with, "Well, um, people, we have a special treat in store for Roger and the rest of the senior leadership. Just bear with us as we get set up here." The blomers – two cats, three hawks and several pigeons – moved into place, but then quickly rearranged themselves and traded places in the goofy manner of people putting on a play they hadn't thoroughly rehearsed. Brennan said something to the group off-mic, and they gleefully rearranged themselves once more. "Okay," he said, coming back on, "Are we . . . are we . . . okay, okay. We're ready. We're ready!"

My intestines roiled, and I clenched both my mouth and my butt cheeks to prevent a ghastly borborygmus from escaping me. I looked at Morgana. She was all awkward-but-patient smiles as she waited, along with the rest of the table, the rest of the room, for the show to begin.

It became clear within the first twenty seconds that these blomers possessed none of the theatrical talent of the crows and bears that Morgana was working with on a now-daily basis. The "story" began with Brennan, in the role of a vip who had thoroughly embraced pullulation's societal changes, leading this group of blomers, like a Pied Piper, into the Percussive Insurance family. *How bloody autobiographical*, I thought as I stifled a burp and watched them prance and mince around in front of us. They began singing a song that someone had clearly written in haste about how wonderful it was, and how grateful they were, to work for such an "awesome" and "generous" and "innovative" company. I cringed as they tried to get the room to join in on the song's chorus, clapping their hands in broad, swinging arcs of their arms and hollering, "Come on, folks. Come on!"

A slug of gas moved like hot lead through my intestines, and I clutched myself and shifted awkwardly in my seat. I noticed then that there was one blomer in the group who had not joined in on the skit's elaborate gambolling. This individual, a hawk, held a histrionically puckered expression on his face, a mien of disapproval over what he was seeing. Then, at the appropriate cue, he stepped forward to put a halt to the proceedings. His gestures and mannerisms conveyed an attempt at playing – *badly*, I thought – a very stuffy and stuck-up vip. Ah. So this was the role that Brennan had pegged for me. The audience chuckled as the hawk moved around the stage, trying to break up the celebration and telling people what a disgrace it was to have blomers carry on like this in a place of business. The Hector character went goose-stepping from cluster to cluster of blomers, wagging his finger and singing his own stilted song about tradition and decency. More chuckles. Then, two cats seized him by the arms, spun him around and forced him into what was quite obviously a simulated threesome.

The large pellet of gas now rode down the pneumatic tube of my colon. "Ughhghhh . . ." I moaned, and Morgana turned to me.

"Sweetie, are you okay?"

"I think I need to step out for a minute," I said, and got up. "The food."

She gave a sympathetic nod but then turned back to the play.

I felt like a grenade with the pin already pulled as I made a beeline through the tables and toward the back of the room. Slipping through the labial curtains and dashing down the corridor of ice stages, past the go-go dancers now milling on their break, I soon found myself back out in the convention centre lobby. I frantically searched for and then found the men's room and pushed my way inside. I barely had time to ensure I was alone before I finally let loose, the noxiousness unfurling out of me like a parachute as I leaned to the left against a stall door. "Ughh . . . fuck!" I grunted as the room filled with the stench of a broken sewer pipe. When I felt well enough to move again, I washed my hands needlessly and then headed back out to the foyer. I wanted to loiter a moment to ensure that the skit would have wrapped up before I returned to the party. Looking across the lobby's marbled expanse, I saw what seemed briefly like some kind of mirage – two familiar faces coming toward me up the escalator that led from the street. Alanna and Mitch! I began to walk in their direction.

"Well, hello there!" I called over, and they perked up at the sight of me.

"Oh, hey," Alanna said as I approached. I shook Mitch's hand and gave her a hug. "What are *you* doing here?" she asked.

"Corporate event," I replied, and gave a roll of my eyes. "You?"

"Same," she sighed, and nodded toward a conference space on the opposite side of the lobby from ours. "The post office was able to transfer me, and I've never been to the corporation's big downtown soiree. This is," and she eyed the elaborate foyer a moment, "different."

"So, you're all moved into your new place?" I asked.

"Yep," Mitch responded. "We're in a condo over on Laird." He said *condo* as if it belonged to a foreign tongue, a term foisted onto him by an occupying force. They suddenly stared at their feet, as if embarrassed that things had come to this. As we stood there, I noticed that the two wore what I could only describe as hastily chosen dress clothes: she an ill-fitting blue and black frock, he a dress shirt and slacks chosen right off the rack, stiff and starchy and cheap. The attire accentuated their awkwardness here in this lobby, in this convention centre, in this downtown core of the city they had spent their whole lives avoiding.

"Is Morgana here?" Alanna asked, looking up.

"Yeah, she's in there," I said, and gestured to the ice vagina. "I slipped out because some colleagues are putting on this ridiculous skit as part of the entertainment. I couldn't hack it."

Alanna nodded as if she understood. "We're expecting our night to be equally awkward."

Indeed, indeed. A queer tension swelled between Alanna and me then, like whorls of sadness kicked up from a rank and festering swamp. In one stark second, I could see a dozen extinguished desires brooding in her round face. In that moment, I wanted to ask about her miscarriage. I wanted to ask, *Are you okay?* and mean it in the broader sense. Perhaps she wanted to ask me the same thing, wanted to know about the prodding, probing angst, the fear, that teemed just below the surface of my eyes. It was as if we needed to cling to each other like life preservers then, but something came between us – something more than just her husband standing there, uncomfortably rubbing at his hairline, or my wife waiting for me back at the table.

I was just about to open my mouth when one of the blomers from our party, a pigeon, came cruising past us with two of the go-go dancers on his arms. Less than ten feet from where we stood, the trio stripped off their clothes and arranged themselves onto a plush leather bench that sat against the railing near the escalators. We all turned reflexively to glimpse their loveless, mechanical fucking as it commenced before we turned our gazes back to each other. I had the sudden urge to take Alanna's hand.

"Look," she said, "I'm thinking we're not going to stay long. This really isn't our scene. Why don't you text me when you guys are about to leave and maybe we can come out and join you."

"I'll do that," I said.

"Okay."

"Try to have fun in the meantime."

"You too."

And then we parted company, Alanna bracing Mitch's arm as if to drag him along, and me drifting with an almost aimless saunter back down the corridor of ice stages.

I returned to the table to discover that the skit had finally, blessedly wrapped up, and Morgana had returned to chatting with her neighbours. "Oh, hey, you're back!" she said as I sat down. "You missed the end of the play. It really was quite . . . something."

"Yes – something!" the blomers at our table agreed.

"Where were you?" Morgana asked.

"Well, strange thing: I ran into Alanna and Mitch coming back from the bathroom," I replied. "They're at their own event next door."

"Oh, weird!"

"Yeah. They said to text them when we're leaving and they'll come out to join us."

With meal and skit wrapped up, people began to wander off from their assigned tables. Sure enough, Otis and Ellen soon arrived at ours. "How was your meal, folks?" Otis asked before he got a look at my green face, and then said with a chuckle, "Oh, Hector, dude!" I was just about to reply when the next inevitable part of the evening began: the room suddenly filled with a DJ's booming club music, and people – mostly vips – began to make their way to the dance floor. The blomers, meanwhile, headed back toward the catwalks that led up to the sex cages dangling above us.

"Let's dance," Morgana said, and hauled me to my feet.

"You wanna come?" Otis said to Ellen as he joined us.

"Oh, no thanks," she said, and slipped into the seat I had just slipped out of. "I think I'll wait here. But you guys have fun."

I was tempted to stay behind to keep Ellen company, but Morgana was already pulling me along by the wrist. There, on the congested dance floor, I put in a good effort even though I hate dancing. I tried to maintain an arm around my wife's waist, but she kept slipping from my grasp to do her own thing, strutting and shaking and smiling among the crowd. Otis, meanwhile, shimmied about in his own manner, sort of waltzing with himself out of sync with the music. I looked back at Ellen, now alone at our table, sitting stiffly in her turtleneck. I watched as she examined her cuticles, scanned the room, glanced up at the ceiling.

Finally, when I felt we had put in enough of an appearance, I pulled Morgana close and asked, "Are you okay if we go now? I'm still not feeling a hundred percent."

"Oh," she replied, her voice tinged with disappointment. But then she shrugged and said, "Oh, okay. That's fine. If you want to get going, we can go."

"Great," I chimed, and moved over to Otis. "Hey there," I yelled over the grating dance music. "We're going to head out. You want to come?"

"Absolutely," he replied.

So I pulled out my phone to text Alanna while the two of them collected Ellen. To my relief, she texted back right away to say they'd meet us in the lobby.

When the six of us convened there, Morgana made some quick introductions for the two couples who didn't know each other, and then we headed down the escalators and out the glass doors into the cool November evening. We decided to stroll through the footpaths that ran along the lake before heading back up to the subway. Prior to pullulation, this area of the city – long beautified with knolls and park benches and scenic views of the water – would have been all but deserted, especially at this time of night and at this time of year. But now, the lakefront parks and pathways were utterly choked with crowds – large, loud, inescapable clusters and constellations of blomers. In fact, I felt a strange and sudden anxiety grip the air as we meandered. Behind me, beneath a stark thick oak, came a blomer-sparrow's distinctive squeal, and I could not tell if it was a sound of pleasure or of pain.

Alanna was just filling us in on the construction job Mitch had managed to land in the first five minutes of their move to the city. His welding skills, for so long an albatross around his rural life, had become hotly desired now.

"What's it like working with dogs all day?" Otis asked.

Mitch, true to form, took a long time to answer. "They don't say much," he said, not saying much. Then, very reluctantly, he added, "I guess they're okay." Alanna chimed in then about how, despite them both finally working full-time and the "whole whack of money" they'd received for their land in Hope Mountain, they were still struggling to make ends meet in the city.

Three blue jays came zipping past us as we ambled, one of them clipping the side of Mitch's arm. "Hey, slow down!" he yelled after them. "Where's the fire?"

"Oh, us too," said Otis to Alanna. "I mean, we're making more money than ever and we're still cutting costs all over the place. This inflation is fuckin' cray-zeee."

"Speaking of such things, how's the play going?" Ellen asked Morgana, somewhat slyly. "You actually *quit* your job to do it full-time, didn't you?"

Morgana sort of staggered under the remark's weighty sub-text. "Um, yeah. I mean, yeah. It's been a real struggle, but we're managing. It'll be totally worth it, though – the play's going to be *awesome*."

"And when's the big debut?" Alanna asked.

"Oh God, I have no idea. If the production keeps growing as it has, we won't –"

More blomers came tearing past us then, cutting my wife off. They seemed to appear from behind trees and over the board-walk in droves. We looked over and saw them congregating just north of us in a parking lot that had been a beautiful green space less than a year ago.

"What's going on over there?" I asked.

"Another orgy?" Mitch asked with a grunt.

"No, I don't think so." I moved toward the assembled crowd. "It looks like . . ."

A scream pierced the air then. There was no mistaking *that* for an orgiastic cry – someone in the gathered crowd had hollered out in deep pain. "What the hell?" I asked, moving through the bollards and up onto the sidewalk that bordered the parking lot.

I felt Morgana's hand touch mine. I sensed my friends col-lecting behind me. "Oh, Hector, you haven't seen this before, have you?" my wife said. "You haven't . . ."

No. I hadn't. I had heard rumours about this sort of thing, perhaps even caught distant echoes of it on my walks to work. But no, I had never witnessed it myself.

There were about fifteen or twenty blomers gathered in a circle in the centre of the parking lot. They were all jeering and barking and stomping their feet. Through their swaying bodies I could see another blomer down on its knees on the asphalt. It had been stripped to near nakedness and was bleeding from its mouth, its ears, its broad, tuberous brow. Every couple of seconds, one of the standing blomers would move to the centre of the circle to deliver a kick or a punch. I cringed at each sickening thud. Some of them had makeshift weapons – a tire iron or a broken piece of pavement – and moved in with a viciousness that defied description. The blomer on the ground raised its hands in a plea for mercy, but to no avail. I say "its" because the gender of this poor creature was indeterminate – a perfect amalgam of female and male. Its soft, feminine face was marred by chin whiskers, its plump, almost sensuous breasts framed by broad shoulders. I spied both sets of genitals peeping from its torn pants.

"Should we . . . should we *intervene*?" I asked with a cringe. A few other vips had gathered around the edges of the parking lot, curious bystanders attracted by the same hubbub we had been. But I caught something immediate and horrifying in their expressions. I couldn't believe it. It was that same cautious indifference – the long glance toward, the quick glance away – that vips often showed toward the blomers' public acts of group sex. Except this wasn't sex. This was torture, this was *murder*, right out in the open, below the glittering new condo and office towers overlooking the lake, and all the wealth and opportunity they promised. These vips could bring themselves to do nothing.

The tortured blomer took a sudden, beefy knee to the mouth, its head snapping back in a whiplash, its shattered teeth spraying like aerosol around its head.

"Shouldn't we intervene?" I asked again.

"No, we shouldn't," Morgana replied, and tried to pull me away. "It's okay, Hector. That one's a hermaphrodite."

"*Morgana*."

"What? That's what they're called. The term isn't politically incorrect anymore. It's what the blomers themselves call them."

"But we . . . we should . . ."

"No, we shouldn't. This is what they do, Hector, when they discover a hermaphrodite among their numbers. It's what they *do*. We just have to leave it alone."

I turned to look at my friends. Morgana was more concerned for me than she was for the tortured blomer, her soft brown face all teeming with love and wifely solicitude. Ellen, meanwhile, was actually staring at her cuticles like a bored teenager. There was no horror in her pretty face, no disgust, no desire to intercede in the assault. I thought, *What the fuck is the matter with you?* But Mitch's expression was the worst. I saw him lick his lips as he watched the violence unfold in the parking lot, and he got this lunatic glint in his eye, one I could only describe as heightened curiosity, as if this beating were but a spectator sport to which he had gained a free pass. I had never felt so alone as I did in that moment, as I took in the two of them and their reactions.

But then I turned to Otis and to Alanna. They too seemed utterly alone in that moment. Alanna had brought a hand to her mouth and her eyes were swimming in tears. Otis's face, looking as shocked and impotent as I was sure mine did, had turned as pale as milk.

There was a revolting series of sounds then, like someone stabbing at a large, torso-like bag of fertilizer with a knife, and I spun back to the parking lot. One of the blomers, a dog with thick and heavy features, was driving his elbow between the hermaphrodite's shoulder blades in quick, frantic smashes. The poor thing fell to the pavement and did not get up. The crowd of blomers swarmed it then, kicking and punching and ripping once more. There rose an almost sonorous cry, a beautiful cry, as the hermaphrodite turned its broken face up at us, at *me*. The mouth, full of blood and devastated teeth, gave off a horrible grimace, and its eyes were full of an intangible fear.

I turned my face away.

"Oh, Hector," Morgana said. "We should go. We should just go." And she took my arm and started to pull me away, with our friends trailing reluctantly behind us.

CHAPTER 7

There was another delay with *Harpies: The Musical!* Carolina told my wife and the rest of the cast and crew that the play would not debut until at least after the new year. The show was morphing into a three- or possibly even four-hour musical extravaganza, a massive orchestral sex epic, the Wagner's Ring cycle of shagging.

I began to wonder if Morgana could sense my unease with this now convoluted stage show and her role in it. I thought I'd grown adept at hiding my alarm – about the production and about many things – from my wife. It wasn't that hard. Up was now down. Right was now left. Wrong was, it seemed, now right. Was it right for a husband to listen to his wife describe the things that Morgana was describing to me after returning from her marathon rehearsal sessions to our now abbreviated condo unit? (The spare bedroom's transformation into a mini bachelor suite was finished, and six strangers, blomers all, were living in there – we could hear them through the new wall as if they were mice.) Was it right to listen to such cheeky descriptions of staged sex while our walls rumbled with the muted sound of actual sex? Was it right to try to make love to my wife at night in the midst of all that racket? To make love in *our* way – tender until it wasn't, quiet until it wasn't, and followed by a lengthy afterplay of gentle, self-congratulatory words – while the blomers banged and thrashed at each other and screamed such lurid obscenities just beyond our headboard? It was about as right as anything – as right as the normalization of violence on our TV or in our streets. It was about as right as feeling constantly strapped for cash even though I was working harder than ever.

But Morgana could sense all this. It explained why, during a rare meal we ate together on a weekend shortly after the onset of winter, she suggested I come by Theatre 647 some evening after work and take in one of the rehearsals. "You've started looking so tense whenever I talk about the play," she said. "I think it would be good for you to see first-hand what Carolina and the rest of us are up to."

I agreed, so the following Monday, after I had worked through lunch so I could leave the office relatively early (at least by post-pullulation standards), I made my way through the fresh-ly fallen snow to Theatre 647's massive barn-like structure on Alexander Street, right off the gay village. Morgana and I had tak-en in a few tasteful plays in this space over the years, a smattering of Chekhov, a bit of Beckett, a few things by Ibsen. But when I arrived in the lobby and kicked the snow from my boots, I could tell that the influence of blomers had taken the theatre's brow from high-middle to the lowest of the low. Posters for upcoming shows hung framed along one wall of the lobby, all of them mu-sicals and featuring blomers in garishly coloured costumes with overwrought expressions that hinted at some kind of onstage sexual hijinks.

I texted Morgana to let her know I'd arrived. Before long she came flouncing out to the lobby. "You made it!" she exclaimed, leaping into my arms. She wore her usual rehearsal garb: comfy black yoga pants stretched across her wide expanse of hips, black tank top and a kerchief that bound up the coils of her hair. After I let her go, she rubbed her exposed triceps and shivered. "Ooh, it's cold out here, Hector. Let's get you inside."

I followed her through the doors to the stairs that led down to the large, cavernous rehearsal space below the theatre. Unlike the lobby, this area – which resembled a mini underground school – was utterly sweltering. Blomers pushed past us in droves as we worked our way down a hall lined with costume trunks and clothing racks on wheels to the room where Morgana was rehearsing. We stepped inside the large space to find who I assumed was Carolina standing atop a plastic chair in one corner – a tall, swanlike woman dressed in a denim gown, her long straw-blond hair laced into an imposing braid that went down the length of her back. She had a wire-bound booklet resting on her forearm, which I assumed was the ever-growing script for *Harpies: The Musical!* Morgana invited me to sit in a chair set up discreetly on one side of the room, which I did.

"Where's my story editor?" Carolina called out loudly but not unfriendly over the room. "Is my story editor here today?"

A cat standing near the back of the throng raised an immediate hand to get her attention. She too held a copy of the booklet. "Right here, love," the cat said, eager, it seemed, to gain favour. "What do you need?"

"Can you please tell me," Carolina said with a flourish, "what the plural of *phallus* is?"

"Uhh . . ." the cat dithered, lowering her eyes briefly to the script. "Umm . . ."

"Well, I can tell you," Carolina went on, "that the *Canadian Oxford Dictionary* provides two answers: *phalluses* and *phalli*. I looked it up last night."

"Right," the cat replied with a nod.

"Now. If both are correct, then I don't really care which one we use. But I *do* care that we are consistent. And as you can see, here we are, in Act 3, Scene 4, using *phalli*, whereas –" and she flipped maniacally through the booklet, "– in Act 14, Scene 7, we use *phalluses.*"

"I'll fix it right away," the cat said.

"Excellent. Very good. Now. Speaking of phalluses, or phalli, or whatever we're calling them, can I please have the Spartan and Athenian soldiers in this scene step forward."

The crowd parted and ten crows came up and arranged themselves in two groups of five in front of Carolina. While this was by no means a dress rehearsal, I could see that these men were, for the sake of the scene, already sporting large codpieces, and one imagined the phalluses, or phalli, therein arcing upward with ridiculous, blush-inducing length and girth. Each of the crows had also taken up a sword from the prop table that rested against the far wall. These toy weapons were quite a bit shorter in length than the phalluses, or phalli, which, I thought, made for a very deliberate visual statement.

"Okay," Carolina continued, "I want us to work on the transition in this scene to the Spartan harpies' entrance. So, can I please get Perkins to pick up 'War Is What We're Good For' at, say, bar eighteen?"

This Perkins, a bear seated at a small piano in the opposite corner, threw a *No problem, boss* salute at Carolina and then rolled his dexterous fingers across the keys. Carolina gave a snappy count-up – "A-five, six, seven, eight!" – and then the soldiers launched into the tune. "War Is What We're Good For" had a dark, foreboding melody, full of portent and sinister undercurrents, but even I, with my untrained ear, could tell that it was an expertly composed arrangement. The two armies circled each other as they sang, the pending violence looming large between them. The men held their swords taut in their fists, their cocked elbows splayed out like wings as they stomped and marched around, threatening to do one another a villainy. The tension was palpable. But then, just as the two sets of men looked ready to strike each other down, the music shifted suddenly, billowing upward into a major key. Three scantily clad vixens came prancing into the space between the two armies. *Scantily clad* was perhaps an overly generous description: the girls wore translucent lavender teddies as light as gossamer, and through each purplish veil I could see a skimpy bikini bra and the wishbone-shaped shadow of a thong. The girls, all three of them, were vips – vips! This didn't seem right. *Does . . . does this play contain vip-on-blomer action?* I thought.

I was about to find out. The girls sang and minced and waggled their pert little bottoms around at the blomer boys. The tune now shifted into a completely different song, as such things were wont to happen in musicals. I had no time to absorb this new number's elaborately torqued rhyme scheme because I was distracted then by the choreographed striptease that ensued. Indeed, the girls removed an article of clothing at the end of each burst of lyric: first their open-toed high heels; then the bangles that hung from their wrists; then the teddies, slipped from shoulders as smooth as cream; then the bras, unhooked at the back with a burlesque faux coyness; and then, finally, the thongs, lowered slowly, sensuously, over jutted hips at the song's charged climax.

Perkins went absolutely rogue at the piano then, pounding at it to produce deep, guttural chimes. The girls, now naked, made short work of the blomer boys' clothing, pulling apart cod-pieces and removing shirts and pants as the lads pretended to be stunned and paralyzed by the girls' beauty. Soon everyone was in the buff, and then the ten men, liberated from the simulacrum of their phalluses, or phalli, turned around to expose to me their very authentic erections – veiny, menacing bats that rose over their navels. The feuding armies comingled then, their quarrel instantly forgotten, and positioned themselves to have a real good go at the girls. I clenched awkwardly in my chair. Perhaps I was expecting nothing beyond the abominations I had seen on my daily walks to and from work since pullulation, the curbside orgies between blomers. But this was something different. I struggled to grasp what I witnessed. Somehow, below the dull and soulless fluorescent lights of that theatre basement, these thirteen people emulated an intimacy so intense as to stagger the mind. Whereas blomer-on-blomer group sex always struck me as robotic and loveless, this display unfolded as if between people very dear to one another, best friends for years who had decided to just take a plunge, to leap deliciously out of the realm of the platonic and into the ravenous. The girls went places they had seemingly never gone before. The men grunted in gratitude at each new position and manoeuvre. I thought: *Simulated sex, my arse! Have they no shame?* But as I leaned forward to look closer, I did begin to doubt whether these acts were in fact real. I couldn't quite see for sure whether each tangle of limbs had crossed the threshold beyond staged coupling. Was that the enamel gleam of semen along someone's backside or just a trick of the light? What was truly happening there behind the chestnut curtain of that girl's hair? I tried to look and not look at the same time.

"Okay, that's great," Carolina called out.

And just like that, the orgy ended as fast as it had begun and the actors climbed to their feet. In one hot second the girls had resumed an air of dedicated amateurs, a trio of workaday vips – office dwellers or housewives or whatever – who were partaking in a bit of community theatre for the sake of a hobby. The blomers, meanwhile, were rapidly deflating before my eyes. They all nodded in clinical agreement as Carolina walked them through what went well in that scene and what still needed work, speaking of the segment as if it had been out of some Edwardian drawing-room drama. Were they serious?

I lost track of Morgana briefly as the crowd of actors shuffled around to prepare for the next scene. But then she re-emerged, stepping forward into the centre of the room. I took a long, deep breath. My wife had donned an elaborately woven salmon-coloured wimple, the defining costume trait of her character, Titania. Two other actors soon joined her – both blomers, one male and one female. I clenched up in my seat. What the hell was I about to witness? Was this why my wife lured me here, so I could watch as she . . . ? But no. The scene consisted almost entirely of dialogue, a bit of interstitial exposition between what I presumed to be two segments of sexual free-for-all. The only variant was near the end, when Morgana took her mark and broke out into song as Perkins accompanied her on the piano. Oh my. I had forgotten what a lovely singing voice my wife had, lush and full and ascendant. It fluttered through the air of that drab rehearsal space like a chickadee freed from its cage.

When the scene ended, Carolina called a break and my wife came over to where I sat, she all smiles and pride in her work, and I struggling to suffocate the conflict of feeling that threatened to overwhelm me.

"So, I'm done for the night," she said. "We can go now if you like."

I stood up, perhaps too quickly. "Sure thing," I replied. "We should give these people . . ." and the right word dangled just out of my reach, "their . . . privacy?"

Morgana furrowed her brow. "Oh, Hector, they don't care that you're here. Anyway. Just come with me to the dressing room so I can gather up my stuff."

So I followed her out into the hallway and into a small chamber on the left-hand side. It was a cramped room with a row of vanities and stools along one side and a jumble of props and costumes on the other. Morgana headed to one of the vanities in the middle, where I could see her purse and knapsack, her winter coat and boots piled before it. While she squatted to gather up these belongings, I allowed my eyes to wander to the vanity's mirror, framed by its grand, pearl-like necklace of light bulbs. I was struck then by a sudden flash of memory. In my mind, it was twenty-five years earlier, and I was getting ready to perform in some community play of my own and sitting at a vanity just like this one. What did I remember? What thoughts and sensations saturated my head? Of course. I was getting my makeup done, the most delightfully intimate experience of my young life. The person doing it was one of my co-stars, a pretty, brainy girl in her mid- or late teens. Being a boy right on the cusp of puberty, I was overcome with the near-illicitness of this act, the immediacy of her body so close to mine as she dusted my cheeks with rouge or artfully drew lines over my eyebrows. I tingled all over at the feel of her touch. Her face seemed so kind, so wise, so *kissable*. Her sweet breath was right on my skin as she worked on me. If I lowered my eyes, I would catch a glimpse of her breasts resting like freshly risen bread there, so close to where my legs dangled off the canvas-and-wood chair in which I sat. And looking through the vanity's mirror, I could see the most intoxicating thing of all – other co-stars behind me in various states of undress. Pulling off their street clothes. Putting on their costumes.

Of course. *Of course* the theatre was sexualized. It was *sexualized*. And it had always been thus. You couldn't escape it. And now, perhaps the blomers knew this better than we did. Perhaps they –

Morgana, dressed and reassembled to go outside, grabbed me by the arm. "Come on, let's get out of here," she said, snapping me out of this reflection. "It's been a loooong night. What were you thinking for dinner? Do you just want to pick up some shawarma on the way? I know it's not Friday night, but oh, Hector, you do look like you could use a treat!"

❧

And still, more reading. I couldn't explain where I found the time, couldn't explain why I kept landing on this trite and well-trodden genre. Oh, I was consuming some real trash now – zombie apocalypse novels and vampire apocalypse novels and novelizations of disaster movies from decades gone by. I couldn't get enough. Even the worst of these tomes felt like a palliative to what I saw on our streets, in the world around me. The more engrossingly absurd the premise, the easier it became to ignore the real absurdity that cast its palls of destruction and change: the endless construction that left our city pocked and cratered; the streetside orgies barely fazed by the winter winds that came; the wanton murder of hermaphrodites (a term that still twanged with archaic, hateful connotations) that we all just chose to ignore. *Bury your nose in a book and forget about it*, I thought. I made a point of leaving the living room during the late-night news when those new segments, introduced after pullulation, came on. Sports, weather and . . . your mass shooting report? Really? Yes. Sure, these missives came strictly out of the gun-loving USA, and perhaps they were necessary. But was it necessary that they be sponsored by Snickers? I caught a whiff of the commentary as I left Morgana and headed to our bedroom to read.

"And now Steve-O's here with your mass shooting report."

"Yes, that's right. It's your mass shooting report, brought to you by Snickers. Snickers: take a bite out of your hunger! We start in Northampton, Pennsylvania, where sixteen people were killed in a trailer park just west of . . ."

No, turn it off. Turn it off! But of course, I would never yell this at my wife. She looked so content there on the couch, unwinding with the news after her busy day of rehearsals. She'd just say, "Heading to bed, Hector?" and I'd say, "No, just going to read for a while." And a moment later I'd be splayed out on our duvet with another paperback as our thin condo walls rumbled with the sound of our neighbours' coupling.

❧

Brennan Prate had been made a director.

A new year dawned bright and cold, and the email announcing his promotion arrived on the Tuesday after we all got back from the Christmas break. The city beyond the windows of Percussive Insurance appeared to be made entirely of crystal now, in the white gleam of winter, with all those new condo and office towers rising to the sky like immense shards of ice. Coming back from the holidays, I was not surprised by the fresh throngs of foot traffic that impeded my strolls to work. (I was now leaving the house a full fifteen minutes earlier than usual to compensate for crowded sidewalks and long waits at traffic lights.) Nor was I surprised by the two new subway stops that had opened along the route, seemingly overnight, which disgorged even more crowds, more unfamiliar faces, into this part of downtown. But I was certainly shocked when I came into the office and discovered that my arch-nemesis had been invited to join the company's senior leadership. It looked as if all his scheming and sycophancy – not to mention the M.B.A. he'd been earning in the evenings and on weekends at the local business school since before pullulation – had paid off. When I received the email announcing Brennan's promotion – a message praising his initiative and leadership skills, his mentoring of dozens of blomers and, surprisingly, the fact that he was a proud member of the wide-o community – I was having my morning coffee with Otis. I turned my computer screen around to show him the news that had arrived in my inbox like a premonition. Brennan's new job title was as ominous as it was convoluted: Director of Informational Strategy and Operational Expansion. What could that even mean? Otis and I glanced at this notice together, and together we frowned.

"Maybe it won't be so bad," he said.

"Yeah, maybe," I replied.

Of course, neither of us believed this; and sure enough, less than a month later, there came an announcement of a major restructuring. A tremor of shock passed through the organization when people learned that, despite our nearly year-long bout of exponential growth, the company had decided to lay off a string of employees. I had been at Percussive Insurance for my entire career and had never had to deal with a major downsizing. As the associate HR director, I was once again flung into the role of chief pacifier as these sackings occurred. Thankfully, Otis was not included among those fired, though (I noted dourly) the majority of them *were* vips, like us.

And then I was summoned to what was labelled a post-restructure planning meeting, which Brennan Prate himself would chair. It turned out that the *operational expansion* part of his vague new job title meant that he had direct jurisdiction over the HR department, over me.

The atmosphere was already thick with shit disturbance as I arrived at the conference room for this get-together and noted Brennan's place at the head of the boardroom table. Before we had all even settled into our seats, he called the meeting to order and launched into a dizzying array of PowerPoint slides projected on the screen. I and the other managers listened as Brennan began to unwind the multiple changes coming to the company. Each new slide revealed another breathtaking bullet list of org chart modifications.

". . . and as a result of *that*," he was saying, "IT will now be known as Informational Services. Now, as for *your* department, Hector," and he turned his wide, baggy face toward me, "Human Resources will now be known as Human Capital –"

"Human *cattle*?" I asked, incredulous.

"Human *capital*," he stressed. "Jesus, Hector, why do you need to be such a shit disturber?"

Going flush, I harrumphed and turned to my fellow managers, hoping to see a gram of solidarity in their silent faces. But my fellow managers – a few of whom had actually been cattle prior to pullulation – looked at me as if my dig at the new nomenclature was a shocking act of corporate sedition. I wondered then if Brennan was mulling over how he might get me included in the next round of firings.

"Look, I'm not trying to cause trouble," I said, "but I have to admit, I'm a little disturbed by these random, arbitrary changes to how we do things around here. I mean, does it really matter whether we call my department *Human Capital* versus *Human Resources*? I'm asking this out of genuine curiosity."

Brennan's eyes bulged and his mouth puckered into a sort of moue at my insolence. He was about to unleash a tirade when a hawk sitting down at the other end of the long boardroom table raised a hand. "Maybe I can stickhandle this one, Brennan?" he asked.

"Ah, yes, Warren, please. Thank you."

And so, Warren rhymed off a series of points about departmental relabelling that was so convoluted, so labyrinthine with business jargon that I found myself zoning out almost right away. This slurry of nonsense did exactly what it was designed to do, which was to get me to stop caring about whatever half-hearted point I was attempting to make. In a nutshell, the renaming of departments was to align them with new industry standards and conventions, which in turn would make Percussive Insurance more attractive to future investors whom we'd need to help fund even more aggressive expansion plans for the next fiscal year, blah blah blah. The last thing we wanted was to appear bush league, to seem like small potatoes as investors tried to decide whether we were worth financing.

"And *this*," Brennan Prate chimed in, "is especially important considering the capital we'll need for our new building."

New building? I thought.

"New building?" I said. "Wait – what? We're getting a new building?"

Brennan's face gyrated in the affirmative.

"Why the hell doesn't anyone tell me anything around here?" I snarled.

There was a great stirring at the table. Apparently, the other managers hadn't known about this either. But whereas my murmurs and gurgles arose from a sudden and disquieting alarm, theirs emerged from a more pleasant sense of surprise, as if they had just learned that they were all receiving a gift.

"Well, we're telling you now," Brennan said. "In fact, I received the new floor plans just this morning. Let me see if I can punch them up."

With a few keystrokes of the laptop in front of him, he was able to access the shared drive and then open a large PDF containing the new floor plans. He maximized it so that its looming, faint-blue shape consumed the whole of the screen, stretching across our gazes like its own galaxy. It was clear, even from this vantage, how much larger these new office digs would be over our current arrangement, but something else was obvious, too.

"So this sort of open-concept style," Brennan was saying, "spread across all floors of a thirty-storey skyscraper with advanced technology inlays and GreenFriendly-certified heating and cooling systems will require –"

"No offices!" I found myself shouting. "No offices at all! And . . . and barely any walls?! Is that right? We're just . . . we're just all out in the open now?? And . . . and . . ." There were more burbles and whispers around the table as I sounded off. My eyes had wafted up to the top left-hand side of the screen, where the address of these new digs was printed in faint Courier New font – an address that caused a great gulp to escape my throat as I realized that our new home would be nowhere near downtown. "And . . . and . . . I'm sorry, but *where is this new office located?*"

CHAPTER 8

lanna's text message was tinged more with mystery than desperation, but it still caused me to raise an eyebrow.

Any chance you could come by here after work some night this week?

This request seemed so incredibly strange in the age we now lived in. True, it would have been absurd, back when Alanna and Mitch had lived in Hope Mountain, to pop over on a work night, but it felt equally ridiculous now. Their condo was only eight, maybe ten subway stops away, and yet our friends felt farther away than ever. I chalked this up to a major shift in the mentality of our city, and indeed the wider world. Travelling between two points, even of a short distance, had become so taxing and time-consuming – what with the traffic, the crowds, the transportation infrastructure stretched to the breaking point – that nobody wanted to do it, especially after putting in a full day at work. All you wanted to do was make it home to your increasingly smaller abode for some "me time." For us vips, this meant a lot of television, a lot of streaming Internet. For blomers, this meant a lot of fucking.

Is everything okay?

This seemed like a reasonable question to ask. It was the kind of question you asked a friend if, for example, he or she wanted to speak to you on the phone rather than send a text.

I just need your help with something. Is it okay? I'm sorry to be so vague. Feel free to say no.

No, I can come over. How about tomorrow night?

So, we set it up. It wasn't going to inconvenience Morgana if I didn't come immediately home, as she had another evening full of rehearsals. The commute from work would take just shy of an hour on the new subway line that had opened in the neighbourhood. I took the book I was reading to keep me company, though there was barely enough room to free it from my bag and steer it close enough to my face to see the words. The subway car was like its own vast megalopolis: two thousand arms raised to the hand grasps formed their own skyline in both directions as far as the eye could see; four thousand earbuds emitted faint, discordant chatter like the honking of traffic; and the seated people all around us were like the suburbs, comfortable but trapped.

Reaching Mitch and Alanna's neighbourhood, I bobbed and deked my way along the congested sidewalks as if on an obstacle course and used my Google Glass to find their condo tower, its shape rising into the sky like a huge steel peg. The footman in the lobby – an impeccably dressed goat in long coat and cap – called up my arrival and then buzzed me in, the security door screaming upon its release. I rode the elevator up and arrived at Alanna's abode. One knock was enough for her to throw open the door.

"You're here," she said swiftly. "Come in. Come in."

She led me into their unit and closed the door. I noticed that the lights were off for the most part; just one lonesome lamp glowed on an end table at the far side of the living room. There, in its luminescence, I spotted what I considered to be a rather strange sight for this household: a giant stack of books, a tottering pile of paperbacks and hardcovers, was arranged around the end table's feet. As Alanna took my coat, I thought, *When did she and Mitch become such big readers?*

"Thanks so much for agreeing to come over," she said. "I know it's a huge inconvenience." Her voice was clearly tinted with distress.

"No problem. What's going on?" I craned to look around. "Is Mitch home?"

"No. He's on a construction site late again tonight. Those dogs are working him like, well, a dog."

"And Isaac?"

"He's in the other room, watching TV. Hang on a sec." She went over to the short hallway leading to the back of the condo and called out to her son. "Isaac? Hey, Isaac, sweetie, can you guys come out here?"

You guys? I thought.

Sure enough, Isaac appeared before us with some company in tow. My eyes widened at the sight of this unfamiliar person, my breath catching in my throat.

Alanna moved to stand behind him, or her, or it, and placed her hands on his, or her, or its, shoulders.

"This is Lesley," she said.

Lesley was, beyond a doubt, a blomer. The brow ridge swelled bulbously over downcast eyes, the ears and lips disproportionately large. Lesley was also clearly a cat, evidenced by the way that she, or he, or it, stood with one foot folded bashfully over the other. A wine-dark scab, I could see, had coagulated into a paste on the chin, and bruises as green as the ocean ran along the inlets of the throat. When Lesley's mouth twisted open to give me a short, traumatized "Hi," I could see that several teeth in the front were missing – not in the adorable way that children lose their baby teeth, but in the violent way of being kicked or punched or wrenched out.

"I had to do *something*," Alanna said quickly when she saw I was about to speak.

"Alanna . . ."

"I had to do something, Hector. I just . . . I just couldn't leave . . . leave . . ."

"Leave . . . ?"

It was as if neither of us knew how to proceed, but then Lesley helped us out. "Them," they said in a barely audible whisper through that broken mouth. "Them, please."

Them? I thought. *Okay, fine. Them. Them.*

"Oh, sorry, sweetie, I forgot already," Alanna said, and kissed the top of the child's head. "Them. I just couldn't leave them to be beaten to death in the street like that, Hector. I just . . . I just couldn't do it. I couldn't do it. I just couldn't. She . . . they, *they* are only a child. A child."

"Okay, slow down, slow down," I said. "Everything's going to be fine. Let's start at the beginning. When did this happen?"

"Four days ago. I had to run out to a little bakery around the corner to pick up these buns we really like to go with some clam chowder I was making for supper. But the bakery was closed. It's run by just this one guy – a nice enough fellow, you know, for a crow. Anyway, there was a sign on the door saying he was on vacation and the store would be closed for the next week. So I had to go to the supermarket instead. The place was, you know, packed as usual, but I managed to get what I needed."

"Alanna?"

"Sorry. I'm babbling. Sorry, sorry. I'm *babbling*. Anyway. I was coming out and walking through the parking lot when I saw it. It was just like that night after we left our staff parties at the convention centre. About seven or eight blomers were gathered around in a circle. At first I thought it was just another orgy, but then I could see they were all kicking and punching and choking poor Lesley to death. I mean, they were just a little kid! I wasn't thinking. There were no other vips around, not that it would make much difference. But I just couldn't take it. They . . . they were just a little child, Hector. I ran into the group as they took a break and grabbed Lesley by the wrist and pulled them away. These blomers weren't very tough. I was able to fend them off with my bag of buns."

"Alanna."

"Anyway, sorry. We ran like the dickens together and got back here as soon as we could. The concierge downstairs was having his dinner, thank God. I don't think he would have let me in . . . let me into *my own home* otherwise."

"What does Mitch think about all this?"

She began to cry. "Oh, Hector, he's so pissed at me. You have no idea. I mean, I lied to you just now. He's not working late at the construction site because he has to. He's there because we've been fighting for two days straight over Lesley, and he doesn't want to deal with all this right now."

In that moment, I could easily imagine Alanna and Mitch fighting. They'd been together pretty much their whole lives, since elementary school really, and now more than ever, I wondered if they'd gotten together not because they loved each other – because who could fall in love, in real love, at such a tender age? – but because the pickings had been so slim in those days. Very few people had chosen to have children for decades, and your options were limited, especially if you grew up in a rural place as they had. If you didn't want to end up alone, you latched onto whomever you found at least halfway agreeable, even if, in the end, they were not the right person for you. And so you fought with this person more and more as time went on. This might have even been the case with Otis and Ellen. They fought a lot. Had they paired up with the same *Oh, I suppose you'll do* kind of attitude? And even Morgana and me – we didn't squabble that much, and when we did, it took on a kind of jokey quality, and we were mostly kind to each other and supportive of each other and knew all kinds of inane details about one another, and we tried our best to have sex at least a couple times a week, and the sex was always sweet and playful and usually very good. But what about us? Would we have ended up together if the world hadn't been so sparsely populated prior to pullulation? Or would she have gotten a better offer?

"Alanna, what are you going to do?" I asked.

At this question, she gruffly wiped the tears from her eyes and turned to Isaac. "Okay, Isaac, you guys can go back to watching TV if you like."

It was Lesley who spoke up. "No," they said. "No more TV." They raised an arm and pointed ghostlike to the stack of books on the other side of the room.

"Oh, of course," Alanna said. "Sweetie, I keep forgetting, you're a cat. You just go over there and help yourself to another one, okay. You don't even have to ask."

Isaac rolled his eyes. "They're *always* reading."

Together we watched as Lesley crossed the room and squatted at the bounty of books. They pawed around for a bit before making their selection, then stood back up and clutched the tome to their chest.

"What did you pick?" I asked.

They turned the book around to face me. It was an old non-fiction work from what looked like decades ago. The title read, *The History of English*.

"An apt choice," I commented.

The kids left us alone then and Alanna turned back to me. "It's remarkable," she said. "I managed to teach Lesley to read in less than ten minutes. They were insatiable. They blew through my copy of *Chatelaine* and all my Maeve Binchy books in the first couple of nights. I had to go to a used bookstore with tote bags. I dropped four hundred dollars in that place. Yesterday alone Lesley read *To the Lighthouse* and *Huckleberry Finn* and *No Logo* and *A Clockwork Orange* and two Shopaholic novels and about half of *White Teeth*."

"That *is* remarkable," I said. My eyes panned around the room. "Look, do you mind if we turn on another light or something? It's very dark in here."

"No, we can't," Alanna replied. "All these condo buildings are so close together, and we don't have any curtains for the balcony windows. If the neighbours were to look over and spot Lesley, it could be very bad. I don't know what would happen."

This brought me back to the question I had asked. "Alanna, what are you guys going to do?"

"Well, I'll tell you what we're *not* going to do. We're not just going to hand Lesley over to the authorities so they can cast them back onto the streets to get beaten to death for the simple fact of being a . . ." and here she hesitated on the term ". . . for being a hermaphrodite?"

Indeed. Yes. That nomenclature still jarred, still clattered with an unsavoury ring in our old-world ears. I could tell it bothered Alanna to say it, and she could tell it bothered me to hear it. Somehow, this mutual understanding drew us together, allied us to one another. She took a step toward me.

"I feel responsible now," she continued. "I mean, I saved their life, so am I not responsible for them now?"

"Alanna . . ."

"And frankly, Hector, after losing the baby last year, I . . . I just . . ." Here she began to cry once more. "I just think, would it be so wrong . . . to adopt one of them?" She saw my face flicker. "I mean, to adopt this one. This one. Lesley. To adopt them. To protect them, to love them, to try to help them find a place in the world, or at least help them be ready for when the world is ready to accept them. I know this is probably hard for you to understand because you and Morgana, like most vips, don't really have a parental instinct. But I do. I have it in spades. I just want to be a mother. I just want to *mother* someone." She wiped tears off her face. "Oh God, that sounds awful. It makes me sound like I just picked Lesley at random, that it was premediated and that

I planned to save a hermaphrodite, any hermaphrodite, from a beating death. But I swear I didn't. I didn't, Hector."

Somehow, our fingers had entwined. I gave hers a reassuring squeeze.

"What can I do to help?" I asked. "What do you need from me? You wouldn't have asked me to come up here for no reason."

"I knew *you* would understand," she squeezed back. "I could see it in your face that night after the convention centre. I knew you felt the same way I did, a way that Morgana and Mitch clearly didn't. So I just wanted you to come up here and see this for yourself, and to assure me that I'm not off my rocker. That what I've done is normal and right and good."

"And you're saying Mitch doesn't see it that way?" I asked.

With that, she let my hand go and took a step backwards, her head shaking. "He's livid," she said. "He thinks I've lost my mind. He watches the news like a zombie and listens to the dogs at the construction sites and just accepts their hatred of . . . of herms like Lesley at face value. It's like he and so many other vips we know have just been hypnotized by it."

Herms, I thought. *Herms. Yes, that's probably as good a term as any.*

"We've had so many screaming matches over this," she said. "I've told him that none of this makes any sense. Their animosity toward herms isn't based in reason; it's just another by-product of pullulation itself. So much of the pullulation process was random, right? I mean, why did cats become such voracious readers while blue jays are really good at painting? Or why did eagles make for such kind, empathetic social workers while goats just became louts who work as doormen in condo building lobbies and *can't mind their own fucking business.*"

I stepped forward and, prepared to tell her verbatim what she wanted to hear, put my hands on her shoulders as she wept into the finger tucked under her nose. "You're not off your rocker," I said. "What you've done here is normal and right and good.

It is. But you know as well as I do that you can't go skulking around your own home with the lights turned off and avoiding the windows forever, or forcing your family to do the same. If you want to help Lesley, then you need to help h– them, *them*. Okay? Go online, do some research. Find out if there are groups of like-minded people out there dealing with the same thing. I'm sure there are. Write a letter to your city councillor or your MPP, or the fucking prime minister herself. Tell them that this kind of random, pointless violence just won't stand. I'll do the same." I didn't actually think this would make a difference. Blomer violence against these herms had become normalized almost as quickly as their public acts of group sex, and to hear blomers describe it on talk shows and in op-ed pieces, the desire to harm herms was as baked into their chemistry as a cow's photographic recall or a sparrow's propensity toward science. Our current PM and her Conservative majority government had swept into power on a mildly progressive Red Tory platform five years ago, but she had done an abrupt about-face after pullulation and adopted a staunch laissez-faire attitude toward all things blomer. This made sense considering what a huge voting block they now represented, and any grassroots movement from vips would have little chance of swaying her, as she and her provincial counterparts were riding high atop a booming economy.

"And if you want to adopt Lesley, I think that's a great idea," I went on. "You are so much a mother, Alanna. Anybody can see that. But if you're going to do this, then you and Mitch have to be on the same page about it. You do. You'll make each other miserable if you're not."

Alanna stared wet-eyed at the floor for a bit, but then nodded. What I had said seemed to make a lot of sense to her.

"You know, I'm very envious of you and Morgana," she said, looking up. "You guys seem to be on the same page with each other way more than me and Mitch."

She must have seen something waver across the transom of my face because she furrowed her brow then and paused as if waiting for me to refute her observation. "Everything *is* okay with you guys, right?"

How could I answer that? If I told Alanna that I thought my wife was cheating on me with another man, she would be shocked and horrified, not to mention furious at Morgana. But if I told her that I thought she was cheating on me with fifteen other men, then it wouldn't have been so bad at all. Somehow, it would have seemed like just another unfortunate but inescapable aspect of the culture that blomers were foisting onto us all.

"We're fine," I lied. "We're just really busy. Like a lot of couples, we don't get to see much of each other these days."

"Oh my, and here I am asking you to come all the way up here and listen to me blubber about what's going on with us."

"No, it's okay. That's what friends are for. But I really should go. I'd like to get back and have at least a bit of time with Morgana before we both collapse into sleep tonight."

Alanna nodded, then turned her eyes with a brief glance of longing to her condo unit's door. "Yeah, tell me about it," she said. "Anyway. Come say goodbye to the kids before you go."

We moved down the hallway to Isaac's tiny bedroom, made tinier now by Lesley's presence. The two kids were engulfed in beanbag chairs and engaged in their respective distractions: Isaac with earbuds in and watching something on his tablet, his face glowing in a kind of seaweed green, and Lesley coiled up like the cat they had been with *The History of English* open and resting on one forearm. Even in the narrow blaze of their reading lamp, I could see they had finished nearly a third of the book in the time Alanna and I had been talking. Watching the kids from the door's threshold, I couldn't help but notice how different the two were in physical appearance and yet how ... *related* they seemed, there in that little room. It was as if a strong, lively current of sibling relationship was already humming between them.

"Guys, Hector's going to go," she said to them. "Say goodbye."

Isaac came up for air for all of a nanosecond, but Lesley raised their eyes from the page and held their gaze up to me like a torch. "Goodbye," they said, their voice meek and yet gravid with gratitude. What they were thanking me for, I had no idea.

❧

One thing about reading all these postapocalyptic yarns and dystopian warnings was that I had started to believe in other dimensions of reality. Everywhere I looked I saw portals now, doorways through which I could glimpse a world that wasn't quite ours but could be, that might one day yet be, if fate awakened something dormant in us, in the world, in the trajectory of time. These books, these novels and stories, taught me how easy it was to not only look through those doorways but to pass through them, to step into another dimension, to become a different person. How easy it was to allow a singular event to transform you, to nudge your course, to open that portal and have you sucked through it.

I certainly felt that way about pullulation. Look at what it had awakened in Morgana. How had I ever thought that teaching music to kiddies would ever be enough for her? She was such an entertainer, a pure exhibitionist. Now the play had become everything for her: more important than the career she was so lucky to land, more important than even me. It was as if pullulation had shoved me through a door and said, *Here is a version of your wife, but not the same version you know. Teaching is not enough for her. You are not enough for her. This version needs what only blomers, this new world order, can give her.*

And what was I becoming? How had pullulation changed me? I felt so many strange impulses and desires tremoring through my staid self. I thought thoughts that I had no business thinking. *Tamp them down,* I told myself. *Put them out.* This is not who I am. This is who I am. This is not who I am. This *is* who I am.

Who was I? Oh God, did I even know?

❧

By late spring, Percussive Insurance had completed the move to its new digs in the high north end of the city, and life became unbearable to me.

I knew on some level that I had been spoiled, had been anomalous in my twenty-minute commutes on foot through our downtown. *Surely this could not last*, I told myself. Surely I would, as a working stiff, a primary breadwinner, a bringer-home-of-bacon, have to join the masses who twice a day poured like effluence into our rapidly expanding subway network. One could not stop change. One could not stop progress. The city, indeed the entire world, was bending to the will of pullulation, and I would have to bend with it.

Those first few weeks getting used to that new commute were awful. How does one describe what it felt like to be led with millions of others onto those platforms below ground and wait for the shiny new trains to pull up, except to say that it was prison? *Prison.* We were like cattle down there, like internees, like human data being poured into a human spreadsheet, huge, unknowable and orchestrated from afar. On these treks, I had come to learn just how brief twenty minutes truly was. In my old life, twenty minutes got me all the way to work if I walked fast enough. Now, twenty minutes got me only to my first transfer point. Five other twenty-minute periods awaited me as I made my immense, ridiculous slog through the subterranean maze of our city's new transit system.

The worst part was what I saw when I finally climbed from the subway station up to street level not far from the glittering thirty-storey shard of glass that Percussive Insurance now inhabited. One would think that after such a long and torturous commute, one would be relieved to see the rich azure sky, to smell the outside air and to walk relatively unencumbered along the sidewalk. But I grew troubled by what I glimpsed, morning in and morning out, after my arrival at work. It was as if the city were made entirely of crystal now. Yes, crystal. There was not, it seemed to my pessimistic eyes, a cubic inch of spare space between the icy, soulless steeples of industry that now surrounded me. They were like mountains of quartz reaching for the heavens, glass and steel stretching endlessly, eternally into the firmament. Not a breath of green, not a skein of nature anywhere to be found. And this wasn't even downtown! It was what they now called *uptown*, or *midtown*. Fifteen short months ago, this city district had been a forest, a jungly ravine. But no longer. The apocalypse had come, and the science fiction writers, with their awful Hawaiian shirts and their awful allegories, had gotten it completely wrong. The apocalypse was not an empty world, a burnt-out husk, a population wiped out by disease or war or poor planning. It was the opposite. It was a crystal world. It was a subway world, a three-hour commute world, a two-hundred-and-fifty-square-foot condo unit world, an open-concept, no offices for anybody and you can never *ever* be alone with your thoughts again kind of world. We had reached, through the marvels of pullulation, the apotheosis of human achievement, which was the eradication of solitude, the normalization of crowds, the acceptance of relentless suffocation.

To be inside our new digs, to move through its floors and aisles, its alcoves and vistas, was to feel under perpetual surveillance. There were no walls anywhere now. Just thousands of small, squat desks made mostly of glass lined up in identical rows that spread out across the floors, across the vistas, right to the tall pure-glass windows that surrounded us on all sides. Through these windows we could see directly into all the other buildings that surrounded us. There, strangers went about their own automaton-like business in their own wall-free spaces. We were insurance people; they were, perhaps, accountants or lawyers or business consultants or government bureaucrats. For us, they looked like fish in their aquaria, and I was certain we were the same for them.

Needless to say, this new set-up bred an entirely different culture at Percussive Insurance – or, more accurately, it created an absence of culture, a vacuuming up of any smattering of charm or personality the place once had. Our new corporate ethos certainly precluded any notion that Otis and I could still gather for our daily coffee and have our gabby gossip sessions about all the people we didn't like. Nope. That time of our lives was over now. I barely saw Otis anymore. He was on a different floor than me, and it was all we could do to meet up in one of the so-called break rooms (*rooms* having become a euphemism around here; they were basically just a small corner section on floors four, eight and eighteen that included booths and a glass island in the centre containing a microwave and a fridge) during the occasional lunch hour. We had to limit our kvetching to the confines of email. He probably wouldn't have felt comfortable sharing what he shared in those notes with anyone other than me, since, as the associate director of "HC," I was the one who ultimately brought the hammer down on any staff who shared inappropriate things over email. This double standard felt like the last pillar, the last bastion of all the privilege and comfort I had lost under this new regime, this new order that had squeezed my life into such awful and unfamiliar shapes.

Otis and I reached a breaking point. He sent a note one Friday afternoon pointing out how long it had been since we had done anything fun, anything spontaneous.

Let's go to the Cajun Cage, he pleaded. Ellen hasn't seen you in forever – she misses you! She's been such a sourpuss lately; you could probably cheer her up way better than me. Besides, Thursday Banana is back playing tonight and we should go see them.

A warm, agreeable thought briefly burned in my core when I read that, but I pushed it away, the inappropriateness of it, this notion of catching a glimpse of my best friend's wife, of how just seeing me might "cheer her up." Mulling things over, I knew I wouldn't see Morgana tonight because she had another late-evening rehearsal as *Harpies: The Musical!* inched ever closer to its long-delayed opening night. If I didn't go out with Otis, I would face another Friday with a stack of household chores to do after I had finally made it back to our condo.

Fuck it, I thought.

Fuck it, I emailed him. *Let's do it.*

So we did it.

⮑

"Man oh man, there's a traffic jam
from here to Louisiana.
It stretches for klicks and traps all the chicks,
including my girl, Pollyanna."

Despite everything, Otis and I found ourselves belting out this tune like drunken university students as we climbed from the subway stop and made our anxious way toward Markham Street and the Cajun Cage. One could not deny the catchiness of this earworm that had become a kind of anthem for the cats and cows and foxes in this part of the city. Despite all the strife that blomers had brought into my life – at work, with Morgana, in the very state of the world – I was powerless to resist the song's hypnotic charm. Poor Otis, he seemed on edge, not quite himself, as we worked our way into the long line waiting to get inside the club, and our ridiculous duet only heightened rather than allayed the twitchy nervousness that plagued him. I thought about what he'd said about Ellen earlier – she's been such a sourpuss lately – and I wondered if that had something to do with it.

Taking a gander over the people standing in front of us, I tried to judge how far we were from the door. "Do you want to call Ellen?" I asked him. "See if she can't help us jump the queue again?" A few heads turned to give us a dirty look.

"I can try," he said, taking out his phone and bowing his head over it, "but she hasn't been answering me all day. I actually haven't spoken to my wife in over a week."

I gave him a surprised look as he moved the phone to his ear. When he caught it, he said as way of explanation, "We've just . . . we've both just been working a lot lately." He waited, then lowered the phone. "Voice mail," he sighed. Then he tried again, and again said, "Voice mail." He puffed out his cheeks. "Maybe I'll send her a text."

"She . . . she does know we're coming tonight, right? I mean, you emailed her or something?"

Otis turned his eyes up to mine in what I interpreted to be a guilty look as his thumb padded around the screen. "Nope. Nope, she doesn't. But . . . you know, I have an open invitation to come out whenever I want. Right?"

I was about to say something more, to entreat him to divulge additional details about what was going on, but then the line moved suddenly and before we knew it, we were very near the door. After a brief but pregnant silence that loomed between us, the line moved again and then we were inside, paying our cover charge at the desk and stepping into the packed club.

"Let's just try to find a table," Otis said.

We got lucky: we spotted a freshly abandoned two-seater against the far left-hand pillar of the room and hustled together to nab it. The table was still loaded with a metropolis of empty, filthy glasses from the previous occupants, but we didn't care. Someone (perhaps even Ellen) would eventually come by and clear them; and besides, if we craned our necks from this vantage point, we could get a pretty good sightline to the stage.

The band, which apparently had been playing sets since the late afternoon, was on what felt like an extended break, and a great energy and tension vibrated through the air as the audience waited for them to take up their instruments once more. I glanced up at the club's high ceilings and noticed a new addition to the decor there: the owners of the Cajun Cage had installed, perhaps due to popular demand from its blomer clientele, sex cages not that dissimilar to the ones in place at the staff party last year. Through the gloaming shadows above the stage lights, I could see groups of what I assumed were blomers grappling with each other in those steel confines, the cages swinging lazily through the dark. I turned back to Otis, who looked pensive, wary. The air's distant grunts and moans and screams seemed only to exacerbate his now-curdled mood. He hadn't said anything in quite a while.

"Do you know," I ventured, looking to say something, anything, to break the silence, "where the word *Cajun* comes from?"

"Huh?" he said dreamily. He looked at me as if he had just realized I was there. "Oh. No. No, I don't."

"It's a bastardization of the word *Acadian*," I told him. "Yep, it's true. Something to do with Acadians escaping persecution in the Maritimes and fleeing to Louisiana to restart their lives there. Hence the French influence."

"Ah. Interesting," he said, uninterested. But quite clearly my mention of this had put tonight's earworm back in his brain because Otis began to murmur it below his breath. "*Man, oh man, there's a traffic jam / from here to Louisiana . . .*" He took out his phone, perhaps to check if there had been a text from Ellen in the last five or ten seconds.

I was just about to try something else when our waitress finally came by. It was not Ellen. This server was a nervous little chicken who looked new to the serving profession. "Hey, fellas, sorry to keep you waiting," she said automatonically, gathering up the dirty glasses off our table with a clutch of her hand and placing them on her tray. "Super busy tonight. Can I get you guys some drinks?"

We ordered margaritas and then Otis asked, "Is Ellen around right now?"

"Ellen?" The chicken rolled her eyes toward the ceiling to think about it, then rolled them back down. "Oh yes, she's hanging out somewhere."

"Could you send her over to our table when you get the chance?" he asked.

"And you are . . . ?"

"I'm her *husband.*"

"Oh. *Oh.* Of course. Right away."

She scurried off and we turned back to face in the general direction of the stage. The room seemed to grow more swollen with people; the bouncers must have admitted another wave from the street. A buzz began to stir in the air, and the cages above our heads gave a sudden, mad lurch. I looked to my left. Through this darkness, I thought I saw members of Thursday Banana descending the catwalks that had been installed along the walls leading up to the ceiling. It was hard to tell; the room was so full, so shadowy, a vast chamber of anticipation. Thousands of conversations seemed to clog the air.

"It looks like the break is coming to an end," I called out to Otis, and he nodded without emotion.

We waited in silence.

The waitress came by with our drinks, setting them before us in haste. Otis raised a chin, a questioning eye to her.

"She's on her way over," the chicken said as way of answer, and dashed off again.

We waited in silence.

And then Ellen did appear, looking both flush and ghostly. Her butterscotch hair was stacked without strategy atop her head, her cheeks and throat were a slick and clammy rose colour, and her server's uniform lay twisted on her lithe frame. Though appearing very worn out, she also held a certain vitality in that moment, a dewy élan that I couldn't peel my eyes from.

"I didn't know you were coming tonight," she said, a hint of curtness in her tone.

"Yeah, no, kind of spontaneous, last-minute decision," he replied. "We wouldn't miss a chance to see Thursday Banana. I tried to get you on your phone, but you didn't answer."

"Well, it's really busy, as you can see. I wish you'd told me you guys were coming." And here she paused, as if to ruminate on the reason why. "I would have gotten you a better table than *this*."

"It's okay," I chimed in. "The table's fine. It's great. We can see perfectly well from here." All this was my attempt at sweetening that sourpuss.

"Anyway," she said. "You got drinks, I see. That's good. The band'll be starting back up in about two minutes."

"In the meantime, can I talk to you?" Otis said. "Is there somewhere we can go?"

"What? No. I've got, like, ten tables I'm serving right now, and I –"

"It'll just take a sec."

With a sigh, she folded her arms over her breasts and looked off into space. But then she motioned with her head for him to follow her. Otis slid off his seat to do so, and they disappeared together through the mob of people.

Whatever it was they were discussing, it certainly took longer than a sec. I sat there alone, waiting for them to return, growing impatient with Otis's absence.

The band took to the stage. A great, thunderous applause rolled up from the crowd, buttressed by shrill whistles and loud cheers. The group launched immediately into "Traffic Jam," much to the joy of the audience, and we all joined in and belted it out along with the band. I felt sad that Otis was missing out on this moment of musical communion. I didn't recognize the next two tunes, but they were lovely enough, and I bobbed my head and sipped my margarita as the chords and lyrics unfurled across the room.

At some point near the start of the fourth song, Otis slipped discreetly back onto his seat. I swivelled around to look at him. His face had turned ashen but his eyes were wide and very alert, very saturated with what looked like a thousand angry thoughts. I waited for him to start, but when he didn't, I decided to take the initiative.

"Everything okay?" I asked.

He said nothing for a moment. Just picked up his margarita and took a brief sip from it. Then, without removing his glare from the stage, he asked: "Why does my wife hate me?"

At first I thought I'd misheard him over the din of the music. But I hadn't. The question lingered in the air between us before sinking like a rock. I swallowed hard and tried to come up with a response, a retort. It would have helped had Otis given me something more, a bit of context around what he and Ellen had just discussed. But he remained committed to his brooding muteness.

"I'm sure she doesn't hate you," I said. "Whatever's going on, she's probably just ... ?"

I held out the question like a relay baton I hoped he'd take up, but he didn't. He just shook his head, moistened his lips, ran a hand through his long, sandy-blond hair. "Let's just watch the show," he said with a sigh.

So we watched it. Thursday Banana rolled through forty-five minutes of rowdy, carefree tunes, and we absorbed them like a pair of passive sponges. At one point my eyes drifted over to the deep right of the stage, where I thought I caught a glimpse of Ellen. She was not hustling between the tables serving drinks. In fact, her tray was nowhere to be seen. Instead, she was crushed up against the edge of the stage, the corner no doubt poking into her flat, tender midriff. Her eyes were closed, her hips swaying, her arms up, her fingers splayed and waggling to the beat of the music. She was a groupie at the band's feet. Whether Otis had spotted her or not, I couldn't tell.

When the set ended, the band descended the stage and disappeared, and Ellen seemed to disappear with them. Our chicken came by and we ordered another round of margaritas. The drinks arrived and Otis and I sipped from them, barely speaking. By the time we finished, I could feel all the fatigue of the day clinging to my muscles. There was an awkwardness in the air now that we had nothing to listen to, nothing to talk about.

"Wanna go?" Otis asked.

"Sure," I said. "But don't you want to . . ." and I motioned vaguely in the direction of the crowd, to the place where I thought Ellen might be.

"No, I'll talk to her when she gets home," he said, and slid dejectedly off his chair.

It felt so strange, so mean and deliberate, to leave the Cajun Cage without seeking her out and saying goodbye. But there we were, on the sidewalk outside, among a new crowd looking to get in. Otis and I hugged briefly, malely, and gave each other a nod.

"I'm sorry tonight was such a bust," he said.

"No worries," I replied. "I hope things will be okay with you guys."

He nodded again, then turned and just strolled off toward the subway. And I turned and headed for home.

As I began hiking back toward my condo tower, I observed that the streets on the way had grown creepily quiet. This struck me as bizarre considering that, since pullulation, it was as if the city had refused to sleep. Even in the middle of the week, it was not uncommon to look out one's window and find sidewalks and thoroughfares choked with blomers at 2:00 a.m. But not tonight. Tonight, the avenues and boulevards were so empty that they appeared to gleam. En route to my neighbourhood, I passed just two foxes copulating vigorously against a Canada Post box. As I turned onto Isabella Street for the final stretch home, a gaggle of roughnecked and dust-covered dogs, still in their bright orange safety vests from their day on a construction site, came hooting and hollering toward me before veering off into the night. Otherwise, I encountered no one.

That is, until I arrived very near the base of our condo tower. I was waiting for the red light there to change so I could cross the street when I heard what sounded like singing, a plaintive and desperate croon, coming from the laneway on my right. I turned to face it, furrowing my brow. I was struck by how that noise, that resonating hum, could at once seem both pained and melodious. I doubled back and moved toward the lane. It ran between a squat brick building – a municipal hydro station – and another sparkly new condo tower climbing into the sky. I stood at the lane's mouth. There in the shadows, crumpled against the red brick wall of the hydro station, sat a blomer. Its head was turned up to the night sky as if in benediction, but its legs were twisted and scattered beneath it at unlikely angles. This close by, I could tell the voice, that singing, was all gargled and moist. The sound chilled me to my core.

"Hey there," I called out. "Are you . . . are you okay?"

I took a step forward, and it was like the shadows receded under the gleam of a street lamp on the other side of the lane. This close up, I could now see that the person was a gopher, one of those blomers obsessed with the rarified attitudes of duty, bravery, courage. Indeed, this gopher was partially dressed in what looked like a Canadian military uniform. The khaki pants were torn at the knee, and the collared green shirt loomed open like a mouth halfway to the sternum. "I say there, are you okay?" I asked again, taking another step forward.

That was when I nearly walked into the pond of blood gathered on the asphalt around its splayed hips.

The gopher, blinded by bruises that swelled like fruit around its eyes, stopped singing and turned toward the sound of my voice. Despite the face's marring injuries, I could tell it was a male – or, at least, mostly male. The brow was gruff, the jaw lantern-like, the chin sporting a tasteful soul patch. But the nose. The nose. It curled up softly, sensuously, at the tip. It had a prettiness to it. It reminded me of Morgana's nose.

I looked down at the shirt that yawned open. Ah yes. *You nearly got away with it,* I thought, *what you were hiding from your eventual assailants – and, no doubt, your comrades in the military. You, my friend, could have almost passed for a straight-up man. But no. No, no.* There, in the pale splash of the street lamp's light, I could see a pair of women's breasts gawping out from the torn shirt. They were, to be fair, small breasts, incipient breasts, like those of a teenager just entering the sadistic funhouse that was puberty. But they were breasts just the same. An eggplant-dark gash, brightly weeping, ran along the rack of ribs below the left one.

"You're going to be okay," I said, though it was obvious this wasn't true. As if to answer my falsehood, the blomer's breath grew very shallow and hitchy then. I squatted to be at eye level with . . . with . . . them, *them,* and they reached out their hand to me. In one self-hating moment, I considered rejecting it. I thought about all the anguish blomers had caused me, and all the animus I felt toward them. But then I thought of poor Alanna, cradling her Lesley to her bosom and protecting them from all the violence and chaos that this new world had wrought. It wasn't right. It wasn't right.

I placed the hand in my own and squeezed it.

Things did not take all that long. The breathing started to gurgle, like the soft percolations of a coffee maker. When it ended, I placed the hand gently, respectfully, back on the blomer's lap.

I looked at my palm. It was covered in blood.

There was no way to know what compelled me next, but as I stood back up, I felt an abrupt urge come over me. I raised my hand to my face and, after a moment's pause, dragged my index finger along one cheekbone and then the other. I was like a football player putting on that black gunge before a game, or maybe like one of the kids in *Lord of the Flies.* Either way, I wanted to mark myself with this blomer's blood as proof that I had done what I had done.

I left the laneway. I crossed the street. I entered our condo building and rode the elevator up to our unit. I went in and immediately headed to the bathroom. I popped on the light and, there in the mirror, stared at the two streaks of blood on my face.

I looked like a warrior.

Immediately, I felt ridiculous and washed them off. Silly, silly, silly. What did I think I was doing?

I went into our darkened bedroom. Morgana was already there, already asleep on her side of the bed. I stripped off my clothes and climbed in next to her. Moved up against her wide, soft rump and wrapped my arms around her.

As usual, she smelled of other men.

PART 3: ROAD-TRIPPING

CHAPTER 9

I'd had just about enough of Brennan Prate and his shit disturbing, and I wasn't going to take it anymore.

Something had come over me in the weeks since that night at the Cajun Cage with Otis, when I had stumbled upon the dying gopher. It felt as if a major shift had occurred within me, like a core part of my personality had been altered, broken off, compromised. Normally, what you saw with Hector Spencer Thompson was what you got. I'd always been, if I was anything at all, pleasantly predictable. My appearance, for example, was anodyne to the extreme: I was of medium height, medium build; I wore small, slight spectacles, neatly ironed shirts, pressed pants; I was always clean-shaven and kept my silvery hair short. My attitude was equally inoffensive. I thought of myself as warm-hearted and eager to help others, even if I was a touch reserved and private. I knew that I didn't always have the best sense of humour, often feeling as if jokes that others enjoyed went sailing over my head. No question, I was very wrapped up in the structures and protocols of my job at Percussive Insurance, and I tended to tamp down confrontation whenever I could. But I considered myself a peacemaker, a consensus seeker, a bridge-builder. I had been, during this whole growth-obsessed period in the company's history, a bureaucrat in the best sense of the term.

No more. *No more*, I thought as I watched Brennan Prate hurl his way toward me across the oceanic open-concept office in what looked like a deep-seated need to disturb shit. *Bring it, motherfucker*, I thought. Had he already noticed (and noted?) the changes that had come over me in the last little while? The fact that I was shaving only about twice a week now? Or that my shirts were wrinkled more often than they were ironed? Or that I had grown curt with people – especially blomers – in the break areas and bathrooms? Or that I had taken to silent sulking during management meetings, not volunteering ideas even when the problem at hand would've benefitted from my expertise? I was downward spiralling, and I sensed that he knew it.

Brennan arrived at my desk and immediately hauled out from under it what we called a toadstool – basically a little cabinet on wheels with a thickly cushioned top (this abomination had replaced the now-rescinded guest chairs that had come standard with my now-rescinded office) – and planted himself upon it in a sort of bowlegged manoeuvre that revealed in one horrifying flash where his gut ended and his groin began.

"Two things," he growled in that nasally voice of his. "First, we need to have a little talk about the intranet."

Oh fuck. Of all the topics that touched my role in HR, my least favourite was the company's infuriating employee portal. It had been a somewhat labyrinthine puzzle even when Percussive Insurance had had just two hundred employees; now that we topped out in the thousands, the site was a like a giant gag puzzle, a massive online scavenger hunt. The portal had four separate navigations – top, left, right and bottom – with the tabs in each chosen and arranged seemingly at random. The text's varying font types, sizes and colours made the homepage look like a digitized ransom note. The badly pixelated clip art was about fifteen years out of date. And the search box appeared to be strictly decorative.

"What about it?" I asked.

He glared at me – we both knew that, as the HR – sorry, *HC* – manager, I was more or less to blame for the intranet's sorry state – and then nodded at my computer. "Can you punch it up for me, please?"

I did so, then turned my monitor round to face him.

"See that banner image at the top?" he asked. Which, of course, I did, as it took up a full quarter of the screen. "'Kay, that design is, like, *three* colour palettes ago. And *that*," and he pointed to the image's bottom left corner, "isn't even our logo anymore. Hasn't been for six months."

"Yeah, I know," I said with a kind of faux mea culpa. "We want to update it, we do, but it just keeps getting pushed down the priority list. You know how it goes, Brennan."

"Oh, yeah?" he asked. "And what about the rest of it? Don't you realize that nobody can find anything on that fucking site? I mean, I'm a *director* and I can't even locate my own department's documents anymore. And the other day, I tried to use the search box to find expense forms for the finance department, and do you know what result it coughed up? An e-vite for a bake sale from *four years ago.*"

"Oh, Brennan, you probably just didn't use the right key-words," I replied with a smirk. At that his jowls jiggled with in-credulity, and I cleared my throat. "Look, everybody knows the intranet is quirky. It's got quirks. But you know, you learn the quirks, you make them second nature, and eventually you're able to find what you're looking f–"

"Not good enough," he interrupted, and when I piqued at his insolence, he offered an olive branch. "Look, I got a fox down on eighth. Name's Raymond. Good guy, great guy, only takes two or three sex breaks a day. And he's a whiz when it comes to informa-tion architecture. He designed us a microsite for the Clarington rollout and I couldn't have been happier. All very logical and easy to use. I want him to design a new intranet for you."

"Well, I'll take it under advisement," I said. "You know, we have a lot on our plates right now, but I'm sure –"

"No, you're not taking it under advisement, Hector. You aren't stonewalling this one. I'm moving Raymond up here to work with you on it. Two months and he'll be done. No argument. I outrank you now, and if you can't make this happen, then *I* will."

He and I stared at each other like two cowboys engaged in pistols at dawn.

"And the second thing?" I asked.

"Well, while I was trawling around in the back end of the system – I get access to that now – I happened to take a peek inside your own personnel file."

"Really?"

My stomach coiled like a snake, though I fought hard not to show it. What was he doing in *there*? Was he mucking around for dirt on me? Surely there was none to be found – I was squeaky clean, just squeaky clean; hadn't so much as received a "met goals with some exceptions" performance evaluation in all the years I'd been with the firm. Yet I could tell by his expression that Brennan did have something on me, or thought he did. He raised an eyebrow and tilted his meaty face forward, as if inviting me to come clean. I shifted uneasily in my seat.

"Do you realize how many vacation days you have banked?" he asked.

"Oh. Oh, *that*." A sense of relief coursed through me. "Well, Brennan, what can I say? It's been an incredibly busy ti–"

He began rhyming things off on his heavy fingers. "You had three days left over from two calendar years ago and four from the year before that. Then, last year, with the exception of your short-term disability after your car accident, which doesn't count, you took zero days. Understandable, I *guess*, considering we were in the throes of pullulation. But you've also taken no days in the first quarter of this year. If we prorate that, it means you're now owed thirty-two days. That's almost seven weeks' vacation."

I looked at him, then shrugged in a *Whattaya gonna do?* gesture.

"Can I be honest with you?" he went on. "You look like shit, Hector. No, I'm sorry, but you do. You look like you could use a good long break. You've been dropping balls right, left and centre, and you've been snappy and unresponsive with people. I've noticed it, and others have, too. So might I suggest you use some of those banked days to take an extended leave from the company?" I opened my mouth to protest but he raised a hand to stop me. "I'm not talking the full whack. Not by a long shot. You ain't gettin' seven weeks. But maybe four? Or even five? Think about it."

I swallowed hard and flared my nostrils at him. "Brennan, I'm fine."

"Are you? Tell me, when was the last time you replied to an email within twenty-four hours? When was the last time you laundered that shirt?"

"Brennan . . ."

"I want you to think about it, okay? Take your wife someplace sunny and nice. Go chill out on a beach where the drinks come with little umbrellas in them. Maybe by the time you get back, Raymond will have the new intranet all wireframed and ready for your approval." He slid off the toadstool then and mounted his feet. "Think about it."

"Brennan . . ."

"Just think about it."

❧

When you're as obsessive as I am, it's very hard to let things go.

I knew I needed a break. I knew I was, as Brennan Prate had put it, dropping balls. I was losing my grip. I also knew that this place wouldn't necessarily fall apart without me. With whole squads of chickens and goats (not to mention two cats and a pigeon, God bless her taut, analytical mind) working under me, the Human Resources – check that, Human *Capital* – Department would not collapse if I took a short sabbatical from the company. But it was very hard to let things go. It was hard to admit that I had a problem, that something fundamental about me had changed. I wasn't normally a bitter person. I rarely dwelled in the darker corners of human nature. But every time my mind conjured images of that dying gopher, that herm, clasping their quavering, blood-damp hand to mine as they took their final breaths, I would grow overcome with acrimony. I would see my blomer colleagues as the potential murderers they were and my fellow vips as the accomplices who blithely ignored it all. It felt as if the entire structure of this post-pullulation reality, what every-one had come to accept, needed to be torn down, but I also felt powerless, utterly impotent, to do it myself.

Matters grew worse. Somehow, I became even snappier and more belligerent with people. I began rejecting meeting invitations outright, providing no corresponding explanation for my absence. I began misfiling peoples' personnel dockets or even logging an incorrect performance evaluation score on their re-cord. I began stealing mugs.

There were other acts of subversion. Example: I made up my mind that I would begin keeping more – how shall I put it? – *Parisian* hours at the office. I would stroll in at nine thirty, take an hour and a half for lunch, leave the office by four. When I got dirty looks from my underlings or colleagues, I gaily ignored them, whistling through my now-abbreviated day as if this be-haviour were perfectly natural. I decided that, should Brennan Prate make a crack about what I was doing, I would counter that this was just me acknowledging his point that I was spending too much time at the office.

Unfortunately, I failed to keep Morgana abreast of these changes. The first week wasn't so bad: she had been harried enough by the play's rehearsals (its debut had once again been delayed; now it seemed it wouldn't open until the summer) that she failed to notice that I must have gotten home earlier than usual to get dinner on the table so soon. But then, halfway through the second week of this scheme, my new schedule tripped her up. Indeed, one could say that it tripped her up royally.

It occurred on a night when I'd managed to arrive back at our condo even earlier than my previous earliest time. I had somehow slipped away from the office a few minutes before four o'clock, and on the commute home, I hit all my subway transfers perfectly, stepping onto each car just seconds before the door closed and the subway pulled away from the platform. Consequently, it was still daylight by the time I was strolling down the street toward our condo tower. This hadn't happened in months! I greeted our building's doorman and then rode the elevator up to our unit. As I unlocked the door with my watch, I expected to find the place cast in silent darkness. But instead, I came inside to discover all the lights on and Morgana standing in the middle of our living room with two of her blomer co-stars, both male. The descending sun was blaring across our windows, lighting the three of them in a fiery late-afternoon glow.

The first thing I noticed – which should *not* have been the first thing I noticed – was that Morgana wore upon her head the elaborately woven wimple that had become the distinct element of her character Titania's costume. The garment was of a deep and lascivious purple, with rich, velvety folds and lacy webbing, and was sort of a cross between a nun's habit and a leonine mane. Below it, she had donned a skimpy, satiny, salmon-coloured negligee, which rippled with surprising flattery over her short, stout frame. The second thing I noticed – which should have been the *first* thing I noticed – was that the blomers standing on either side of her (two tall, strapping young crows who did not seem to have a gram of body fat between them) wore nothing at all except a pair of tight boxer briefs that hugged their firm and chiselled hips. Arching upward from these briefs, much to my dismay, were two huge, intimidating, Aristophanic hard-ons that aspired toward my wife with rigid longing. They were club-like, cudgel-like, but did not, I thought in that one short moment, look like prosthetics at all.

"Hi, sweetie!" I exclaimed from the doorway, making sure to drop my briefcase with a pronounced thud. She was just in the middle of belting out one of her numbers and stropped abruptly when she saw me.

"Oh, Hector! Hi. Hi." She did this sort of cringing, embarrassed manoeuvre that involved bearing her weight down on one foot while pressing an index finger under her nose and turning her face away. But she recovered fast and came bounding up to me for a hug, her face blushing. "What are you, what are you doing home so early?"

"Things are a bit slow at the office," I lied, "and I thought, *What the hell, I've been working so hard, I'm going to jet at four o'clock today*. So I did. What's, um . . ." and I eyed the two acromegalic, half-naked studs standing in my living room; their erections raged on as they waited for my wife to return to them ". . . going on around here?"

"Oh, sorry. *Sorry*. I should have said something this morning before you left." She gave an uneasy, apologetic laugh. "We've totally overwhelmed the theatre's rehearsal space. *Harpies: The Musical!* is getting out of control. So Carolina encouraged us to practise certain scenes at home if we could. Sorry, sorry. Where *are* my manners? This is Sean and Raphael."

"Hiya, fellas," I said, and gave them a stiff, salute-like wave. One would think that in the presence of their co-star's husband, a drab man of insurance in tweedy slacks and a rumpled dress shirt, those sprouting exclamation marks would calm themselves a little. But this was not the case. As I stepped into the living room, my eyes flickered involuntarily to those black boxer briefs and saw that they had grown wetly blacker at their tented tips. The lads returned my impassive wave and then folded their arms loosely over their chests in what I considered to be a very thespian way, an unsubtle act of impatience.

"Anyway, we need another, what?" Morgana looked at them. "Maybe an hour or so?"

"Probably more like an hour and a half," one of them replied stonily.

Morgana turned back to me. "Yeah, maybe an hour and a half. But then, with you home so early, we can actually cook supper together. Just like old times. Won't that be *nice*?"

"And will your friends want to join us?"

"I don't know. Why don't you ask them?"

I turned to the blomers. "Lads?"

"Can't," said either Sean or Raphael.

"Me neither," said the other.

Something in their tone struck me as slightly sarcastic, even snarky – as if they'd be happy to stay had dinner involved just Morgana.

I decided to ignore it. "Oh well, maybe next time." I turned back to my wife. "Anyway, I just realized I didn't even bathe before I went to work this morning. I think I'll go take a shower."

"Okay, sounds good," Morgana replied. "Like I said, we won't be much longer."

I stepped closer to her then and fingered the soft, silky fabric of the negligee. "This is nice," I remarked, but to my surprise she blushed again and coiled away from me, as if I'd made a faux pas.

"It's not mine," she said somewhat sternly as she looked at the floor. "Hector, it's . . . it's just a *costume*."

"Of course," I replied. "Of course." The three of them stared at me, and I stared at them. Ah, yes. I got the cue and left them to their work.

Later, I stood alone in front of the large, counter-wide mirror in our bathroom. Through the walls, I could hear the muffled sound of blomers banging and thrashing away at each other above and below me, which may have drowned out the sound of any banging and thrashing coming from our unit. Having stripped off everything except my Y-front briefs (no longer tighty and whitey but more of a sagging near-death grey), I stared down at my own comparably un-Aristophanic loins and sighed. The sight of my near-nakedness, of all the vulgar alcoves of my body, sent an emotion coursing through me that I could not name. *Yes, yes. There, there.* Whatever this feeling was, it seemed fuelled by those random thatches of hair, the concaving chest, the convexing gut. God, I was getting old. *When are you going to turn this emotion around?* I thought. *When are you going to turn it around and call it what it is – anger? When are you going to start getting mad?* But the truth was, it wasn't quite anger. It was something else, something akin to anger but far less kinetic.

I sighed again and slid my undies off. I was just pushing aside the shower curtain and reaching for the tub's faucet when a sound, as crisp and transparent as water, came pealing through the tiled walls. It was Morgana, in our living room, giving up the most uproarious laugh, a shrill-yet-warm guffaw, a generous jag of hysteria. It rang out like a bell. And for the first time in our marriage, the sound of her unfettered joy made my skin crawl.

❧

I got summoned down to the fifth floor. A cat had bitten somebody.

In the pre-pullulation age, this would not have been unusual; though, of course, there were no cats in a corporate environment back then. Back then, cats bit. Cats were biters. We all knew this. It was especially true when you attempted to pet them on their little heads or their soft, furry bellies when they didn't want you to, or if you made a sound they didn't like. Cats bit. Just like dogs barked, gophers burrowed, goats bleated and pigeons shat on everything. That was then. Now, cats, dogs, gophers, goats and pigeons – not to mention scores of other mammals and birds – walked among us in human form, or near-human form. They wore blazers and slacks. They carried file folders and smart phones. They sat in meetings and said things like, "Yes, but what's the profit margin if we delay the launch till August?" or "I'd order the

Waldorf salad except, you know, it's got walnuts in it." They took Caribbean vacations and went to spin classes. They were just like us, or mostly just like us. So when a blomer engaged in a bit of pre-pullulation behaviour, we vips found it terribly unnerving.

I stepped out of the elevator onto five and hurried to the site of the commotion. A group of employees had collected around a workstation in the northeastern corner of the floor, and I could already hear elevated voices arguing with each other about what was going on. Steeling myself, I raised my hands in an *Okay, okay, let's all just calm down* sort of gesture as I approached. Faces turned, and I was relieved to see there was still a small sliver of deference offered me as the head of Human Capital.

"All right, all right," I said. "Let's start at the beginning. What happened?"

"Josephine bit Tara on the hand!" someone called out.

"Tara was about to steal her Fitbit."

"It's not her Fitbit. It's Tara's. She left it here last night by accident – right there on the edge of her desk."

"No, it's Josephine's. She couldn't find hers at home before she left for work. She's certain it's hers."

"That doesn't mean she can bite somebody on the hand!"

Everyone began talking at once again, but I soon parsed the particulars of the situation. Josephine, a cat working in the Contracts & Deeds department, and Tara, a vip also working in Contracts & Deeds, were involved in a desk-sharing arrangement. Desk-sharing had become increasingly common here at Percussive Insurance, despite my protestations; upper management believed it helped cut down on costs and optimize space for those departments that had so much work as to run two shifts per day. This was definitely the case for Contracts & Deeds. So, Tara and Josephine shared a single desk: Tara used it for her workday, which ran from 7:00 a.m. until 3:00 p.m.; then Josephine used it for hers, which ran from 3:30 p.m. until 11:30 p.m. The rule around shared workstations was that you were not allowed to keep any personal effects whatsoever on the desk, and you were to keep the station neat and organized for the other person. This, I knew from my many years of working in human resources, would become a breeding ground for conflict. I mean, how demoralizing can you get when you won't even allow a worker to keep a family photo or personalized coffee mug on a desk overnight? And "neat and organized" was certainly up for interpretation. It bothered me to no end that in less than fifteen months, the company had gone from everybody having their own office to this madness, but upper management wouldn't listen. So, sure enough, Contracts & Deeds had called a rare department-wide meeting for two thirty today, and Josephine had agreed to shift her hours a bit so she could attend. For the first time in months, her and Tara's days overlapped, and all the tension, all the passive aggression that had been brewing between them as they treated each other like a malicious poltergeist in their workspace, erupted over this one misplaced personal item.

"Give me the Fitbit," I said to no one in particular. When no one in particular came forward, I said again, "Would someone please just give me the Fitbit?"

A neutral third party stepped up and handed the item to me. I examined the wristband briefly, turning it around a couple of times in the hope that it might contain an identifying feature. Of course, it did not. The Fitbit was indistinguishable from every other Fitbit in the world. I then summoned Josephine and Tara to stand before me, eyeing them up as they did. It was remarkable, I thought, how feline Josephine seemed – it was rare for a blomer to exhibit so strongly the qualities from his or her animal antecedent – and I was slightly unnerved at the way she looked like she'd lick her whiskers then if she still had them. Tara, meanwhile, displayed downcast eyes that had gone puffy from crying. She was in her mid-thirties, so it had probably been decades since someone had bitten her (at least, non-consensually), and the shock of it all was just too much to bear.

"Okay, here's what's going to happen," I said. "You two are going to go home right now and think about what you've done." A supervisor for Contracts & Deeds raised a hand of protest, but I cut her off. "Nope, nope. I'm sorry, Kathy, but I don't care. You can just email them the minutes from the meeting." Then I turned back to Tara and Josephine. "And while you're home, I want you both to look for your respective Fitbits. One of you no doubt left it there and just forgot. When you find it, I want you to call me, okay? And when you do, I will give *this* Fitbit," and I raised up the black-strapped device like a torch, "to the other person tomorrow. Deal?"

When neither answered, I answered for them. "*Deal.* Now, I want the rest of you to go have your meeting. And tomorrow, after we've solved this whole Fitbit mystery, I want Tara and Josephine to write an apology email to each other and for everybody to move past this." I turned to the two women. "And I'm also going to figure out a way for you two to have your own desks from now on."

This seemed to satisfy people enough for them to begin dispersing. I tucked the Fitbit into the pocket of my slacks and then took in a long, languorous breath. Since I was already down here on the fifth floor, I decided to pop by Otis's desk for a visit, as I hadn't done so in a while. *He won't believe the shit I have to deal with,* I thought. His workstation was on the far end of the floor, on the other side of the elevator banks, so I began strolling toward it at a leisurely pace. As I did, I passed row after endless row of small, open-concept desks – home to investigators and account assistants, directors and project managers, lawyers and salespeople, all working under self-surveillance, its great panoptical grip. I soon came upon Otis's area: because his desk was squeezed right up against the windowed corner of the floor and there was a frosted glass partition there to demarcate space for a photocopier, he was afforded the slightest modicum of privacy.

Faces full of concern or even panic turned up at me from desks leading to Otis's as I strolled down the aisle. I creased my brow in confusion. People were staring at me as if I, Mr. HC Manager, had come to resolve yet another crisis afflicting the fifth floor.

The crisis in question? I saw it as I rounded the glass partition and stood at Otis's desk. There in his chair, he sat hunched over his station with his work phone pressed hard against his ear while his free hand clamped his skull in a kind of death grip. His face had turned a frightening fuchsia, and his eyes were pissing tears.

I was just about to speak when he stood up abruptly. He removed the phone from his ear and began striking it down upon his desk as if it were a hammer. He pounded the receiver into its console with terrifying thrusts of his hand, again and again and again, until finally he released it and let it rest there in its cradle before cupping his tremulous mouth in his hand.

"Otis . . . dude?" I asked.

He jumped, startled at the sound of my voice, and turned to face me. He said something like, "Hey," or "Hi," or "Oh, hey," and then began pressing at his damp eyes with the balls of his palms.

"Brother, what's going on?" I asked.

He tried to speak, but his breath went all hitchy and his face turned an even deeper red.

"Okay, okay," I said, stepping forward and putting an arm around his shoulders. "Come with me. Let's find a quiet place to talk."

Easier said than done. As I led him away from his desk and cast a brusque *Mind your own business* glare at the people who were staring at us, I realized that there were virtually no private places I could take Otis. Meeting rooms, break areas, even the café down in the lobby, were all open-concept spaces. So I led him instead toward the men's room in the hopes of finding a vacant toilet stall (preferably one designed for people in wheelchairs, so we'd have the extra room) where he and I could stand and talk.

We were in luck. As I shepherded him into that brightly lit and tiled space, we saw that a hawk was just exiting the wheelchair stall on the far side. In his impeccably tailored suit and air of entrepreneurial smugness, the hawk made his able-bodied way over to the counter of sinks, where he gave his hands a quick, cursory wash. To Otis's leaky and enflamed face, the hawk tossed a glance more suspicious than empathetic and then pushed his way past us and back out to the office.

I took Otis into the stall and shut and locked the door. Oh, my. The air still held the fecund aromas of a fresh shit, and despite my attempts not to, I couldn't help but cast a quick look down at the golden skid mark at the bottom of the bowl.

"I'm sorry, brother," I said.

"That's okay."

"It's the only place. This fucking office."

"I know. It's fine. It's fine."

He slumped against the wall and I leaned against the door, my hands descending into my pockets. I could feel Tara or Josephine's Fitbit in there, the strap cold and impersonal. "So, what's going on?" I asked.

He took a moment to compose himself, inhaling deep, almost angry breaths despite the stench, and shook his head as if in disbelief.

"She's left," he said.

"Who?" I asked, though I could already guess.

"Ellen. She's left."

"Left where?"

He rotated his eyes up to me. "No, she's *left*. She's left *me*." His voice turned all hiccupy again. "I don't know where she is. This all started last night when she packed a bag but wouldn't tell me where she was going, wouldn't talk to me, wouldn't even look at me. Then I called her cell just now and I could tell she was on the road . . . heading somewhere. She refused to talk and told me not to call back, that . . . that her cell phone would stop working soon . . . and . . . and . . ." He lost his composure then, punching the wall behind him with a bunched-up fist.

"Hey, it's okay, it's okay," I said. "Just take your time. Start at the beginning. What happened?"

He stood there trembling a bit but then began again. "Well, as you know, she's been spending extra time at the Cage, even when she doesn't have a shift. Which was fine. Which was fine. It was just fine. I know she has a lot of friends there, and –"

Just then we heard someone enter the bathroom, and Otis stopped. We stood in silence as we heard the unzipping of a fly and then the deep dribbling sound at the urinal. Whoever it was, he wrapped up quickly but then, unlike the hawk, took his sweet time at the sink, scrubbing his hands maniacally while the water ran and ran. Then, finally, the automated tap turned off and we heard him dry his hands and leave.

Otis proceeded. "I know she has a lot of friends there and I'm not trying to keep her from them. I'm not. I'm not. I said to her, 'If you want to hang out with your friends, then go. Go! Be with them. Have fun!' I never once tried to restrict how much time she was spending at the Cage because I'm not that kind of husband. That's not what you do. Right? *Right?*"

"Right," I murmured. And I agreed with him, at least in theory. "No, right," I stressed.

"Right. But if you're not going to be that kind of husband, then the trade-off is that she's not going to . . . going to . . ." And here, his eyes began pissing again. "She's not going to fall in love with somebody else. And that's what's happened. She's fallen in love with the band. She's fallen in love with Thursday Banana."

"Everyone's in love with Thursday Banana," I assured him.

"No, I mean she's literally fallen in love with them. They've got this new long-term gig somewhere down south, I don't know where, and she left with them. She just . . . left. She told me –"

Someone else entered the bathroom. Christ. We stopped and listened in stony, cringing silence as the person took up residence in the stall next to ours. Everything became sound then. The unbuckling of a belt, the dropping of pants, the nestling of buttocks onto the toilet seat. The pause. The soft grunt. Then the wet, snare-drum rollick of the bowels letting go. Christ. It went on and on, the noise attenuating only slightly with each percussive sputter. *Does the human body really take this long to do this?* I thought with eyes squeezed shut. Time moved as if through thick mud. Finally, we heard the thunderous rattle of the toilet roll dispenser. More unpleasant listening. Then, mercifully, up went the pants, followed by the toilet's vicious sneeze, followed by the stall door unlatching and opening. Much to my horror, this individual, whoever he was, didn't make so much as a perfunctory visit to the bank of sinks before exiting the bathroom. *Dammit*, I thought, *I should have made note of his shoes or something, so I don't end up shaking hands with him later.*

I turned back to Otis as if coming out of a sleep. "She told you what?" I asked.

"She told me she wasn't sure if this meant the end of our marriage or if she'd ever come back. But she told me she *had* to do this, and if I loved her at all I would understand that." Again, he pawed at his soggy cheeks with the ball of his hand. "Which is bullshit."

"Total bullshit," I agreed. My stomach clenched and my shoulders tightened as I waited for him to say more about this betrayal. It seemed very immediate, very serious, this notion that one's spouse could just run off with a merry band of blomers promising adventure and high times and . . . and . . . ?

My whole body felt saturated with dread.

I was about to say, *Go on*, when he said, "I'm sorry to go on like this. And I apologize for what happened at my desk. I managed to get her on her cell but then she just hung up on me and I freaked out. I'm sorry."

"No need to apologize," I replied. "It's totally understandable. Only . . . what are you going to do, Otis?"

"I, I don't know." He looked at me as if *I* might offer a suggestion.

"Well," I sighed, "there's the whole *If you love a thing, let it go* business. You could just try to chill out, play it cool. Give her a chance to come back. And then, if she does, see if you can't salvage your relationship."

His stare turned to one of incredulity.

"Or," I went on, ". . . you could . . ."

"Or I could . . . ?"

The unspoken words dangled there in the stall. Neither of us were quite ready to articulate what we were thinking. We just stood in silence for a bit.

"I should get back to work," he eventually said.

"Yeah, me too."

"Thanks for this, Hector. You're a true friend."

Nodding, I patted his shoulder.

I unlatched the door then and we exited the wheelchair stall together. But just as we did, someone else came pushing into the bathroom. He stopped and we stopped. I turned my eyes up to see who it was.

Oh God.

Oh *God.*

"Another chapter in your bromance, boys?" he asked as he eyed us up and down, then barked a guffaw of unmitigated cruelty.

"Oh, just shut your trap," I told him. His face clicked audibly as his jaw fell open. I just shoved past him with Otis trailing behind me.

CHAPTER 10

have decided to fight for them, began Alanna's email.

The note arrived late in the evening on the day after my toilet stall heart-to-heart with Otis, and I was once again home alone, unaware of when Morgana would return or, I supposed, even where she was. Alanna's sentence struck me like a flint, creating a brief but powerful spark that jolted me out of my malaise and cast me upward toward a truer and more vivid consciousness.

My muscles tensed as I read what my friend had written.

Dear Hector,

I have decided to fight for them. Even as I write this, I feel the incredible (and incredibly important) burden that your advice back in February foisted onto me. I will fight for them. And by them, I don't just mean Lesley, who has become a full member of our family now, much to Mitch's chagrin. I still struggle with the plurality (pluralness?) of Lesley's desired pronoun, since I see them as such a singular, indivisible being and love them like the second child I never got to have. No. By them, I mean all of the blomers who are like Lesley – the hermaphrodites or herms or whatever we're calling them now. I want to fight, not just for Lesley, but for all of them who are like them.

As usual, Hector, your advice to me was sound. I did go online and find a collective of like-minded people. Surprisingly, these activist groups are few and far between. There's one here, two in San

Francisco, one in Mexico City and one in Johannesburg. That's it, as far I can tell. Not surprisingly, these groups are composed entirely of vips. No blomer wants to have anything to do with them. But it doesn't matter. We are small, but we won't be small for long. And we will not let this stand. Some news reports are now saying that as many as one in ten blomers who emerged during pullulation is a herm. One in ten! How can we stand by as they are beaten and tortured and killed all over the world, right in front of us? If blomers are full persons under the law, and herms are blomers, then aren't herms full persons? They are. They are!

Mitch is *still* beside himself with rage at my newfound sense of social justice. He spends all day and half the evening working on construction sites with dogs, and they fill his head with lies. Dogs are terrible. They are the worst, and they're brainwashing my husband. He resents Lesley's presence in our home, and he hates every minute I spend trying to kick-start a movement to defend their right to exist. He's even threatened me with divorce. Divorce, Hector. But I don't care. This is more important than my marriage, and if it rips my family apart then so be it.

I want to thank you, again, for coming all the way up here that night to talk to me about this stuff. I really felt encouraged by what you said. You know, my parents always taught me to fight hard, not only for what I knew was right but also against what I knew was wrong. And I will. I just didn't realize that what I know to be wrong could be so wrong, and on such a scale.

Anyway, I hope you're also fighting against whatever you believe to be wrong. I know, or at least sensed, that you and Morgana may not be on the same page about everything going on in your lives either. I hope you guys are okay, but I also hope that you are picking your battles and fighting the good fight.

Thank you again for what you did for me. You're a true friend.

Lots of love,

Alanna

Yes, I wanted to scream. *Yes. Exactly* that. It startled me how much she and I were on the same page. It startled me how, by the mere acknowledgement of the gift I had given to Alanna, she in turn had given the same gift back to me. As I closed her email, I felt closer to her than I had since . . . since when? Well, since that first week of teachers' college before I had learned about Mitch, before I had latched onto Morgana.

I knew what I wanted to do. The truth of it, that realization, swirled around inside me like an eddy of wind. *Yes, yes,* I thought. *Cast off who you were, Hector Spencer Thompson, and embrace a different self. Sure, the idea you're contemplating is radical, completely out of character for you and, perhaps, even a bit dangerous. But do it. Put the wheels in motion.*

I picked up my cellphone then and began a lengthy text conversation with Otis.

❧

Our city announced that it would start expanding into the lake.

The future had come: Due to the limitations of land space, underwater communities were becoming all the rage now. *Submerged living,* they called it. In our city, you could now pre-purchase a condo unit in a building slated for erection beneath the sloshing waves of Lake Ontario. Advertisements for these were all over the newspapers and the internet, on the sides of buses and above the urinals in trendy gastropubs. Studio bachelors were going for as low as two-seven-five; deluxe three-bedroom, two-bathroom penthouses (*Just eight feet below the surface!* the ads screamed. *A full 45 minutes of daily natural light in summer!*) sold for five-eight. These prices did not include taxes, maintenance charges or submarine fees. Yes, indeed: submerged living residents' daily commute would involve a forty-five-minute ride on a fleet of decommissioned Canadian military submarines, retrofitted with Wi-Fi and even a "quiet car" for sleepy office workers. Due to the looming increase in submerged traffic, the Canadian and US governments agreed to set up an underwater customs checkpoint, as the border ran right through the middle of the lake. From what I read, the duty-free shopping down there was going to be fabulous.

Meanwhile, the air of unfettered savagery that seemed to permeate daily life now was getting out of hand. If we thought we had lost our minds up here in Canada, our neighbours to the south had gone completely bonkers. The United States of America had, more than ever before, adopted violence as its second official language. Whereas we Canadians would politely look away if a gang of blomers tortured and killed some sorry herm in the street, Americans had given birth to a new and unsettling fad: crucifixion block parties, co-sponsored by the Catholic Church and the Baptists. The theory went that if blomers were going to murder their "sexually malformed" comrades anyway, why not do it as God intended – with a colourful array of marshmallow salads served on folding tables to participants, beanbag tossing for the kiddies and hip hop booming from large Bose speakers set up on the sidewalk? If blomers were going to engage in acts of mass torture, why not introduce them to Christian iconography in the process? The churches saw these crucifixion block parties (or CBPs, as they were called online) as just another form of community outreach.

Yes, violence had, in the good ole US of A, become as normalized and forecastable as the weather. Some chalked this up to the fact that following the recent mid-term elections, blomers now held the balance of power in the House of Representatives, claiming many seats in the more liberally minded northern states, and no amount of future gerrymandering could hold them back. This caused many vips, especially those in the hitherto rural areas of the American South, to lash out in senseless acts of carnage. And we were not talking about a relatively minor incident like the shooting up of a movie theatre or first- and second-graders at an elementary school. No. Bombings took place that wiped out entire city blocks. Near the end of winter, a ninety-thousand-vip militia, heavily armed and deeply inebriated, descended upon the

Alabama State Capitol in a surprise midday attack, overwhelming the small, sorry cadre of gophers set up to defend it, and burned the building (and everyone inside) to cinders.

And this, *this* was the environment that my plan was going to take me and Otis into. I must have been out of my mind.

❧

Thursday Banana had one of the worst websites I had ever seen. They had obviously designed it themselves, and it was so bad that I had to wonder if blomers possessed an anti-aptitude to go along with their pullulation-assigned aptitudes and theirs was the inability to organize online information in a logical and easy-to-use way. It was so bad that Otis, even as a seasoned investigator, still needed my help to find out where those fuckers had taken his wife, and so the two of us sat with our respective laptops in the open-concept café in the lobby of our building over the lunch hour, hunting for the band's schedule of upcoming gigs. The website – eight-point white text on a black background – appeared to have no navigation, but it did boast lots of pop-up ads, a video embed of a recent show and an audio player on the right-hand side that blared their music as soon as you landed on or refreshed the homepage. Yes, there was a tickertape-like widget scrolling across the bottom of the screen, but was it a list of impending shows? No! It simply provided another way to play the exact same songs featured in the audio player. This was almost as bad as our company's intranet. At one point, I was certain I had found what we were looking for, but it turned out to be a page of all their *past* shows, going back months, including dozens of gigs at the Cajun Cage.

Finally, Otis let out a yelp of excitement, and his eyes lit up like fire across our table.

"Success?" I asked.

"Oh, you're not going to believe this," he told me, looking up from his laptop. "I mean, it makes perfect sense in hindsight, but . . ." And his eyes ignited again.

"What?" I asked.

"They're in Louisiana," he replied. "They have a regular gig in Louisiana now." And he began humming the tune to the band's signature song.

"Do you know where?"

Otis cast his gaze back to the screen. "They're in Troy," he said. "They've taken Ellen to Troy, Louisiana."

"Where the fuck is Troy?" I asked.

We googled it right away and found its Wikipedia entry. Prior to pullulation, we learned, Troy, Louisiana, had been a near-empty rural crossroads about a two-hour drive north of Baton Rouge. Now, we could see from the pictures and numbers under Quick Facts, Troy had become a steamy, grimy little metro of about three hundred and fifty thousand blomers spanning one hundred and eighty-five square kilometres east to west. In its halcyon past – i.e., five months ago – the city had been a bustling bureaucratic hub as the US federal government set up various authorities there to service the increased shipping traffic along the Mississippi River. But rapid wage inflation caused the call centres and regulatory bodies to pull up stakes and move across the border to Jackson, Mississippi, where labour was cheaper. With a precipitous spike in its unemployment rate, Troy quickly fell to crime and poverty, soup kitchens and boarded-up shops. But then, out of this brief milieu, something emerged to fill the gap: a raucous music scene sprang up, we read, seemingly overnight. This small city now bragged at least fifteen to twenty clubs that offered live music seven nights a week and two matinees on the weekends, as well as four or five major up-and-coming record labels. Whole new genres of tunes were coming out of Troy; one paragraph of its Wikipedia entry likened it to early 1990s Seattle. For any band looking to earn some underground cred, Troy, Louisiana, had become the continent's hottest music destination.

"Can you see where in Troy they're playing?" I asked.

"Yeah, I got it here. It's a club called . . ." and weirdly, Otis paused. ". . . the Carrion."

"The Carrion," I echoed. There was a kind of spooky, disquieting quality to that name. For a reason I couldn't quite know, my skin broke out in goose pimples.

"Yep. Looks like it's right in downtown Troy. They haven't posted the exact dates and times yet, but that's where they'll be playing."

"All right," I said. "Easy peasy. Just fly in there, rent a car and –"

"Okay, here's the problem," Otis said. "And I've never told you this about me, but . . . well . . ."

"Well what?"

He gave a diffident shrug. "I'm afraid of flying."

"Oh?"

He nodded. "I hate airplanes. I just . . . I just can't do them." He looked embarrassed to admit this to me. I sensed then that this phobia, more than anything else, had played a chief role in his own music career not working out. I mean, how do you become a rock star if you're afraid to fly?

"Okay, okay, no problem," I assured him. "So . . . road trip? Let's google how long it would take to drive there."

We did so. The results showed twenty-one hours.

"Twenty-one hours," Otis said. "So that's, what? Pretty much three days of driving?"

"Pretty much," I said. "With breaks and stops and all. To do it safely."

"Three days," he repeated. "Three days there and three days back. That's a long time in a car."

"But I could come with you!" I said, experimentally. "Divide up the driving and provide you with company and, you know, moral support as you confront Ellen. I mean, upper management wants me to use up my vacation time, and I really would like to get away from here for a while. This would be perfect."

"Well, that's the other thing," Otis said. "I don't actually have a lot of vacation time banked. Maybe two days, max. I took a whole chunk for a staycation this winter."

I furrowed my brow. "Hmm," I said, thinking hard about it. "Okay. Okay, I have an idea."

꙾

"You want to do *what*?" Brennan Prate asked me. The stress he put on that last word, the emphasis, made colleagues' heads pop up at us as it reverberated across the open-concept floor.

It was mid-morning of the next day. I had sauntered over to Brennan's desk without a meeting invitation, as he had done to me so many times before. I now sat perched on his toadstool, my spine stiff as a yardstick as I stared him down.

"I would like to give some of my vacation days to Otis Tanton," I repeated.

Brennan's eyes went all buggy. "I've never heard of such a thing," he said, puffing out his cheeks and tilting his head. "I don't think we have a policy for something like that."

"But we don't have a policy against it, either," I told him. "I checked."

"Well . . ." Brennan gasped, squirming in his chair. It pleased me to no end to see his shit so thoroughly disturbed. "This is highly unusual."

"It is. But you told me I had to use up my vacation days, and this is how I want to use them. Otis and I are planning a big road trip down south and he doesn't have the days for it, so I want to give him some of mine."

"Highly unusual," he said again, and fidgeted. "I'm sorry, but I'll have to run all this past Tahir. Let me call him now. Maybe he's free to come down for a chat."

My stomach clenched. Tahir was a recent acquisition of Percussive Insurance, a camel whom we headhunted away from a financial services firm in his native Egypt to become our new Executive Vice-President of Human Capital. Needless to say, while I wasn't surprised that the company hadn't promoted me internally to the post, I still felt slighted and threatened by his presence. As camels were not indigenous to the continent, I had never met one before; but over the course of a three-hour management meeting that Tahir called less than a week after he arrived, I learned that camels possessed a weird mix of aptitudes from other blomers. Indeed, within the first handful of minutes of the meeting, it became evident that Tahir had the analytical mind of a pigeon, the business cunning of a hawk and the ability to speak in the dulcet, nurturing tones of an eagle, even when shooting down your ideas or crapping on the company's long-standing traditions. In other words, he was ideally suited to a career in human resources. I sat there like a seething cauldron as he used this "introductory get-together" to criticize or tear apart all the HR policies that I had built my career upon. Vacation and bereavement allotments, the pension plan, flex-time arrangements, the departmental party budgets – none of them, I learned, was safe from his ruthless expertise.

That night in bed, lying next to a half-asleep Morgana, I stewed in my own rage. *He's been here less than four days*, I thought as she curled a comforting arm around me in the dark, *and already I've had it up to here with Tahir!*

Brennan Prate now had his phone against his face. "Uh-huh ... uh-huh ... great." He hung up. "Okay, Tahir's on his way down."

When the camel arrived, I couldn't help but stand up from Brennan's toadstool, as if at attention. Tahir, I noticed, engendered this kind of reaction in people. He held an aura of officialdom, of authority, like you felt compelled to salute him whenever he entered a room. In pure bureaucratic flare, he was dressed in four different shades of brown, a tasteful medley of seersucker that I could never get away with. His face was long and greyish, his eyes somewhat sad, his Brylcreemed hair parted brutally down the middle in a style that struck me as very nineteenth century. The effects of his acromegaly were confined almost exclusively to his mouth: the lips were like slabs of thick meat, the teeth behind them about three sizes too small for their gums.

"Have a seat, gentlemen," he said in that deep, commanding baritone of his, and we complied. "What can I do for you?" he asked as he remained standing.

"We're just talking about all those vacation days that Hector here has banked."

"Ah, yes," Tahir said, turning his face toward me with a look that I could only describe as *camelish*. "They're a real problem. You simply cannot have that many days banked, Mr. Thompson. You really need to start using them up."

"That's what *I've* been telling him," Brennan went on. "But now he says he wants to give a portion of them to his boyfriend, Otis Tanton."

"Brennan, shut up!" I barked petulantly, open-concept office be damned. "Seriously, shut the fuck up. God, you're such a shit disturber!"

Tahir's face puckered with surprise at my outburst. His ensuing glare seemed to say, *What is the meaning of this? Do you gentlemen not realize that we blomers now cut the tongues out of employees who speak to each other in this way? I mean, it's just not civilized.*

I was fairly convinced he was about to give me the what for, but then he turned his laser-like gaze onto Brennan. "Mr. Prate," he said, "am I to understand that Mr. Thompson here would like to transfer some of his surplus vacation days to another employee?"

"Exactly," Brennan said.

"And what is your objection to this?"

That caught Brennan flat-footed. "Well . . . Well . . ." He stammered a bit, struggling to recover. "It's just that it's never been done before. We don't have a policy for it."

"But that's hardly a reason to object, now is it? I mean, certainly our Human Capital software will allow us to simply delete a number of vacation days from Mr. Thompson's account and add an equivalent number to his friend's? Do you suppose that would be a problem?"

"No. No, I don't suppose so."

"And do you suppose that a decision like this, however unorthodox, could best be resolved at the manager-director level? I know I'm still new here, and I don't mean to pull rank, but I am a VP. My expectation would be that you could resolve these sorts of issues on your own."

At that, Brennan downcast his eyes in a look of penitence before casting them back up at me. I seriously considered sticking my tongue out at him behind Tahir's back.

As if intuiting my insolence, the camel swooped around to face me. "And as for *you*, Mr. Thompson. Your surfeit of vacation days, you must agree, belies a much larger problem that you've been having. Now, as an experienced HR professional, clearly you must see that you are suffering from an acute case of burnout. I have been made aware by others in senior management of the issues you've been having, and I must say your performance has been falling well short of my expectations of someone at your level."

It was my turn to stare shamefaced at my navel.

"So, if a lengthy vacation is in order, then let's make that happen. And if you need to take this break with your friend, Mr. . . . Mr. . . . ?"

"Tanton," I said. "Otis Tanton."

". . . with Mr. Tanton, then let's make that happen, too. Take a lengthy break. I encourage it. But when you come back, we need you to *be* back – at full strength. I know this company has undergone great change, both in its operations and its culture, and I also know that you've been struggling to fit in with all that change. But if you're going to continue being a member of the Human Capital team, Mr. Thompson, you *need* to fit in with that culture. It's paramount that staff see you as an exemplar of it. So take your vacation with your friend, and when you come back we'll reassess whether this is still the right place for you to be. Do I make myself clear?"

"Yes, sir," I said.

"Okay then, if that will be all." And he gave a very slight, very diplomatic smile, then turned to go.

I raised my face back up. "Oh, Tahir, by the way," I said before he could leave, "about that corporate culture you keep speaking of. Just so you know, it's not Mr. Thompson or Mr. Prate."

He tossed me a quizzical glance. "I'm sorry?"

"We refer to each other by our first names around here. Everybody does it – from the CEO to the guys in the mailroom."

He blanched a bit but quickly recovered. "Well, we'll see about that. But in the meantime: *Hec*tor, Bren*nan*," he said, pronouncing our names as if they were sobriquets, "I bid you both a good day."

∾

"Are you sure?" I asked. "I mean, are you absolutely certain?"

"Of course. Of course."

"You don't mind?"

"I don't mind."

"But . . . but you know what this means, right?"

"What? What does it mean?"

"Well . . ." My hesitancy pushed through the seconds like the prow of a ship.

"Oh, I get it," she said, and tossed me a puckish smile across the dinner table. "You're worried you'll miss opening night of *Harpies: The Musical!*"

Well, that too, I thought.

"Oh, Hector, you're so sweet." Morgana manoeuvred a half-stalk of asparagus into her bright pink mouth. "But listen, it's okay," she said as she chewed. "I won't be offended if you miss the debut. You've shown more patience and understanding with this play than any husband should be expected to show. So what's the big deal if you're not there for opening night? There'll be plenty of chances for you to see the play after you get back. Carolina expects it to have a long, long run."

That was putting it mildly. The director, above and beyond her acumen for creating provocative musical theatre, had had the foresight to hire a hawk to be in charge of the play's marketing campaign. His relentless entrepreneurialism, his chemically prescribed business cunning, had already secured for the show a lengthy guaranteed engagement here; and, provided things went well and reviews were good and tickets sold briskly, he also had a small coterie of investors willing to finance a tour across Canada. And if *that* happened, Morgana would finally, finally get paid for her performance. Not much, at least at first. But if there were more tours, she and the rest of the cast and crew would start bringing in a semi-regular paycheque. It was what they had all been killing themselves for, and it looked like it might just happen.

"Are you . . . are you sure?" I asked again, carving into my chicken breast.

"I am. I think this road trip is important to Otis, and frankly, to you too. I think it's great that you're getting away from everything for a while and having an adventure."

That's one way to describe it, I thought.

"You really need it," she continued, "and Otis will certainly appreciate having you there for backup. *God.*" She made a face then, a wrinkling of her nose as if she'd smelled something bad. "I can't believe Ellen has done this. Why would she leave him? He's such a great guy."

"Well, that's the other thing," I said. "This trip, you know, it . . . it could be dangerous."

"Oh, I don't think it'll come to that," she assured me. "I doubt Thursday Banana will put up that sort of fight."

"No, no. What I meant was, it's the States – and Otis and I will be driving right through the middle of it. Things are so . . . wonky down there right now."

"I'm not worried," she said. "You guys will just have to be extra vigilant. And besides, you're vips visiting from another country. Nobody's going to bother you. I think the news reports down there blow everything out of proportion."

"Still and all, this is quite a gutsy move," I ventured, "especially for a boring old guy like me."

"Hector, you're not boring."

I just gave her a look. "Morgana, I'm an HR manager at an insurance company."

"Ohh," she sang at me in sympathy. She set her fork down and came around the table. Wrapped an arm around my shoulders. Kissed me on the mouth. "I think this road trip will be good for us, too," she said. "It'll be nice for us to have a break from one another. And maybe doing something new will help you gain some . . . some perspective. I think we both agree that you've been struggling with a lot of the change happening in, you know, the world."

I wanted to get angry at that. What's more, I realized I wanted her to get angry at me. I wanted her to say, *How can you go away and leave me? How can you take this big road trip with Otis and miss the debut of a play I've been working so hard on for over a year?*

But she just looked at me with a galaxy of kindness in her face and kissed me again. "And maybe I'll gain some perspective, too, by not having you around."

I couldn't know what she possibly meant by that. Part of me wanted all my anxieties, all my fears to come boiling back up to the surface then. But part of me wanted to believe that she just meant that I was somebody who could be missed, who could be appreciated more by not being around for a while.

I squeezed her back. "We should eat," I said. "Our dinner's getting cold."

CHAPTER 11

We couldn't believe it. There was, just as the song had predicted, a traffic jam from here to Louisiana.

We had decided to use my Camry for the road trip, as it was, thanks to my accident last year, a lot newer than Otis's car (a dim silver Honda Civic with 250,000 kilometres on it) and thus, likely more reliable. Despite the lingering, inexplicable twitchiness that still plagued me from that fender-bender eighteen months ago, I agreed to take the first shift. I knew that traffic coming out of our city, even at nine o'clock on a Monday morning, could prove dicey, and I wanted to spare Otis the stress of driving through it. He seemed out of sorts when I came by his tiny, west-end townhouse to pick him up, lost in thought as he loaded his suitcase next to mine in the Camry's trunk and then climbed into shotgun, discovering the two coffees I had picked up for us on the way. "You okay?" I asked, handing him his cup, and he gave me a solemn nod. "Let's do it," he said with a melancholic sigh before raising the slit in the lid to his mouth and taking a sip.

Our plan was to get as far as Cincinnati, Ohio, that first night. It was a reasonable goal, provided we kept the pit stops and pee breaks to a minimum. Cincinnati had, thanks to pullulation, ballooned to what urban specialists had deemed (perhaps oxymoronically) a mid-size megalopolis of about 8.5 million people. I dreaded the thought of what traffic would be like coming into that city at the supper hour, but in the meantime, I tried to relax behind the wheel and looked forward to the open road as we made our way down there.

How was I to know that *open road* would be such an anachronism? *Man oh man, there's traffic jam / from here to Louisiana.* Thursday Banana, you cheeky buggers, truer words had never been spoken. How had they been so prescient? What was it about pullulation that had, less than a year and a half ago, transformed a ragtag bunch of bears, climbing bleary-eyed and caked in their own shit out of the northern Ontario woods, into such wise shamans of vehicular congestion? How did they know? I was fully prepared for us to take an hour to escape the greater metropolitan area of our city – but not two and a half! Christ. We had barely reached the outer fringe of what passed for the suburbs before we had to take our first pee break, the coffees having found an uncomfortable place to sit inside our bladders. Another hour and we were hungry for lunch. We decided to stop in the city of Guelph.

Before pullulation, Guelph had been a rather sleepy town about an hour away, comprised mostly of website companies and one of our insurance competitors and a small university that specialized in agricultural sciences. No more. A string of New Age educational institutions had cropped up, seemingly overnight, and taken over the city, driving out the insurance company and tech firms and farming professors. These institutions trained blomers for a surprisingly robust growth industry in the post-pullulation age. Indeed, Guelph had become the go-to place to get an advanced degree in this high-demand art form. And what art form was that? I couldn't believe it when I heard about this phenomenon on the CBC and read about it in *The Walrus.* Guelph had become ground zero in the exciting world of – wait for it . . .

Pole dancing.

Yes, pole dancing.

Pole dancing had become all the rage in Guelph. The university now offered an internationally renowned M.F.A. in pole dancing and had received twenty-five thousand applications from all over the world for last spring's semester. There were also, I had read, smaller, seedier technical colleges – housed above pawnshops and restaurants and Guelph's new subway stops – that offered diplomas in pole dancing. There were pole dancing after-school academies for kids. And about three dozen strip clubs choked Guelph's now massive, bustling downtown. Even places that weren't strip clubs provided a training opportunity, an internship as it were, for ambitious pole dancing aspirants. This, Otis and I learned, included the hole-in-the-wall Thai eatery just off the highway where we had stopped for lunch.

In this small, dour, badly lit Asian diner, with its tiled walls and grim brass Buddhas and vinyl seating, I ate the mango tofu, and Otis ate the eggplant supreme, and "Kerri" spun and spread herself and did the splits about eight and a half feet from our table, moving round and round on her pole like a swirl of peppermint. She was clearly a blue jay, maybe one who had failed to cut it as a professional painter or sculptor or graphic designer and was now determined to express her "artistic temperament" through the use of her body itself. She was still an amateur at it – why else would she be dancing in a shitty lunchtime dive like this one? – but she was working hard over there on her slightly raised circular platform. I could tell by the tense, pinched expression on her acromegalic face that Kerri was building toward a big move, one she had practised hard and was proud of. And here it was. Bracing herself with the crooks of her arms, she threw her body out face down and perpendicular from the bar and held herself rigid there, quivering under the strain of gravity. Next, she spread her legs wide, sort of in a V formation, and raised up her small, pert bottom to us, providing an unencumbered view of her – how should I put it? – isosceles of intimacy. Then she closed her

179

legs again before moving a slow, sensuous belly dancer's wave through the entire length of her body, writhing it like a snake's.

"This isn't going to work," Otis said across the table.

"I agree," I replied, poking at my mango tofu with my fork as I stared at Kerri and felt my appetite vanish into the ether. "Do you, do you want to get this to go or something?"

When Otis didn't answer right away, I glanced over and saw that he wasn't watching the dancer at all, or trying to eat, but rather staring into his phone.

He looked up at me. "What? No, no. What I meant was . . ." He turned the phone around so I could see its screen, which displayed a new traffic app he had downloaded. It showed that all the highways between here and Ohio were red – a deep red, a blood red. "There is no way we're making it to Cincinnati by this evening," he told me. "Things are gonzo out there."

"So we need to find a new place to hole up for the night," I replied.

"Okay, okay," Otis chanted as he turned the phone back around, "let me work it out, let me work it out." And his thumb began flying around the screen.

There was something foreboding that loomed between us, now that we realized how little progress we were going to make. We needed to drive; we needed to get down to Troy as fast as possible. Every day, every hour that passed could mean Ellen was that much more lost to Otis, and it would be that much harder to convince her she was a fool for running away with Thursday Banana. But the ominous thing hanging over our table was this: Where were we going to sleep tonight? The next major megalopolis was London, Ontario, and at the rate we were going, we might make it there in time for supper. But then what? We'd want to press on, wouldn't we? We'd want to get farther down the road than that. And so, what was the next big centre? Of course, we already knew.

"So, if we push ourselves," Otis said, "and are willing to have a late evening, we can make it as far as . . ." and his face twisted into a rictus of concern.

"Dude, don't say it."

"Windsor," he said. "We could make it as far as Windsor."

Oh Jesus, I thought. *Not Windsor. Anywhere but Windsor.*

"Are you sure?" I asked. "I mean, there's got to be some better place before that. I thought Chatham was up over a million people now."

"Oh, it used to be. But six months ago, city council voted to level the entire place and turn it into a parking lot for commuters taking the trains into Windsor. And there's nothing between it and downtown except subdivisions. I mean, I've got a hotel app running beside this traffic one," he said, "and there isn't so much as a bed and breakfast in that whole area."

"That's ridiculous," I said.

He shrugged. "Nobody travels *to* Windsor, willingly. You're either passing through to get to the States, or you commute in for a job and then commute back out again before dark."

"I know," I said, and we both sighed. What happened in Windsor after the sun went down was nearly indescribable. Everybody, at least in the circles we travelled in, had heard about the mind-boggling rituals that unfurled there each evening. A shudder passed through me as I thought about it now.

"Do you think we could spend the night there?" I asked.

"Well," Otis said, scrolling through his phone again, "there are plenty of vacancies, that's for sure."

We ate the rest of our lunch in silence, and then Kerri came along with a plastic jug, some sad coins and crumpled bills tucked in the bottom, and Otis and I each slipped her a tip.

"Either of you interested in a lap dance?" she asked in a kind of absent, robotic way, and Otis and I averted our eyes.

"Tempting," I said before she could grow impatient, "but we really should be going."

"Yes, thank you," Otis added.

❧

Ten o'clock. Ten fucking o'clock. That was how long it took to reach Windsor, Ontario. And it was the absolute worst time to be rolling into its streets. By then, the sadistic ritual that had come to define the place had just hit its zenith.

Ten o'clock. Based on the distance between where we ate lunch in Guelph and what time we reached the Super 8 in Windsor that Otis had booked on his phone, I figured that our average speed on the highway had run no better than thirty kilometres an hour. I blamed the vexation I suffered at the sight of so many cars (thousands of cars, *millions* of cars) on the fact that I lived right downtown and, despite the inconveniences of pullulation, or perhaps because of them, still had very little reason to drive. Yes, it was utterly demoralizing to move so slowly down an eight-lane highway designed for top speed. Even the supper we enjoyed at a Swiss Chalet in London could not perk us up; we hit rush-hour traffic coming out of that city, and all our frustrations bubbled immediately back up to the surface. At one point, around eight thirty, I turned to Otis, who had taken a shift at the wheel, and said jokingly to him, or at least half-jokingly – yes, I was definitely half-joking, or quarter-joking, or eighth-joking – "Brother, is Ellen really worth all this?" And the sad thing was, the funny thing was, the sadly funny thing was that he didn't smile or turn his head to look at me but just kept his gaze pinned to the darkening windshield and clutched the wheel at ten and two and grunted.

We could see the macabre ceremonies unfolding along the little avenues and cul-de-sacs of the massive suburb we passed through on our way into Windsor. People were out on their driveways and sidewalks, sitting in circles on lawn chairs and stools, holding up flashlights to their faces – faces that were profanely animated or contorted by a terrifying rapture.

"Look away," I said to Otis. "Just keep your eyes on the road, brother."

"Okay, okay," he replied, his voice trying to hide his panic.

The ritual appeared to be exactly as described to me in the pages of *Maclean's* magazine and on CBC's *As It Happens*. With our windows rolled up we could not hear what these assembled conclaves were talking so vigorously about, but we knew. The hordes did not thin out as we approached Windsor proper, with its massive glittering skyline of condo towers and office buildings. In fact, the throng only grew in multitudes as we made our way into the downtown core. These assemblies of people populated sidewalks and parking lots and whatever green space was left in the city. To the right of the car, I saw a man fly up off his stool and throw his arms into the air as if praising Jesus. To the left, I saw a woman – a grown woman, in a bright floral summer dress – lying supine on the ground and flailing her arms and legs like a toddler having a tantrum at the mall.

"Okay, okay," I said to Otis. "We just need to get to the hotel and rush inside as fast as we can." I swallowed hard. "We do not want to be sucked up into this."

This was something that seemed to plague only towns and cities in Canada that had been major manufacturing hubs in decades gone by, long before pullulation. Nobody, including the journalists at *Maclean's* or *As It Happens*, knew what it was about these places – whether it was something left over in the water or the soil, or the air itself – that made the sparrows and bears and foxes that came climbing out of the woods, or the dogs and cats and parrots that shook off the shackles of pethood, want to engage in such self-excoriating mass ceremonies. Every day these blomers would go to work in offices and shopping malls and construction sites just like the rest of us. But every night, instead of going home and watching TV like normal people (or fucking, like blomers), they would instead assemble outside in the open air, in these gatherings of six or ten or fifteen, and they would take turns releasing the one emotion, the one feeling that had pent up inside them all day long. It was a sentiment that everybody

– vips and blomers – felt at one time or another, a perfectly natural opinion of the self that one could hold in moderation. But these blomers, living in these cities and towns, needed to gather together outside in all weather and confess their feelings in great ritualistic ceremonies. And of all the towns and cities in Canada where this phenomenon happened, Windsor was the absolute worst. Nobody knew why.

Maclean's and *As It Happens* (not to mention scores of sociologists) used the same term to describe what the gathered hordes expressed in these great streetside congresses: imposter syndrome. Every blomer in this megalopolis, all the dogs and crows, all the blue jays and gophers, even the hawks in their entrepreneurial smugness, wanted to express how much they felt like frauds at the end of the day. Of course, everybody experienced a pang of imposter syndrome from time to time, perhaps even daily. But we vips had always been conditioned to suppress this feeling, to not vocalize it all that often. We were taught to think: *I'm good enough. I may not be perfect. I may not be living my best possible life. The self I'm presenting to the world may not match the person I feel like on the inside. But I'm workin' hard. I'm doing my best. I'm trying.* Not here. Here, the evening air would chime with the wails and screams and warbles of pure, abject failure, the confession of every lie told, every compromise embraced, every short-, medium- and long-term dream left to fester unrealized in the deepest chambers of one's mind. The dog who wanted to be a painter. The hawk who wanted to play the bongos in a ska band. The gopher who wanted to set his rifle or policeman's gun down and stay home to raise children. These blomers felt hampered by the rote, prescriptive aptitudes assigned to them at pullulation and wanted to profess their unhappiness about it to the heavens. And why had such a ritual taken hold only in Canada? Had it something to do with our national habit of remaining in a perpetual state of apology? Such behaviour, for example, did not occur in the writhing Gomorrah that was Detroit, just on the other side of the river. Over there, blomers were happy enough to torture and kill herms all night long for sport. The contrast with Windsor was stark. Every night in Windsor, it was a "Kumbaya" moment writ large.

And God help you if you were a vip caught on the streets of Windsor after dark when these massive group therapy sessions began to unfold. The blomers wanted nothing more than to catch you and force you to participate under threat of violence. It gave them a profound sense of validation if they could get you to take part, to express your own deeply guarded imposter syndrome, to join in these circle jerks of misery.

The Super 8 was right in the middle of Wyandotte St. East, and Otis and I grew tense as we approached. "Okay, okay," I said. "We just find a spot in the parking lot, get our gear out of the trunk as fast as we can and make a beeline for the lobby. Everything will be fine."

"I dunno, dude," he replied. "Maybe we should try to cross the border. I mean, we're so close."

"But we're not – not really. You saw the traffic. Lineups at customs could be another three hours. And besides, do you really want to take our chances spending the night in Detroit? That place is fucked up – we could run into some real violence, some *actual* violence there." When he still seemed hesitant, I pressed on. "Look, we've been driving for thirteen hours. We're exhausted. We have a reservation. Let's just get in as quickly as we can."

He finally nodded his agreement and steered the Camry into the Super 8 parking lot, the car jostling over the raised sidewalk as he did. Our hearts sank when we saw there were no empty spots near the door. "Damn!" Otis snarled.

I sat up tall in my seat to gander out the windshield. "I think I see one over there," I said, pointing to two rows over. "Just go around and pull up."

He followed my instructions, guiding the Camry to the end of our row and around to the one I had pointed to. There were plenty of spaces there, and he manoeuvred us between a pickup truck and an SUV as quickly as he could. As he killed the engine, we looked out the window together – and had our worst fears confirmed. Beyond the Super 8's parking lot was a knoll that sat between us and the chain-link fence that led to the next parking lot over. On that knoll, we could see a gathering of about eight or nine blomers camped out on lawn chairs, their flashlights turned upward as if for the telling of ghost stories. The blomer whose turn it was to disclose his daily failures was standing, his face contorted, his free hand gesticulating madly, pounding and tearing at his chest as if he were a repentant sinner – which, in a sense, I supposed he was. The person sitting to his left turned her gaze to our abruptly extinguished Camry. At first her squint through our windshield was of mere curiosity, but then her gaze changed to one of suspicion, her beady eyes narrowing into a diaeresis beneath her brow.

"Oh fuck," Otis said. "Oh fuck, fuck, fuck, fuck, fuck."

"Stay calm," I told him. "Just stay calm. Listen to me, okay. Here's the plan. Just pop the trunk. The lever's at your left foot, by the door. We'll get our bags and then run as fast as w–"

"No, I'm fine sleeping in these clothes," he said. "I'm fine with not brushing my teeth. Fuck the bags."

"Okay, fine. Me too. Are you ready? Are you ready?"

"Yep. Ready. I'm ready."

We threw open our doors simultaneously and rushed out of the car like a couple of cops on a cop TV show. As I slammed the door and pivoted on my heels toward the Super 8, I could see via my peripheral vision the group of blomers rise en masse from their lawn chairs at the sight of us.

"Frieeeeeends . . . frieeeeeends!" they called over in a zombielike drawl.

"Oh, Christ," I said to Otis. "Run!"

We bolted like a couple of scared deer, but it was too late. We could hear the patter of their feet behind us as they descended the knoll to give chase. The Super 8's bright, bumblebee-coloured awning – LOBBY WELCOME it read ungrammatically on the front – seemed so very far away. We nearly made it, though; we nearly got under that awning to throw open the glass doors and find sanctuary inside. But then a second group of blomers appeared from nowhere, tearing up the parking lot's entrance toward us and cutting off our escape.

❧

"No. Fuck off."

"Please sit."

"Yes, sit. Sit and unburden yourselves to us."

"No. Fuck off."

A knife was produced. It didn't look real. It looked, there in the shadows of the Super 8 parking lot, like a toy switchblade that a kid might beg his mom to buy him at the Dollarama. But as the blomer who held it waved the thing in our faces before pointing downward and saying again, more menacingly, "Please sit," I began to have my doubts. So, Otis and I flopped into the offered lawn chairs and cast our arms over our chests like querulous children.

Then one of them asked, "So which of you would like to go first?"

Otis made a great display of clamming up, which was his big mistake. They zeroed in on him then, nudging and pushing him, determined to pry that nut open, convinced he had lots to share. This was probably true. I knew that thoughts of Ellen had not been far from his mind all day long, and wasn't the whole situation with her a kind of imposter syndrome? Otis just shook his head in short, manic darts and said, "Nope, nope, nope," as the blomers bore down on him.

Someone grabbed a fistful of his hair and yanked his head back. The guy with the knife stepped up then and rested the blade under Otis's exposed chin. No, no. It was definitely not a toy.

"Okay, stop," I called over. "Leave him alone. Please? Look, I'll . . . I'll do it." I swallowed hard.

They turned their attention to me.

"I'll do it," I repeated, "but I'm the only one. Not him. You either get just me or nothing at all. Deal?"

They fell silent for a moment.

"Highly unusual," said one of them, a cow in a polo shirt.

"*Highly* unusual," stressed another, a cat in a tank top and skort.

"But..." and here they seemed to deliberate on it with a mere twitching of their eyes "... we'll allow it," said a third, a bear in a Tilley hat.

The tension eased slightly then as they gathered round me like children anxious for storytime.

I sighed. "I, I'm not sure how to begin."

"Why don't you start," said one of them, "by telling us what you do for a living?"

"I'm an HR manager at an insurance company."

"Whooooooo-oooooooo!" they all sang in unison, a great anticipatory chime, as if such a career choice would be rife with dejections and regret.

"And what did you want to be when you were a little boy?" asked a deep-throated fox. "No vip grows up wanting to work in HR."

"Or insurance," a sparrow pointed out.

How would you *know that?* I wanted to ask. *Two years ago, you were both still shitting in the woods.* "Well, I suppose when I was very small," I went on, "I wanted to be a fireman. I mean, what little boy doesn't? But then, when I got a bit older, I thought I might try my hand at..." And here I paused, because this was that small part of me that I never really talked about, not even with Morgana. Especially Morgana. "... at acting," I finished.

The blomers' faces all swelled. Even Otis, still a touch distressed there in his lawn chair, raised an eyebrow.

"Well, there was this show on TV when I was a kid that I really loved, called *Pixie and the Saints*."

"I remember that show," Otis said.

"Yeah, yeah. It was about this girl named Pixie, who was very plucky and charming, but also a bit bossy, and she had this group of friends, made up mostly of boys, and she led them around their neighbourhood, which was like a cross between Sesame Street and Candyland, getting into all kinds of mischief and adventures. It really wasn't targeted at guys, but I watched it anyway, in secret, because . . . well, I had a terrible crush on the actress who played Pixie."

Whoa. Where was this coming from? I hadn't thought of this stuff in literally decades.

The blomers' expressions egged me on.

"She was roughly my age," I continued. "I guess we were eleven? And her name was Luna. Luna Morrow."

"Luna," someone in the back knelled out, as if the word held the most exquisite novelty.

"I know, I know, her parents must have been New Age hippie types or something. Anyway. I read somewhere that she lived with them in Burbank, California, where the show was filmed. So, at eleven, I decided I wanted to run away to Burbank and get a job on the show as one of the saints, and also become Luna's boyfriend-slash-husband. I figured the best and most efficient way to do that was to get involved in acting. So I did, and I took a real liking to it.

"My parents were very accommodating," I went on. "They sent me to theatre camps, got me involved in community plays. They even hired me an acting coach for a time. This went on for three or four years, which is a long stretch when you're that age."

"And then what happened?" asked a spellbound cow.

"I don't know. Life happened, I suppose. I enjoyed acting well enough, but I wasn't any good at it. I got a bit older and started to think about what else I might want to do, you know, for my career."

"You mean," piped up a plover, "when the weight of the world began to crush your soul?"

For a moment, I wanted to laugh at that. But then suddenly, I didn't. Suddenly, those words seemed to set off a strange resonance, a tiny depth charge of longing inside me.

"Um, hardly," I said. "I just . . . I just started to think about doing something a bit more, you know, practical."

"What about your love for Luna?" someone called out from the back, and Otis couldn't help but guffaw.

"What? No." I shook my head. "No, no, no. The crush only lasted a few months. The show got cancelled long before I lost the acting bug. Luna sort of dropped off the pop culture radar after that. I heard that puberty had not been kind to her: she needed to have a boob reduction at, like, sixteen. It got botched, and the trauma of it sort of wrecked her acting career. She eventually grew up to be a stay-at-home mom." Oh, wow, I was really nattering now. Otis appeared concerned. "Look, look, none of this is the point."

"Then what is the point?" someone asked. "What happened next? You can't tell us you went from acting to HR in one step."

"No, no. I, I, I . . ." I was stammering. *Fuck it. Stop stammering.* "I ultimately wanted to be a teacher."

"Ooooh, a teacher!" several of the blomers chorused.

"That's right. You know, maybe high school math, high school biology. I figured it would have, you know, a performative quality to it. It would be fine. It would be just fine." I gulped. "Except . . . except it wasn't fine. Several decades of plummeting birth rates – I mean, that's the whole reason all of *you* were created in the first place – and enrollments were down. Way down. There were no jobs. There were hardly any jobs in teaching. So I got one in HR instead. It's kind of like teaching," I remarked. "You're teaching adults, in a way. You're teaching them not to be dicks at work."

"So it was a compromise of a compromise," stated the plover emphatically. Several heads nodded, as if they too understood the pain, the numbness that came from making multiple concessions to life.

"Well, thing is ... the thing is ..." I wanted to refute such a basic summing up of my career, but I struggled to find the words to do so. I felt hollowed out, weak, almost childlike as these strangers forced me to boil my existence down to its most essential failure. A slight tickle of tears came to my cheeks then, and I batted at them absently. Otis's look went from concerned to alarmed. He attempted to rise from his lawn chair to come comfort me, but a meaty hand fell onto his shoulder, holding him in place.

When I couldn't find any words, someone to my left said, "Let's move on to another topic." I turned and saw that a pigeon had spoken. She nodded at my wedding ring. "We see that you're married."

"Yes, yes," someone else said, "you must have resigned yourself to the fact that things were never going to work out with Luna."

Oh, for Christ's sake, I thought.

"Why don't you tell us about your wife?"

"My wife? Oh ... oh, okay. Well. Her ... her name is Morgana."

"And what does she do?"

My throat constricted then, trapping breath and mucus and all my words, every last fucking word. The blomers' eyes grew big as I hesitated.

"Okay, look, this bullshit is over," I said. "You've gotten what you wanted out of me, so just let us go. Let us go."

The guy with the knife, still standing behind Otis, raised it wordlessly at me, pointed the blade like a conductor's baton toward my face and tossed me an intimidating grimace.

"Okay, fine," I said. "Fine! But I'll tell you right now, you're all going to make a really big deal out of this."

The blomers leaned in together, excitedly, as if this were the plot twist they were waiting for.

"She's a teacher," I murmured.

They all gasped, a great collective intake of air.

"That is, she *was* a teacher," I went on in a kind of trance. "She gave up her job last year ... so she could be an actor in a play."

"OHHHHHH!" they all cheered, their voices booming upward into the night sky. They began hopping around, hooking arms and swinging each other around in a kind of freakish square dance. It was as if they had finally cracked the spiky, awkward knuckle of a lobster and had gotten at the succulent meat inside.

"So she's living the life *you* want!" someone called out.

"And you are, day after long day, just bearing with it," someone else said, "working in your pointless, soul-destroying job in HR!"

"Look . . . look . . ." I tried to say.

"Have you told her how you feel?" the cow asked.

"Have you told her about your past ambitions?" chimed in the fox.

"Does she know about Luna?" called out the person in the back.

"Would you shut the fuck up about Luna!" I screamed. Otis made another attempt to climb out of his lawn chair and get to me, but several arms now held him back.

"Answer the question," the cow said. "Does she know about all this?"

"Look, look, look," I sputtered. I didn't know what to say. I didn't know how to feel. My hands were twitching, wanting to cast themselves upward.

"Does she know?"

"No," I said. "No. No, we . . . we never talked about that stuff."

"So you've been keeping it from her."

"You've been keeping all this from Morgana, masquerading as a happy, satisfied husband the whole time while secretly resenting her."

"No, no, no, that's not . . ." I was hyperventilating now. I felt like I was being skinned alive.

"What else have you been keeping from her?"

"Nothing, nothing."

"Tell us," said the pigeon.

"Yeah, tell us," said the fox. "How did you feel when she quit her job? Were you upset by that?"

"No, I wasn't," I said. "Not at all. I wasn't upset by that. I wasn't upset by *that.*" The fact that I had put stress on the last word had opened up another can of worms.

"Then what were you upset about?" someone asked.

"Yeah, tell us."

And the thing was, by that point I really wanted to. I really wanted to unleash on them what I was so enraged over, so terrified by.

"It was you," I snarled. "It was you fucking blomers with your ... fucking orgies!"

They all gasped again and leaned back, a little offended.

"What do you mean?" asked the cow.

So, quite involuntarily, I began describing the premise behind *Harpies: The Musical!*

"So yes, I'm worried," I said. "I'm worried that my wife is having sex with a bunch of strange men. I'm worried that my wife is fucking a whole crew of them *right now.*"

"So you have a problem with sex?" asked the plover. "You have hang-ups about sex?"

"Poor Morgana!" cried the pigeon.

"I don't have a problem with sex," I said. "I have a problem with my wife shagging a bunch of people who aren't me."

To the blomers, this of course sounded like Martian.

"Maybe you don't like sex," huffed the fox.

"Fuck you, I love sex," I said. "I do. In fact, thanks to you guys slobbering all over each other in the streets, I think about sex way more than I used to. I think about sex all the time. I do, I do – both with Morgana and ... and ..."

Whoa. *Whoa. Careful now. You're entering unchartered territory, Mr. Thompson. You're thinking thoughts that you never, ever admit to – even to yourself. You are thinking thoughts that you don't ever mention, even when you're narrating the story of your life to yourself.*

Otis could see the precipice on which I stood. "Okay, enough!" he barked, struggling to get out of the lawn chair as they held him down. "You've gotten what you wanted, so let him go. Just let him go."

But the blomers' faces, glowing at me like moons in the sky, were expectant, pre-climactic. There was something in their leers that revealed great furrows of feeling within me. This was it. This was *it*. I got it. I got what all this was about.

"Fine. Fine!" I snapped. "You want me to be honest? You want me to cast off the charade? Fine! I see you guys doing what you do in the streets and at work and I think – *why the hell not?* You guys do it, so why not us? Why not *me*? Huh? Is it because I'm a coward? Is it because I'm just a buttoned-down sod, just a stammering chickenshit with a yardstick up his ass who is too timid to admit what he's really thinking sometimes? Hmm? Now don't get me wrong, I love my wife. I do. But if that's all sex is now, thanks to you, then why not? There are lots of women I wouldn't mind taking a poke at if Morgana and society were cool with it. Sure. Sure. Like my friend Alanna." Yep, I went there. I was in for a pound now. "I'm not all that attracted to her, but sure. Sure. I'd be curious. We're very close, very intimate with each other in our way. So why not? Or this guy's wife!" And I stood up from my own lawn chair suddenly and trawled my hand out toward Otis in a great sweeping gesture. "I mean, his wife, Ellen, is fucking *hot*."

Otis managed to get one arm free so that he could slap his forehead into his palm. The blomers, meanwhile, hooted and cheered and threw their arms in the air. I followed suit. I spread my fingers and flailed my hands and danced around as if trying to flag down a car.

"I mean, he's my best friend in the whole wide world," I said, stomping my feet on the asphalt like I needed to pee, "but I would fuck his wife in an instant if he was cool with it. I would. Again, don't get me wrong. Morgana's cute. She's spunky, spirited. But if Otis said to me, 'Hey, Hector, wanna trade, say, every third weekend?' I'd be down with that. Why not? Why the hell not? If that's all that sex is now!"

"Oh, Jesus," Otis muttered, turning his palmed face away.

"Yes!" chanted the blomers.

"Yes!" I chanted back. "I'm tired of always pretending, goddamnit!"

We thrashed around and swung our arms into the air and turned our faces up to the deep night sky. It was only then that I noticed vaguely that it had begun to rain.

◇

In the borrowed dreariness of our Super 8 hotel room, Otis lay on his queen-size bed and I lay on mine, and together we conducted a staring contest at the ceiling's harsh stucco. I could see, thanks to the urinous glow of a street lamp blaring across the room through the parting in our thick hotel curtains, that Otis's eyes were wide open. My gaze flickered toward his a few times, but his never flickered back to me. We just sprawled there, on our respective beds, in rigid silence. The blomers, thankfully, had allowed us to return to the Camry to retrieve our bags. Yet, despite having brushed my teeth thoroughly before coming to bed, my mouth still felt pasty, unclean.

"Brother," I said through the gloom. "Brother?"

"Hmm?"

"I'm . . . I'm sorry. I'm so sorry I said those things . . . about Ellen. I mean, I mean, *Jesus*. It's ridiculous. Just fucking ridiculous that I would say that stuff."

"It's okay."

"No. No, it's not okay."

"Look, don't worry about it," he said, which felt like the worst possible thing he could say. I waited to hear the packety sounds his crisp hotel sheets would make as he shifted in his bed to face me, but they never came. Finally, after a long pause, he said, "You were under duress. You did what you had to. They were going to cause us serious harm, maybe even kill us, if you didn't."

"Otis . . ."

Another interminable pause.

"You were very brave," he said finally, still staring at the ceiling. "You saved us."

I hadn't thought of it that way. I didn't think of what I'd done as brave. Indeed, I felt sort of the opposite, as if it took a special kind of cowardice to scrape off the veneer of social decorum and be that baldly hurtful toward someone. I *was* sorry – for having said what I said about Ellen, and for having felt it. And yet, maybe Otis was right. I had been brave, hadn't I? Yes. Yes, I had. And the fact that I engaged in such an anomalous moment of courage had spawned something new within me, as if I had sprouted a queer sort of tendon that hadn't been there before, a newfound strength that would serve me well in whatever fate had in store for us now.

"So . . ." I said after a while, "you and I . . . are we cool?"

"Yeah, we're cool." He did turn then, but only to face away from me. "Don't worry about it," he said again. "Ellen *is* hot. People hit on her all the time. Obviously." He cleared his throat. "I'm sort of used to it. Obviously."

Somehow, shortly after that, we managed to fall asleep.

We rose early the next morning despite the late night. We had learned our lesson re the traffic and decided to skip the Super 8's continental breakfast and get back on the road no later than 6:00 a.m. This decision was a wise one: we managed to clear customs and cross the Windsor-Detroit border in just two and a half hours, the agent logging our iPassports during the brief retinal scan at the booth. By the time we took our first pit stop in the good ole US of A, we had shaken off the previous evening's unpleasantness and were making stilted, desultory jokes with one another. Otis seemed, thank God, to be back to his old self.

❧

We made it to Cincinnati, Ohio, by 8:00 p.m. Nothing of note happened that night.

❧

Except that wasn't true. Around eleven thirty, we were stirred from sleep in our Comfort Inn hotel room when my phone rumbled from an incoming text as it lay charging alongside Otis's on the nightstand between our two double beds. We raised our heads off our respective pillows to look down at it.

"Was that yours or mine?" he murmured in the dark.

"I think it was mine," I replied, and plucked the phone from its charger cord and brought the screen up to my groggy face.

> Sorry to be texting you so late. I'm just at my wit's end here, Hector. I'm sorry, but can I call you? I know this isn't your problem, but I just need to talk.

I moved out of bed and texted back a quick Sure thing as I headed for the bathroom so we wouldn't disturb Otis. I barely got the light on and the heavy door closed behind me before her call came through.

"Hey there."

"I'm so sorry. You were asleep. I must have woken you. Hector, I'm sorry."

"It's okay. No, it's okay. What's going on?"

I picked sleep from my eyes as she said, "God, we just had the most horrific fight."

"You and Mitch, you mean?"

"No. Me and Lesley."

I swallowed. Alanna must have reached a new phase of this . . . experiment in adoptive parenting. "About what?" I asked.

"About them leaving our condo unit. They've blown through the latest stack of books I got them and now they want to accompany me to the bookstore to pick out more on their own."

"Ah, I see," I said. "And you're afraid that . . . ?"

"That we'll go out and they'll be attacked on the street, and I won't be able to stop it like last time. I . . . I don't know if I could face that again."

"But Lesley's bored. Cooped up, right?"

"Of course they're cooped up! They haven't left the house since I brought them here. They've intimated before that they want to go out, and I've always shot it down. But tonight was different. Oh Hector, they've evolved so much as a person, even in the time since your visit. We got into a full-on screaming match that went on for hours. They've only just given up and gone to bed."

"And where was Mitch in all this?"

She made a little farting noise with her mouth. "He went to a pub as soon as we started fighting. He's only now just gotten back, and he's in no shape to talk."

"Alanna . . ."

"What?"

"You can't keep Lesley like a prisoner."

"The hell I can't. What, Hector, am I supposed to just let them loose on the street and watch them get beaten to death by those monsters? Are you telling me I'm supposed to witness that?"

I ran a hand through my hair, now warped with bed-head. "What if you put them in a disguise? Tried to mask their . . ." And here I paused, struggling once more over the nomenclature. ". . . their hermaphroditic qualities. You know, a lot of herms do that. It's how they get around in the world."

"Yes, and a lot of them get caught anyway. Their costumes get torn off and the blomers murder them anyway. Am I supposed to watch that happen? No. Lesley doesn't need to go out. They've got food and shelter here. I'll bring them all the books they want. They've got me and Isaac to keep them company. They can . . . they can be an indoor cat, Hector."

"Alanna . . . you know that's . . . that's not . . ." *Rational*, I wanted to say. But I knew I didn't have enough skin in the game to go that far. So instead I just said, "I understand where you're coming from. But whatever you do, you have to make sure it's best for Lesley and not just for yourself. Right?"

I could practically hear her shaking her head over the phone line. "You don't understand," she said, "because you're not a parent."

Well then why did you call me? I almost replied. But I gulped down those words and just said, "Look, you do what you need to. Okay? I'll support it no matter what. I should get back to bed now, but please keep me posted about what you decide to do."

"Okay," she said in a very mousy voice. "Okay, thanks."

She hung up, and I felt like a complete failure.

It was only after I'd gotten back in bed and apologized to Otis for the disturbance that I realized I hadn't told Alanna that I was on the road.

↬

Another early morning, hitting the highway by six fifteen, and our goal, if the traffic gods showed compassion, was to make it as far as Nashville, Tennessee, by that evening. It was doable, according to the app on Otis's phone: the pixelated highway lines were sprinkled with lots of yellow interspersed with all the red. Staving off the claustrophobia of the car (we'd already come to the morose realization that this trip was going to take a lot longer than we'd thought) involved a steady rotation of entertainment and escape: his iPod, the radio; my iPod, conversation; pit stop; audiobook short stories; thoughtful silence; more conversation; another pit stop; my iPod; the radio. All the while, the long lines of cars went everywhere and nowhere, a permanent congestion, like a heart perpetually on the verge of attack due to all those blocked arteries. We were psychologically prepared for it now, for our progress to become this ceaseless metronome of start-and-stop, start-and-stop, start-and-stop.

What we weren't prepared for was what had happened to the state of Kentucky. As we crossed over from Ohio, it appeared as if the entire place, all forty thousand square miles of it, had been transformed into what looked like one massive boiler room. I knew very little about what Kentucky had been like prior to pullulation – just whatever the left-leaning press up in Canada had told me. I knew it was a place of bourbon, breathtaking rural splendour and rednecks. No more. It now resembled a giant circuit board, with rows upon rows of pipelines running in every direction across the countryside. Pipelines that came down from Alberta; pipelines that came up from Texas; pipelines that ran to the Pacific; pipelines that galloped to the Atlantic. They all connected and intersected here in Kentucky like an enormous assembled Tinkertoy. The state's rustic beauty was long gone. The ground beneath these elevated pipelines was the colour of breaded chicken as far as the eye could see. Grim grey apartment complexes, massive and de-individualizing hulks, dotted the horizon in every direction, no doubt housing refinery workers and lower-ranking petro executives. The air held a permanent canopy of smog. This, I imagined, was what certain parts of China or Fort McMurray must have looked like during its last big economic boom in the years before pullulation. Yes, Kentucky had become ground zero of North America's oil and gas sector, and how could it be any other way? All over the continent, pullulation had caused hamlets to become towns, towns to become cities, cities to become megalopolises, and they all needed fuel. Kentucky had drawn the short straw as to where these millions upon millions of grey tubes, carrying the very lifeblood of progress and expansion, would converge.

Our saving grace was, of course, our eagerness to reach the glowing jewel of the region: Nashville, Tennessee. Neither Otis nor I were country music fans, but we had both read fascinating stories about the genre's capital city, of bears from as far away as the Yukon and even Siberia who had made the long trek to Nashville to seek their fame as country music stars. Their presence had transformed the city into another Las Vegas: riotous with neon and unfettered opportunity, pulsating with people who longed for an abrupt shift in their fortunes. We expected to see bears in cowboy hats and sequined jackets and shit-kicking boots busking on every street corner. We expected to see glowing marquees on every block, to find the very air itself tuned to country music's drawl. In short, we expected Nashville to be *alive*.

And it was, in a sense. As we headed down from the north and passed over the Cumberland River, we gasped a little at the sight of Nashville's massive, manic skyline, at what pullulation had done to it. Enormous, charcoal-black towers, at least a hundred storeys high, huddled around and loomed over the downtown core's older buildings just up from the river's edge. From our vantage, we could spot the landmarks we had read about – the oddly shaped "Batman building" that had once seemed prominent along this cityscape, and all the signs that pointed toward the Grand Ole Opry as you came down off I-65. Fanning out beyond this downtown core, chasing the river along its edges, were scores of gleaming, glittering condo buildings (not that dissimilar to the ones that had infested our city), holding Nashville's now-seething population of ten million blomers.

But where was the neon? Where were the countless clubs and bars and holes in the wall where struggling country musicians could take their shot at the spotlight? Where were the bears? On our way toward the Best Western that Otis had booked for us on his phone, we passed more and more of these black, bleak office buildings and saw that they were, every last one of them, festooned with acronym-laden signage. ING. RBC. PwC. KPMG. K-TEN Global Wealth Management. On and on it went. At this early evening hour, we could see that the upscale eateries and fancy gastropubs at the base of these buildings were packed with blomers, but they were packed with hawks and pigeons and foxes – the males in salarymen suits with ties now loosened, the females in blazer-over-power-skirt ensembles and gravity-defying high-heeled leather boots. Not a single bear among them.

"Christ," Otis said, gawking out the window as I navigated our car through a busy downtown street, "it's become a finance centre. The entire city of Nashville . . . it's just one big bank now."

"But where's all the live music?" I asked, feeling as if our evening plans might slip away.

The front desk clerk at our Best Western had no answers for us as she checked us in. When we told her what we were looking for, she just averted her eyes and kept saying, "I don't know . . . I'm not sure . . . I really don't know . . ."

"C'mon, this is *Nashville*," I said to her, trying to keep my voice jokey. "There's got to be something nearby? It doesn't have to be swanky. We'd settle for a dive with a good band."

"Sorry . . . I don't know . . . I'm sorry . . . I don't know . . . I'm really not sure . . ."

So, Otis and I decided to take a walk after dropping our bags in the room. As we headed down a traffic-choked but otherwise staid thoroughfare, we saw a monorail zoom over our heads carrying what looked like commuters headed home after an evening of drinks. *Well those people found somewhere to have fun*, I thought. And it wasn't as if we didn't pass numerous establishments on our stroll. We did. That place played techno. This place played club. This other place also played club. For variety, that place played dance music. Jesus. We goggled across these bars' outdoor patios and through their glass windows at the revellers. Every last one of them was attractive in the extreme and dressed to the nines, clutching their impossibly elaborate and expensive-looking cocktails in indifferent hands. These bankers and money managers and financiers were not just the new rich. They were the *new* new rich, the *ultra*-new rich. In our blue jeans and T-shirts, with our hair matted and (we imagined) our bodies stinking of three long days in the car, Otis and I dared not cross their thresholds. *How ironic*, I thought, *that we'd be made to feel like a couple of bumpkins down from Canada here in fucking Nashville*. How long ago had these changes occurred? Four months? Maybe five? How could the city transform into . . . *this* so quickly?

The thoroughfare we sauntered seemed to widen with each passing block. Soon we found ourselves in what passed for a suburb: a panorama of shopping complexes surrounded by grey apartment buildings and looming condo towers. Across the street from where we now stood, we could see a seedy little strip mall housing a bowling alley. And above that bowling alley was what looked like the rarest of apparitions – a country and western bar. We thought this because it had a long, horizontal, tired-orange sign out front with the word KICKERS stencilled in black across the centre; and on either end of the sign, done up in a kind of calligraphy, were two images – one of a toothless hillbilly playing a guitar, and the other of a jug with triple-X markings on the front.

"What do you think?" I asked Otis.

"Well, it's either that or head back to the hotel and watch TV."

We crossed the street, passed through the strip mall's parking lot and pulled open the narrow glass door that appeared to lead up to the bar. As we ascended the grimy, steel-braced steps, we could hear all the sounds of the adjacent bowling alley – the hardwood rumble of balls racing down their lanes, the melodic *pong!* of the pins going down, the cheers of the players – but no country music.

At the top of the stairs, we turned right and pulled open a second glass door to step inside Kickers. We noticed that the place, done up in badly outdated orange and brown decor, had not a single patron inside. As we entered, a bald, paunchy bartender looked up from his splayed tabloid on the bar, raised himself off his elbows and gave us a suspicious look.

"Table for two?" I asked cheerily.

He hesitated, then gestured at his empty bar with a sweep of his beefy, short-sleeved arm. We settled in at a round two-seater right in front of the dour, dimly lit stage at the front of the room.

The bartender came by. "Beer?" he queried gruffly.

"Yes, beer!" said Otis.

Beer was produced. It tasted like the urine of a dog with bad kidneys. Otis and I lowered our steins after a grimace-inducing sip.

"Kitchen's about to close if you boys want dinner," the bartender mumbled when he came by again.

We told him no-thank-you, as we'd already eaten at a joint further up the I-65. "Actually, we were wondering," I said, nodding toward the stage, "do you have live music here?"

The bartender blinked at us for a second but then recovered. "Oh, sure, sure we do," he said. "What, you think we installed a stage there for nuthin'? Hang on a sec."

"Actually, it's okay," I replied. "I was only cur–"

"No, no, it's fine. She's about to close up the kitchen anyhow. Hang on." He scooted back toward the bar and opened the swing door there with a poke of his arm. "Laura Lee? Laura Lee! Get your buns out here. You got a gig, girl!"

The bartender returned to us with a look of satisfaction.

Through the swing door with its oval window appeared a short, stocky woman, a vip in capri jeans and a chef's apron, her thinning auburn locks bound up in a hairnet above her jowly, pug-like face. "Leon, whatchu beatin' your gums about?" But then she noticed us. "Oh!"

He gestured toward the stage. "They wanna hear you play."

"Oh!" she said again, and immediately reached behind herself to undo the apron strings knotted at the small of her back. She cast off the apron and peeled away her hairnet and flung them down into a nearby club chair. Her hair fell in her face, and as she turned, I noticed she had a rather prominent bald spot right at the crown. She staggered up onto the riser with a swing of one big buttock after the other, and then hustled to the wings. She came back a second later with a six-string guitar in one hand and a tall stool in the other. Through the floorboards, we caught a raucous cheer rising up from the bowling alley below.

"Now, it's been a while since I played in front of an audience, so you'll just have to bear with me."

"And by the way," Leon said, "there's a five-dollar cover charge for the band."

"Oh, fine," I replied, reaching for my wallet.

"*Each*," he stressed. So Otis reached for his wallet, too.

By the time we paid Leon, Laura Lee had perched herself onto the stool like a chubby falcon and began tuning the guitar as it rested on her thighs. "Now, I'll tell you right off the bat," she said, "I don't do Tammy Wynette; I don't do Dolly Parton; and I do *not* do Shania Twain. I sing my own songs written by my own self right here at Kickers."

"Uh . . . great," I called up.

"Can't wait," said Otis.

"And I apologize in advance for the lack of microphone. Whole sound system got repo'd last Thursday. I'll just have to sing real loud."

Otis and I settled in, sipped our dog piss and braced ourselves.

Staring intently at her left hand as it worked the chords and flicking her right hand to strum, Laura Lee launched into a slow, knuckle-dragging dirge. When she got a good grip on the melody, she turned her face towards us and began belting out her lyrics.

"Kill all the bears, kill all the bears,
kill all them Canadian bears."

Otis and I gasped together in near silence.

She went on, her voice now deep inside country music's warping twang:

"Rape 'em, burn 'em, throw 'em in the trash
for stealin' our jobs and takin' our cash.
Their music sucks, and so does their smell.
I hope they all just go burn in hell."

And there was more of the same. The song really didn't seem to have a chorus, but it did possess a rather distinctive bridge. Laura Lee had to pause briefly to transition into it, her fingers sliding into an unconfident clutch lower down on the frets.

"It's a terrible sit-u-a-tion.
I feel such des-per-a-tion.
It's my dignity's mu-til-a-tion
to deal with this pull-u-la-tion."

Eventually the tune ended, or at least stopped, and we clapped politely. Laura Lee then sang another three songs, all along a similar theme, and Otis and I began to get an inkling of what had happened to poor Nashville, Tennessee.

"Well, that's it for me," she said with a bow, and then slid, somewhat gracelessly, off her stool. "I best get back to the kitchen. I still got dishes to wash."

After she had gathered up her stuff and was gone, Leon came by our table again. "Another beer?" he asked.

Otis and I glanced at each other with what we hoped was an imperceptible look of disdain. "No, I think we're good," I said.

"Say, you fellas ain't from around here, are you?"

"No."

"Where you from?"

"Uh . . . Buffalo," Otis answered quickly. Though vips, we were still deeply unsettled by the violence wished upon Canadian blomers in Laura Lee's first song.

"Well, I hope you enjoy your stay in Nashville." Leon's voice held a slight curlicue of sarcasm.

Otis and I looked at each other again. "Um, about that," I said. "And really, we don't mean this as a dig against Laura Lee."

"Totally not a dig against Laura Lee," Otis agreed.

"But Nashville is supposed to be, like, a major music capital. We searched up and down, and this was the only joint that had anything resembling a live show. What . . . what happened?"

"I'll tell you what happened," Leon said. His voice grew abruptly threatening. "Troy fucking Louisiana. That's what happened."

My stomach clenched, and I assumed Otis's did the same. *Easy does it,* I thought. *Keep a poker face. Don't let on.* Indeed, Leon's explanation seemed almost gratuitous: based on the sentiments expressed in Laura Lee's songs, I knew the last thing he should hear was that we were a couple of Canadians heading down to Troy on a mission involving its music scene.

"The first seven, eight months after pullulation were great, just great," he told us. "We had bears down from the northern states. We had bears down from Canada. We had bears here from frickin' Russia. It was like an orgasm of music. The tourism industry just exploded. And sure, lots of vips couldn't get gigs around town at the time, couldn't compete with all the bears. I mean, look at Laura Lee. Can you believe that woman doesn't have a recording contract?"

"Boggles the mind," I said.

"I *know.* Anyway. Lots of conflict between vips and blomers at that point – fights in the streets, the sabotaging of shows. It was bad. But so what? Confrontation between vips and blomers is the story of America now. And lots of places were way worse than us. I mean, have you been to Salt Lake City, Utah, recently?"

"Can't say that we have," Otis answered.

"It's a fucking war zone there. And I mean twenty-four-seven. We were way tamer. And people really didn't mind the conflict. They just saw it as the price of doing business, and everybody in music was making scads of money. But then just like *that,*" and Leon snapped his fingers, "with no explanation, all the bears just pulled up stakes and left. It was, it was like the shifting of the tides or something. It was so . . . *animalistic,* the way they just ditched Nashville en masse like that and migrated southward, to Troy fucking Louisiana. Troy was America's new music capital, man, and as for poor Nashville, they didn't give a damn. They couldn't be fucked." Having gone red in the face, he took a breath. "And

207

nobody can explain it, but around that same time, somebody decided Corporate America needed another Wall Street, and down-
on-its-luck Nashville fit the bill. Within two months, the bankers
and money managers and stock traders flowed in here like shit
stains. Now, if you're a vip, you can't get a job in this town unless
you got an M.B.A. in fucking people in the ass." Tremulously, Leon
ran a hand through his hair. "And I see it every week, man. I see it
every goddamn week. Bears down from fucking Canada heading
for Troy to take their shot at the big time. Or tourists from all over
hell and creation coming to see what that city has to offer. And if
they're going by road from the north, a lot of 'em pass through
Nashville on the way down. It's like rubbing salt in our wounds.
But what I tell them, if I don't have my shotgun handy so I can
shoot them in the face, is this: stay away from Troy. It's a hellhole
there. And I'm not talking just orgies in the streets or some run-
of-the-mill violence like a normal place. There ain't enough vips
there to keep the place normal. Troy wasn't even a place prior to
pullulation. It was a fucking crossroads, man. And I tell people,
'You ain't never seen a city like that, founded by blomers. It's
. . . it's like something out of the Bible. Just stay the fuck away
from it.'"

Otis and I stared at our now empty, foam-clouded steins, and
I took a fretful swallow. We probably should have pressed Leon to
be more specific, but we didn't. Maybe we feared that, by asking
for details about Troy, we'd blow our cover, and he would threaten
us with violence. Or maybe we thought his perspective on Troy
was so skewed, considering what had happened to Nashville, that
we couldn't trust what he said about it anyway. Mostly, though,
I figured we didn't ask because we'd already come this far, and
nothing he said was going to make us go back now.

"So what did you say you're in Nashville for?" Leon asked.

"Um, just for a boring old conference . . ." I lied.

". . . on mutual funds," Otis added. And I marvelled at how
simpatico he and I could be, how good we were at thinking on
our feet.

"Well of course you are," Leon said. "Of course you are." Then he nodded at our glasses. "That'll be twelve-eighty for the beers, boys."

ॐ

Back in our room at the Best Western, I sat on the edge of my bed and Otis sat on his, each of us deep in our thoughts. I stared at the walls and he stared into his phone, its screen once more casting his face in that milky blue glow.

My own phone suddenly came to life. I took it out of my pocket and discovered an incoming call . . . from Alanna.

"Sorry, I have to take this," I said to Otis.

"No worries," he replied, not looking up.

I stepped into the bathroom and shut the door before swiping the phone's answer bar to green. "Alanna?"

"They're gone!" Her voice was a shriek, a piercing knife that entered my ear and seemed to come clean out of my chest. "Hector, they're gone! They're gone! Lesley's gone!"

I slumped against the bathroom counter. "Oh Jesus, Alanna, what happened?"

She was nearly inarticulate, her words a slopping slurry of anguish. "Isaac got in from school and found the condo empty. He called me at work and I immediately raced home. My closet's all in disarray, and one of my frocks is missing. They must have put it on . . . to disguise themselves . . . and went out."

"Oh God."

"I bolted out of here and went straight to the bookshop I go to for her books. I described the frock to the owner, but he said he hadn't seen anyone come in wearing something like that all day. So I went back out and just started hunting through the streets of our neighbourhood – for *hours*. But I couldn't find Lesley. Hector, I couldn't find them. I couldn't find them."

"Is Mitch there with you?"

"Of course he isn't. He's working a four-to-four shift to-night . . . with those *fucking* dogs."

"Alanna, I'm so sorry. . ."

"Can you come over? Please? I'm just beside myself. Hector, can you please come over?"

I took a deep, guilty swallow. "Alanna, I'm not there," I told her. "My buddy Otis and I are on a road trip to Louisiana. We're in Nashville, Tennessee, tonight. I was in Cincinnati when you called before."

There was a beat or two of silence on the line. "Oh, I'm sorry. Oh. I, I didn't realize."

"It's okay," I said. "Do you want to call Morgana? I'm sure she'd come over and be with you tonight."

"Um, no. No, that's okay. I . . ." She took a big snotty inhale. "I'm going back out there. I'm going to try and find Lesley."

"Okay. Be careful. Send me an update as soon as you can. Please? I'll be thinking about you."

"Okay. Okay, will do." And then she hung up.

I came out of the bathroom and Otis looked up from his phone. At the sight of my face, he asked, "You all right?"

"Yeah, no. That was my friend Alanna. She's just having a bit of a . . . thing back home."

He nodded, and before I could say more, he said, "So, good news."

"Hmm?"

"Thursday Banana finally updated their website. I got the dates and times of their gig at the Carrion."

"Oh?" Once again, the mere mention of the club's name had caused me a fresh outbreak of goose pimples.

As if to confirm my fear, Otis said, "I think you should look at the club's photo gallery." And he handed me his phone.

I began scrolling through the pictures on the Carrion's web-site, clicking on random ones to enlarge them. As I did, I felt my eyes swell in their sockets and all the muscles in my throat go slack. Jesus. Jesus Christ. Was what I was seeing for real? Was *that* what Ellen had abandoned her marriage for? The Carrion, it turned out, was nothing like the Cajun Cage. In these images, I could see throngs of blomers – cows and cats, pigeons and dogs, crows and gophers – not swaying and dancing in front of the stage but rather *brawling* with one another. It was a mosh pit taken to the nth degree, an abject violence done to the rhythm of live music. It made my stomach roll.

Suddenly, I did want us to turn back around and head home. I felt in that moment that, no, not even Ellen was worth this, that Leon's warning to us had been right and true and prophetic.

It was as if Otis had read my mind. "Dude, you don't have to do this," he said. "If you want to back out now, I totally understand. I can buy you a plane ticket tomorrow and send you home. This is my problem, and I can take care of it by myself . . . if need be. Don't worry, I'll get your Camry back to you safe and sound next week."

In light of Alanna's call, I seriously considered it. Should I be there to help her – or stay here and help him? I moistened my lips and looked at Otis again, over there on his bed. He was my best friend in the whole world, and I was still smarting from how I'd hurt him with what I'd said about Ellen back in Windsor. I figured I owed him, and I would stand shoulder to shoulder with him to do what had to be done.

"No," I told him, brandishing my newborn courage. "No, I'm in. I'm *in*, Otis. Let's go convince your wife to get the fuck out of there."

CHAPTER 12

And then we saw something we hadn't seen since – well, since forever: countryside.

We got just a whiff of it, a brief belt of green once we made our glacial way past Jackson, Mississippi, the last of the megalopolises, and then executed a hair-raising, white-knuckled transfer from the I-20 to Route 65 at Tallulah, the turnpikes there coiling and curving around us like slides at a waterpark. Once we had successfully hit our exit (that is, without side-swiping anyone or getting forced into the wrong lane; God, they drove like maniacs here) and headed southward for another twenty minutes, the urbanscape seemed to fall away almost instantly. Before we knew it, we were crossing a terrain that resembled what we imagined this part of America looked like prior to pullulation: tree-lined ditches hiding vast, verdant fields, blessedly free of concrete and glittering towers of glass. This stretch of Route 65 was as rural as rural could be. We passed a truck-stop diner; we even saw a few dusty windmills.

"Well, *this* is nice," Otis said.

"Thoroughly pleasant," I concurred.

It didn't last long. Within another fifteen minutes, the traffic began thickening again and ahead of us we spotted what we assumed were Troy's northernmost suburbs. Even at this distance, we could see those neighbourhoods were made up mostly of rundown or even abandoned townhouses of squat red brick or paint-chipped, weather-beaten clapboard, their lawns weedy and unmowed, their sidewalks overrun with cracks and craters. *Wait – what?* I thought briefly as I drove. *How old are those houses, those streets? I thought there had been nothing out here before pullulation.* But I couldn't bring myself to linger on those impressions, the implausibility of what I was seeing.

The traffic coagulated and then stopped near the city limits. Otis began bobbing and stretching in the passenger seat to glimpse out the windshield at what was delaying us.

"Holy shit," he said. "It . . . it looks like a. . ."

"Like a what?" I asked.

He swallowed and gave a worried grit of his teeth. "A military checkpoint."

It was not a military checkpoint. But it was a group of about twelve or fifteen gophers dressed up in militia-wear – army-surplus camo and yard-sale body armour – with M-16s in their hands and grenades on their belts. These lads had set up a roadblock coming into the city. Some cars they waved through right away. Others they stopped with a brusque raise of their hand. We watched ahead of us as one short-haired woman, a sparrow, leaned out her driver-side window to talk to the gophers. At their insistence, she opened her blouse and exposed her breasts to them. They nodded and let her pass. A few cars later, they hauled a dog out of his vehicle and made him stand there on the side of the road. They ordered him to drop his pants and boxers, which he did, and a couple of the gophers went about examining his junk. It was then that I noticed the man had a rather androgynous face, and it dawned on me. *Oh, of course. They're checking to see that he has only one set of genitalia. They're making sure he isn't a herm.*

When it was our turn, they took one look through our windshield and waved us through without even asking us to roll down our windows. This, I supposed, was the privilege of being a vip in America, and of being just one gender. The shit-eating grins that the gophers tossed at us as our Camry passed were more ominous than cheery. "Enjoy Troy!" one of them called out in a singsongy rhyme just before we sped off.

Enjoy Troy indeed. It became apparent almost right away that we were entering less a city of three hundred and fifty thousand people and more a mystical theme park. Somehow, through the configuration of its cobbled streets, through the span of its granite piazzas and the crouch and nestle of its buildings, Troy created the illusion of possessing a great past, as if it were an old-world city rather than something that had popped up in the weeks or months after pullulation. As we circled toward its downtown, we spotted an enormous church – a church! – that looked like it had been lifted wholesale from medieval Europe and plunked here in northern Louisiana. How was this possible? Who would have built it, and why?

It became clear the instant we passed into the downtown proper that it held the typical blomer trappings: as we passed a park, a giant common in the middle of the city, we could see a ménage of about three dozen people on the grass, all naked, all engaged in some sort of coital entanglement. Still, there was something about the place that struck us as strange. "Look at these homes over here," Otis and I said to each other as we passed through an upscale neighbourhood. We saw beautiful, rambling nineteenth-century-style Victorian mansions with broad, homey porches and three-storey Queen Anne turrets climbing like steeples into the air, or colonial-period manors with white stone pillars out front. We even spotted a few tasteful, low-rise apartment buildings, structures that had become all but extinct in our own city. This, like the sight of Troy's dilapidated suburbs, unsettled me. This wasn't what I imagined a blomer-founded city would look like, and certainly not what Leon back in Nashville had described to us. I had expected an endless parade of new, gleaming, soulless condo towers engineered to within an inch of their lives, like the ones now overrunning our city. Instead, Troy's homes and businesses looked as if they'd been there for decades and were bursting with charm and character – hauntingly so. It all summoned that weird, unnerving sensation I sometimes felt, the one of passing through a window of time, a portal into another dimension of reality. Was Troy even of this world? Had we passed through to an entirely new plane of existence? And, more importantly, would we be able to find our way out again when the time came?

We were soon driving through a grittier, down-market pub district. Even with our windows rolled up, we could hear rowdy, thundering live music pumping out of each establishment – folk and folk-rock, country and Top 40. The sidewalks out front were utterly impassable with drunken, boisterous revellers. Some of them caromed into the street and we had to brake suddenly to avoid hitting them with the car. We spotted a few scuffles here and there, a fist fight or two down darkened side streets, and both Otis and I looked away with unease. We knew – having glimpsed what we had glimpsed in that photo gallery of the Carrion's – that under this raucous party atmosphere was a real and frightening current of violence.

Troy must have been at the height of some sort of blomer tourism season, because Otis attempted to book us a motel room on his phone earlier in the day and found virtually nothing available. No Best Western, no Super 8, no mom-and-pop B & B on the outskirts of town. The best we could do was a single two-bed dorm room at a small college in the west end of the city, deserted now of students on account of it being summer. Offering a two-night stay, this dorm room appeared to be the only vacancy in town, so we snatched it up for ourselves as quickly as we could. Using the GPS on Otis's phone, we found our way to this educational institution, called Queens University College. Thankfully, it was, according to Google Maps, a mere twenty-minute stroll from the Carrion, where Thursday Banana's regular gig would now be in full swing. As we approached, Otis and I expected Queens to resemble the new universities that had cropped up in our own city after pullulation: characterless cobalt office buildings where blomers could earn an honours degree in commerce or a master's in marketing in about a month and a half.

So how pleasant to discover that Queens was not that. We pulled into its quadrangle and were suddenly surrounded by delightful sandstone buildings that exuded an almost Oxonian charm. We parked the Camry, got out and went over to the large but straightforward campus map on a sign at the edge of the grassy courtyard to get our bearings. We grasped the pentagonal layout almost instantly: Arts & Administration Building, Chapel, Girls' Residence, Library, Boys' Residence. Heading over to the latter, we found a small office on the first floor where a young, bored, paperback-reading cat checked us in. We headed up with our bags to the room she assigned us, number 435 on the third floor of the north wing. We unlocked the door to find the simplest of chambers: whitewashed concrete walls and a grey carpeted floor, a chipping black radiator under the narrow, boxy window. Two single beds done up in simple linens lay at either end of the space, their small faux-wood headboards pointing in opposite directions. The walls, I could see, still carried minute smears of blue sticky putty from previously hung posters. Over the room's window were curtains that appeared deliberately outdated: a kind of dark *Frogger*-video-game pattern.

"I think this'll be fine," Otis remarked, setting his bag down.

"Otis . . ." I said, feeling my dread, my sense that we had slipped through some sort of doorway in time, come back. "Does this whole place not strike you as . . . odd? As, you know, like . . . oddly impossible?"

"Hmm?"

I pointed at the other end of the room. "How old is that radiator? What era are those curtains from? Dude, there was nothing here a year and a half ago. How can this place feel so . . . ancient?"

"I don't know. It was probably designed that way to make students feel like they're attending a university of yore."

"But it's not just that," I said. "It's not just this campus. It's the whole city. Do you not sense it?"

But he had already grown quiet, pensive. His mind was clearly churning with other thoughts now that he was once again in the same city as Ellen.

I must have been delusional. I must have been harping on something that didn't really matter. We were here in Troy, and what difference did it make where *here* was? I decided to let all this go – for now. We needed to stick to our mission. "Look, do you want to just chill out here for tonight and get some rest?" I asked. "It's been a long day."

"No," he replied. "If we only have this room for two nights, I don't want to waste time. I want to get this over with."

"Fair enough."

We decided we *did* need a shower and so took turns trundling off to the shared bathroom down the hall. Otis went first, and while he was gone, I took the opportunity to text Alanna, whose crisis had been stewing at the back of my thoughts all day.

Hey there – any update on Lesley? Did they come home?

It took a while for her to reply – so long in fact that I thought I might not hear from her at all. But then my phone buzzed in my waiting hand and I looked down at the screen.

No, they didn't. Isaac and I looked everywhere, but we haven't been able to find them. I'm convinced they're dead. I know in my heart they're gone.

Oh, Alanna, don't say that. Don't give up hope. They may turn up yet.

I don't think so. It would have happened by now. I just have to let Lesley go.

Alanna, I'm so sorry.

Thx. Anyway, Isaac is calling me so I should go. I'll talk to you later.

Okay. Send me an update if there's any news.

Will do.

꙳

Soon Otis and I were clean, dressed for a night on the town and out the door. The residence, and indeed Queens' entire campus, had come alive in the gloaming evening. From the quadrangle, we could see that most of the residences' windows had their lights on, and groups of what looked like tourists – vips and blomers both – were climbing the steps of the A&A building to head inside. Through the building's basement windows, we could hear the clamour of live music from what must have been the student pub. I mused on whether we should pop in, but I could tell by the anxiety in Otis's step that he didn't want to take the time to check it out. As far as he was concerned, we were to get ourselves down to the Carrion as fast as our legs would take us.

Thankfully, it was a relatively straight shot. Queens resided on the south end of Berg Street, and if you headed north for fifteen minutes by foot, Berg Street became Summer Garden Way at Spring Street, which was sort of the main drag of Troy's downtown. Indeed, the intersection of Spring Street and Summer Garden Way had been, we'd learned from the internet, Troy's original crossroads before pullulation. The Carrion was just another five minutes beyond that. At the intersection, we passed a massive public garden, its wrought iron fence and weeping willows and large gazebo exuding an Edwardian feel. In fact, across from the public gardens on Spring Street was a grand, old-timey hotel called The Edwardian. Standing there waiting for the light to change, I was struck by a bizarre jag of déjà vu, a ridiculous sense that I had stood on this corner not once but many times before.

Other sights roiled me along our trajectory. Over here, three people were having sex atop a weather-beaten bench. Over there, the corpse of a herm rotted on a large pike from a recent crucifixion block party, the steel spear driven up through the anus and out through the mouth. This was more graphic than any sight I'd seen in our own city's downtown, but that wasn't what had shaken me. Just behind this pike stood a mint-green statue of a man in eighteenth-century garb, his right hand extended out in a lording gesture. It was as if he had ordered the herm's execution.

Leon had been right: there was something horrifyingly Biblical about Troy.

Before long, the foot traffic on the sidewalk had condensed to an uncomfortable level, and we realized we were walking past a lengthy line of people looking for admittance somewhere. We sauntered along its chattering length, anxious to see where these folks were going. Before long, we realized that this was, in fact, the queue to get into the Carrion. Its entrance, we saw, was guarded by a couple of stern, refrigerator-shaped bouncers in white dress shirts and black slacks.

"God*damn*it," Otis said.

"Line starts back there, lads," someone near the front called out, tossing a gruff thumb in the direction whence we came, and we turned around. As we did, a gaggle of some of the Carrion's patrons came out of the club and jogged excitedly past us on the sidewalk. One held her hand against her nose, the fingers there tacky with blood. Another, I could see, had fresh, vibrant bruises in the shape of fingers all along her throat, and the knees of her jeans had been torn out. A third, a dude, had been rendered into a kind of cyclops, his left eye swollen shut. But far from distressed, these people looked joyous, exhilarated and infinitely pleased with themselves, as if they had just had the night of their lives.

"You realize this isn't our scene," I said to Otis after they scurried past. "We . . . we may not be cut out for this."

"I don't care," he replied. "We've come this far. I'm not chickening out now."

We took up our place at the back of the line, which had grown even longer in the moments since we'd first arrived. It was getting late, and the queue hardly moved at all, and we grew impatient. Twenty minutes passed, then half an hour. We went six feet. Fifteen minutes later, Otis left to go find a public toilet. By the time he got back, we had moved another four feet. All the while, I kept thinking of that photo gallery from the Carrion's website. It baffled me how the cheery neo-calypso tunes of Thursday Banana had found a place in front of what amounted to a mosh pit on steroids. The blomers who populated the dance floor, it was clear, did not come just to sing and sway and dance a jig. They came to be violated, assaulted, roughed up. This was a community of consensual violence. My guts cartwheeled at the thought of us going into the heart of it.

Eventually, one of the burly bouncers headed up our way with a look of apology on his face. He raised his voice to speak to as many of us in the line as he could. "Okay, folks, I got some bad news. There is no realistic way we're gonna get you inside before Thursday Banana finishes its last set."

A collective groan passed through the great crocodile tail of people.

"I know, I know, I'm sorry. Look, this band is new to Troy and very popular. What can I say? My advice is to get here as early as you can for tomorrow's show or come back in a couple weeks after all the hubbub has died down."

Another groan, but then, reluctantly, the line began to disperse.

Yet Otis and I lingered, even after the bouncers began eyeing us with suspicion. The minutes passed.

"Dude, what do you want to do?" I asked.

"I don't know," he replied. "It's not like I expect my wife to come waltzing out that front door."

"If she's with the band, they'll probably go out some back entrance anyway."

He nodded.

"Still, we can wait a while longer, just in case."

He nodded again.

More minutes passed. Eventually, Otis let out a grunt and said, "Okay, fine. It's getting late. We've had another long day in the car. Let's just head back."

"If that's what you want."

As we walked southward along Summer Garden Way and back toward Queens, we realized we hadn't even discussed what we thought might happen once we *did* gain entry to the Carrion. In such an atmosphere of brutality, were we really prepared to put up an actual physical fight to get Ellen back?

"You know, I'm not much of a scrapper," I told Otis as we passed other busy establishments, their own live music pumping into the street, their own queues snaking along the sidewalk.

"And what, I am?"

"Look, I'm just saying – what's the plan?"

He released a long, slow sigh. "Honestly, Hector, I don't know. I guess I just imagined showing up there, and the mere sight of me would convince her that she's made a terrible mistake. Like, she'd see how far I had travelled to get her back, and it would, you know, win her over."

"Do you think that's actually going to happen?"

"Maybe. But if it doesn't, are you prepared to throw a punch?"

"I most certainly am not."

We left it at that. Whatever mysteries tomorrow night might hold – provided we actually gained entry to the Carrion – would have to reveal themselves in due time.

We found our way back to Queens. Entering the quadrangle, we could hear a sound that had become, we now realized, ubiquitous in the city of Troy: that of raucous live music. It was coming from the windows of the student pub in the basement of the A&A building facing the quad, now chockablock with tourists. Otis and I, exhausted, still gave each other a look.

"Wanna check it out?" he asked.

"Suppose a nightcap wouldn't hurt."

We climbed the stairs of the A&A, stepping between its tall, broad stone pillars, and pulled open the glass doors. Inside, we followed our ears across the lobby's marble floor to another set of stairs, padded with a kind of mint-green rubber, that descended into the building's lower level. There, we found a landing outside what was clearly the student pub, the live music throbbing from inside. A bored-looking chicken sat at a table with a cash box outside the door. There was no line to get in.

"Five-dollar cover," the chicken told us.

We paid and then moved inside the pub. A small stage was set up in the corner to our right, where a band of obvious Irish influence was tearing into a song with guitars and a fiddle and a tin flute. The crowd spread through the room, spilling beyond a pool table in the middle to the long, wooden, U-shaped bar on the far left-hand side. We could see that the pub had been done up in an ocean-faring motif – the walls adorned with a ship's wheel, ropes and pulleys, framed photos of navy destroyers, a big brass compass – despite the fact that the nearest ocean was seven hundred miles away.

Otis acquired our first round at the bar while I found us a table near the stage. We drank our beers and took in the music. The band, we saw, was composed mostly of bears – the only exception being the bass-playing blue jay – but there was something different about their performance, or what it engendered, from the ones at the Cajun Cage back home, or what we imagined was happening now just down the road at the Carrion. No one was moshing. No one was brawling. No one was having sex out in the open, crushed against a wall or bent over a table. By comparison, this felt like the sort of show we'd encountered in our old lives, prior to pullulation. This felt like normalcy.

I got that sense again as I got up to buy our second round. Looking over the room as I waited in line at the bar, I thought that a herm could walk into this space, not even bothering to hide their hermaphroditic features, and go completely unmolested. No one here would do them any harm despite the fact that three-quarters of the people in this place were blomers. Perhaps this was what Troy had actually stolen from places like Nashville, this idea that music could be a profound and civilizing force in people's lives rather than the opposite. As I returned to Otis and handed him his beer, I sensed that he was getting this vibe, too.

We got a third round, and then a fourth, which was very unusual for us, as we were not heavy drinkers. The band would, it seemed, play their jigs and reels all night. I felt very much at peace inside these wood-panelled walls with their seafaring gewgaws. I thought: *if Morgana were here, this would be perfect.* I thought: *she and I must be doing something right with each other, because we could take this time apart, put half a continent between us, and still be okay.* We had exchanged just a couple of emails since I'd left home: *How's the road trip going???* she'd asked, and I'd replied with the scantest detail, and certainly said nothing about what had happened in Windsor. And we were okay with that light dusting of connection. We were. Otis, by contrast, seemed to exude a great sense of loss over there in his seat, an impression of missing Ellen profoundly, of having no idea whether they would ever be together again. I could see how those feelings hunched his shoulders and dragged his face downward and made him seem very, very tired. I was overcome then with another jag of guilt. Across the table, I wanted to reiterate: *Dude, I would never hit on Ellen. Those impulses I described in that Super 8 parking lot were so faint as to be practically subconscious, and I would never act on them – ever.* But he also looked like he didn't need to hear that again. He looked like he had much more pressing thoughts rolling through his mind, thoughts of what was to happen when we finally gained entry to the Carrion.

"Should we call it a night?" he asked sleepily as we finished our fourth round of beer. "It's getting late."

"Just one more song," I replied.

Eventually, we left the bar and crossed the quad. The Louisiana night was deep, moist, endless. Staggering up to our dorm room, we unlocked the door and made a beeline to our respective single beds. We collapsed there as if crushed by the burdens of the day, by the weight of everything it had held.

❧

We slept late into the next morning. Too late, in fact. We hadn't risen in time to catch breakfast in the college's dining hall, so we just sort of lay there on our respective beds with our respective thoughts. Eventually we sauntered down for lunch, discovering a cavernous cafeteria of wood panelling and long, medieval-style tables. It was not that dissimilar to the dining hall of my own undergraduate years, with the exception that these walls held no portraits of past presidents because Queens, being less than two years old, didn't really have a past.

After lunch, we trucked back up to our room and Otis went to take the first shower. Not long after he left, my phone burst to life in my pocket. I took it out to look at the screen, and my heart sank when I saw who it was. After a bracing beat of stillness, I moved the slider over and put the phone to my ear.

"Hey there."

"Hi, Hector." Her voice was but a whisper, a near silence, like the last faint reverberation of a tuning fork.

"Hey," I said again, drawing up all the empathy and comfort I could into my voice. "What's the latest?"

That horrible, horrible whisper never left her words. It was so gentle, as if she were sharing the most tender secret with me.

"So . . . um, yeah. Yeah. Lesley's gone. They're dead. I found them this morning."

"Fuck," I murmured back. "Oh Jesus. Oh Jesus."

"Yeah. Their body, um, wasn't all that far away actually. I found it behind our building when I went to put out the recycling."

"Oh, Alanna."

"Yeah. The group of blomers, whoever they were . . . they beat Lesley, stripped them naked and hanged them from a lamppost . . . with my frock."

I had no words. I had no words.

"There was one of my tote bags in the corner of the alley there, and a few books scattered around." Her voice was climbing in octaves. "So they must have gotten to that bookstore after all."

"Christ."

"Yep. I guess . . . um, yeah. I guess it just wasn't something I could prevent. I suppose I'll just chalk all this up to, you know, losing another baby. I'm getting used to that."

When she spoke those words, I felt it briefly wash over me – that strange, foreign feeling of parental instinct. It was so queer. *This must be*, I thought, *what she feels all the time.*

"Anyway, Hector, I just wanted to let you know."

"Alanna . . ."

"Anyway. Thank you for being there for me through all this. I have to go. Thank you. Thank you for everything."

"Alanna . . ."

"I have to go. Thank you, Hector."

"You're welcome."

And then she was gone. I sat on the edge of the bed with the extinguished phone in my hand, not really able to do anything. Eventually, Otis came back into the room, all fresh-faced and damp from his shower. He took one look at my expression and asked, "Hey, you okay?"

I looked up at him. "No," I said with a shake of my head. "No, I'm not." And then I told him everything.

❧

After that, I went to take my own shower, and when I got back, I found Otis on his bed staring into his phone. He looked in the grip of full-on alarm in that moment. His face flew up to mine as I tossed my toiletries bag and clothes from yesterday onto my bed.

"Hector," he said, "what – what day is it today?"

"It's, um . . ." I staggered under the weight of his question. Because the road trip had taken so much longer than we thought it would, my brain now fumbled over exactly when we had landed in Troy. "I think it's, um, Tuesday?"

"No, what date is it?"

"Oh. The nineteenth, I think."

"So then am I reading this right?" He shoved the phone's screen toward my face. On it, I could see Thursday Banana's confusing and badly designed website. "They're only playing a matinee today," Otis said. "Two sets starting at 1:00 p.m."

I looked at my watch. "Oh *crap.*"

We briefly discussed taking the Camry down to the Carrion, but I blanched at the idea of trying to find parking down there. Instead, we opted for the bus and soon found Troy Transit's routes and schedules online. There was a stop right outside the college's gate for the Number 1 bus, and it took a straight shot down Berg Street and into the heart of Summer Garden Way. We rushed out to catch the next one. Otis was quiet and twitchy after we boarded, lost in his concerns as we stood there in that crowded sauna of strangers. As the bus approached the corner of Spring and Summer Garden, we pulled the cord and then shoved our way through the throng to get off.

We arrived at the Carrion to discover that the lineup to get in was even longer than it had been the night before. "Fuck, fuck,

fuck," Otis muttered, and released a groan of consternation. We got into the line but found our patience soon frayed. The queue moved so slowly that there was even a tussle somewhere ahead of us as two groups of fans began arguing over who was ahead of whom in the line.

"This isn't going to work," Otis said.

"We've got to get in," I replied. "We only have the room for another night."

He stretched and strained his head to get a peek at the front of the queue, which didn't seem to be moving. "Nope, nope, nope," he said, his voice filling with panic.

Just then, we did move and were suddenly standing at the mouth of an alley that ran between two buildings next door to the Carrion. We gazed down its deep, concrete throat, past the shadows and a lone green dumpster. There, at the end of the alley, we could see what was clearly a narrow back street. And upon that narrow back street, a white delivery truck was carefully backing up, its slow, robotic beep chirping through the air. We watched it ease its way rearward and out of view. Was it, perhaps, headed for the bar's loading dock? What if we . . . we were able to . . . ?

Otis seemed to get the same idea as me. He pointed with his chin down the alley.

"What do you think?" he whispered.

I shrugged. "At this juncture, what have we got to lose?"

His head bobbed on his neck. "Okay, okay. But let's be quiet about it. Let's be discreet."

We slipped out of the queue, which promptly swallowed up the space we had taken, and made a move toward the end of the line. But we then doubled back and began strolling nonchalantly down the alley's dark, garbage-strewn asphalt. I didn't look back over my shoulder for fear I would make eye contact with the people we had left behind, and they would call out to us, *Hey, hey, assholes! Where do you think you're going?* Thankfully, we made it to the end of the alley and rounded its corner without drawing undue attention.

Sure enough, the white delivery truck had backed up to the Carrion's garage-style loading bay. We lingered unnoticed against a brick wall as two delivery men, a couple of dogs, exited the truck's cab and donned their canvas work gloves. One guy threw open the truck's back while the other greeted one of the Carrion's waitresses, a chicken in a tight skirt and extremely revealing halter top, who was waiting for them. She rolled up the bay door and then the two delivery men began hauling out kegs of beer and lugging them inside. Otis and I crept closer. When the dogs had finished their drop-off, they stopped to chat amiably with the chicken in the darkness of the door. She said something to them that I didn't catch. One of the dogs raised the cuff of his work glove to look at his watch, and then the two men shrugged. They tossed their gloves to the ground like hockey players ready for a fight and then peeled their tank tops off over their heads. The waitress, meanwhile, did this kind of shimmy manoeuvre in her miniskirt and then stepped out of her panties just as the dogs were unbuckling and lowering their pants. One of the dogs got down and lay on his back on the cold loading-bay floor. The waitress climbed aboard him, casting her hips over his as the other dog came looming toward her face, the pale globes of his ass gleaming at us in the shadows.

"Now's our chance," I whispered to Otis, and we scurried like mice along the far wall of the garage. It was easy to go unnoticed, what with the chicken's now bobbling head hooked into the hip of the dog standing with his back to us while the other dog cupped her ass with both hands and ran his mouth all over her now free and flouncing breasts.

We peeped our heads through the loading bay's inner door leading to the back of the club. It stood at the rear of a wide, tiled hallway where harried wait staff hustled around and called out orders and cracked quips at each other and loaded their trays with drinks. About twenty feet from where we lurked, I could see how the hallway opened up into the main room of the club, right next to the swinging doors leading to the customer washrooms. If we could just make it there undetected, we'd be able to blend in with everyone who had stood in line and paid to enter the Carrion.

Thankfully, there was a rack of hanging costumes on wheels – rhinestone frocks and sequined denim coats and a rainbow mélange of feathered boas – about halfway up the hall. I gestured to it and Otis nodded his agreement. We paused briefly, tensely (the three blomers behind us were almost finished, their grunts and gasps building to a frenzied crescendo) and waited for a moment when the hallway was clear. Then we dashed out and over to the costume rack, squeezing ourselves between it and the wall. Then we rolled the rack as casually as we could toward our destination. A few wait staff passed us by, but they were too preoccupied to notice us.

We reached the end of the hall and then leaped like dancers into the club proper. I was awash in relief when I realized we had made it.

The place was packed. We were nowhere near the stage, which was at the front of the club, and yet we had to squeeze our way through mobs of people drinking or making out or heading off to the washrooms. The Cajun Cage back home had nothing on this place. Despite the nondescript facade we had glimpsed from the street, the Carrion had a cavernous, almost stadium-like feel to its interior. The walls were huge and high and done up in gimcrack motifs of pillars and buttresses and Doric columns that lent the space an air of Ancient Greece. The floor seemed to go on forever in every direction. Yet in those first moments, the expanse struck me as no less claustrophobic than a tiny crowded jazz hole or busy lunchtime diner, on account of the throng of people who churned and eddied through this space. My sense of suffocation was aggravated, accentuated by the atmosphere of brutality that became immediately apparent. Already we could see pockets of blomers who had gathered together to wail on and choke and slam into each other to the rhythm of the music. This violence was everywhere we turned: at tables and under tables and *on* tables, against walls and railings and in the narrow – far too narrow – pathway leading to the sole set of doorways back outside.

There was more. Above our heads, up there in the high ceiling, a spiderweb's worth of catwalks led to more sex cages than I had ever seen in a single establishment. They swayed and vibrated through the air like huge, grotesque wind chimes, and the orgiastic noises radiating from them were louder and more extravagant than I'd ever heard, a shrill, communal chorus of pleasure. Yet they could not drown out the music that rocketed through the club, and it was the music that told us we were definitely in the right place. There was no mistaking Thursday Banana's strident, elaborately chipper tunes. One of their familiar B-side songs filled our ears and flooded me with a sudden, unexpected gush of homesickness.

Weaving and shoving through the crowd, Otis and I made our way toward the stage. As we closed in on it, we found a sunken area at its base that held the largest and busiest mosh pit I had ever laid eyes on. I clutched Otis's shoulder as we got a good gawk at it. I couldn't begin to say how many people crowded that railed-off area since, in the throes of their slam-dancing, they were nearly indistinguishable as individuals. Bodies flew through the air in deliberate hip checks; foreheads and faces collided with sickening regularity; elbows and knees arced through the strobing, colourful lights like mandibles tearing apart prey. Otis and I watched the brutality unfold like a pro-wrestling battle royale, the violence striking me as so incongruous with Thursday Banana's cheery, neo-calypso music. How could it inspire such reckless sadism? How could it trigger this need to slam-dance at all costs. I chalked it up to yet another aspect of the pullulation process and its effects on the blomer brain that I simply would never understand.

"Jesus Christ!" I yelled at Otis. "How do people keep from getting killed?"

But he had already begun scanning the manic room for some glimpse of Ellen. We had no hope, it seemed. The Carrion, so much larger than the Cajun Cage back home, was full of strange dark alcoves and cloistered, packed tables on the other side of the mosh pit. A set of velvety red curtains hung at either end of the stage and between them, where the band members stood in their merry calypso formation, unspooled an aggressive mist of dry ice that obscured everything.

"Craziness," I called to Otis over the music. "We don't stand a chance."

"Wait," he called back. "Wait for it." His eyes darted around, seemingly fixated on everything at once.

We waited. Thursday Banana finished a song and then launched into another. A few moshers, either accidentally or deliberately, banged into Otis and me from behind as they headed toward the pit. I took an elbow in the kidneys; someone pitched the crown of his head backward into Otis's. We ignored these jostles and stayed focused on the room. Thursday Banana finished this new song, and then the lead singer called out over the crush: "Okay, folks, we're going to take a short break, but don't go anywhere. We'll be back in about twenty minutes." The lights came up. The moshing ceased. The dry ice clung stubbornly to the air before dissipating. Some revellers headed back toward the tables and alcoves; others made their way to the catwalks that led up to the sex cages. Others just milled on the mosh floor in front of the stage.

"Watch," Otis said, his voice now a whisper. "Watch for it."

It took a couple of minutes, and I felt myself grow impatient. The sensation that came over me then was similar to what I had experienced back in Windsor, like I'd been skinned alive and every nerve was now exposed and jangling. I thought that it would take just one more shove or butt from behind to set me off, and all the turmoil that had been mounting since we had left home would come rushing up like a geyser. I wasn't sure how I could possibly help Otis find what he was looking for in this boisterous place, what with my head now flooding with thoughts of . . . of *everything* – of Morgana in her play, the desperate calls from Alanna, Brennan Prate and his constant needling, my shameful confessions to Otis. It all felt so raw and immediate as I stood there that I barely recognized myself, the sound of my own internal voice.

Thankfully, Otis knew what to look for. He had spent enough time back in the Cajun Cage to know. Sure enough, a few members of Thursday Banana, including the lead singer, came jogging out from the back of the stage, clutching bottles of water in their hands. They trotted down the stage stairs and onto the floor. Moving through the crowd like glib politicians, they shook hands with or winked at or pointed cheerful fingers toward their battered, adoring fans. Someone pulled out a vinyl LP and got them to sign it. Eventually, the band members got across the floor to an alcove table that, in a great fit of irony, was directly across from where we stood. We looked out over the expanse and peered deep into the space where the members of Thursday Banana had gone.

Yes. Yes! With the lights now up and the fog of dry ice clearing, we could see that gathered round a large table with bench seating in the alcove was a caucus of Thursday Banana groupies from back home – including Ellen! She sat three people in on our left, her face small and in profile to us as she leaned over the table to catch whatever the person across from her was saying. When the members of the band arrived, she turned and greeted them with a slight smile and girly twiddle of her fingers.

"There!" Otis said, his voice filling with rage. And then he was on the move.

"Okay, wait, what's the plan?" I called out as I followed him. But the plan was obvious, and I was suddenly saturated with adrenalin. On some level, I must have known that this was not good, that I was no longer in a safe state of mind to come face to face with confrontation. But what could I do? This was what we had come here for, what we had travelled so far to find. I would not abandon my friend at this point. I would have his back, no matter what.

Man, Otis could move fast when he wanted to. He slid and deked his way around the milling mosh-pit dwellers and made a beeline for the groupies, with me barely able to keep up behind him. His long hair looked almost cape-like as he rushed over, and his thin legs pumped and swayed. He arrived and halted at their table a full three seconds before I did, but I still caught what happened. It was almost comical, like some ridiculous and implausible gesture you might see on one of those lame, old-timey sitcoms. Ellen did a double take, looking at him and looking back at her friends and then looking at him again, her face perking with shock. She flew to her feet, her thighs knocking the table and causing the drinks there to wobble. When I arrived at Otis's side, Ellen glanced at me in puckered bafflement. Her surprise at the sight of us was pristine, and it stirred something within her, although I couldn't yet read precisely what.

"Otis?" she said, turning back to him. "Otis! What the fuck are you doing here? What . . . what the fuck are you doing *here*?"

The groupies and the gathered members of Thursday Banana were equally stunned to see us. Most of them appeared to recognize Otis from his role at the Cajun Cage as Ellen's occasional third wheel. They sort of gaped at us like fish in a fish tank, their expressions growing rapidly concerned about our sudden presence, about what it might mean. We had, in one crisp instance, doused their world in the possibility of an altercation.

I glanced back at Ellen and could see now what we couldn't from the other side of the room. Her lovely face had been marred. A fierce black swelling nestled like a small mouse under her left eye, and her bottom lip was split on the right and scabbed over, as if cuffed there by someone's diamond ring. I deduced she must have spent some hard time in Thursday Banana's mosh pit.

Otis himself hadn't deduced this because he asked her, "What happened to your face?"

And for a fraction of a second, we saw it. The softening, the gentling of her expression. His lone olive branch – perhaps the first in their marriage in a while – seemed to rouse something in Ellen without her consent. It was like a flicker of misgiving, of ambivalence, as if this one extension of his worry had caused her to doubt, ever so briefly, the choice to leave him and embark on this crazy adventure. Was this the first moment of reservation she'd felt? As I watched her then, I suspected not. I imagined her trapped inside Thursday Banana's tour bus on their own traffic-clogged road trip down here and thinking twice about what she had done.

She downcast her eyes. "None of your business," she said to Otis, almost shyly. She then rolled her gaze back up and once more tried to appear angry at him. "What are you *doing* here?"

"None of my business? I'm your *husband.*"

The other groupies around the table let out a long *Ooohhh* and began fidgeting on their bench seats. Oh yes, it would seem an altercation was unavoidable. The members of Thursday Banana began to crowd us a little, there at the mouth of the alcove.

"It's okay, it's okay," Ellen said, raising her hands and trying to get them to back off. She motioned to her friends to scooch over and let her out, which they did, and she climbed from the booth to stand at Otis's side. She looked at him again with a kind of half-hearted wifely sneer. "So, what, you finally found the biscuits to board a plane? You came down here to . . . *rescue* me?"

"We drove, actually," he told her.

"You *drove?*" She squinted at him, then turned to me. "You let him do that?"

"It was my idea," I replied, though in that fierce, confrontational moment I couldn't remember if the road trip had in fact been my idea. My thoughts, to be honest, seemed a bit clouded then. No, not clouded. Perhaps the exact opposite, in fact. It was as if everything had turned crystalline, and I had grown hypersensitized to the magnitude, the hostility of our situation. Again, I felt almost exactly as I had back in Windsor, when alien emotions and impulses began whipping up uninvited inside me. I was feeling . . . what was it? Oh, yes. Bravery. I didn't want to tamp down this tension. Suddenly I wanted to stoke it into a big, blazing bonfire.

"I've come to take you home," Otis said.

More ambivalence. It was amazing how much of the stuff Ellen could transmit through that pretty face of hers. I watched as her brow sunk forward and her eyes flickered from side to side.

"Otis, please . . ." she stumbled. "You're embarrassing yourself, okay. Would you . . . would you please . . ." But her voice was chocked with doubt.

Just then, I sensed a group of figures looming behind us. I turned to see that the four remaining members of Thursday Banana had arrived from their dressing room.

"Oh hey, what's up, *bears*?" I snarled. It had become bad form in society to refer to blomers' animal antecedents with that tone of voice, and they tensed immediately.

"Hector, what are you doing?" Otis said without looking at me.

"Everybody be cool, just be cool," chimed in Ellen. "Everything's cool."

"Oh yeah, it's cool," I said, scoffing at the members of the band. "It's cool to just go and kidnap another man's wife."

"I wasn't kidnapped," Ellen said. "It was . . . my . . . my choice." Oh, but her voice was clogged with doubt now. *You'd have to perform the Heimlich manoeuvre,* I thought, *to get rid of all the doubt clogging her voice now.* And in an instant, I had it figured out. She'd been waiting for Otis for months, for years, to grow a pair and do something with the sort of temerity he was showing right now. She was impressed that he'd driven all the way down here to confront her. She had wanted him to show this much conviction about something perhaps ever since he had abandoned his own music career – much to her chagrin, I now recalled – and settled for a quiet life working for an insurance company.

The band members consolidated and began crowding us even more. Oh yes, we were causing quite a commotion. Or were we? I took a brief look up and around the spacious bar. The sex cages above us swung and swung, the savage and hurried gasps from inside raining down on us. Meanwhile, the canned tunes that had come on after Thursday Banana finished its set were causing minor skirmishes here on the floor. Three tables over from where we stood, a couple of girls had begun pulling at each other's hair and speaking obscenities at each other to the rhythm of the music. There was no malice in what they said or did; it was more like a dance, a reflexive, absent-minded groove to the music. On the floor in front of them, two men rolled around in a great tussle, trying to choke each other out. It too seemed almost robotic, a kind of harmless, grappling waltz.

"Look, we don't want any trouble," Otis stressed.

"*I* want some trouble," I said to Thursday Banana, and they tensed even more.

"*Hector.*"

I glared with hate at the band as they glared back at me. My head swooned with so much rancid bitterness, and not just over what these fuckers had done to Otis. I thought about Alanna, and Lesley. I thought about Morgana. Surely all of this was needless, all the change and violence, the anxiety and suffocation wrought by the very existence of blomers. Yes, our world hadn't been perfect before pullation; perhaps the human race had been on a one-way trajectory toward extinction. But was what we faced now any better? I didn't care what behaviours and rituals were born out of the pullulation process, those mysterious chemicals that had risen like radioactive mist into the sky. Were blomers not reasonable, thinking beings now? Did we vips not have a re-sponsibility to condition them to act and think like us rather than allow ourselves to be mindlessly conditioned to be like them?

But we had passed the point of no return. Lesley was dead. My wife could very well be lost to me forever. Ellen would most likely spurn Otis again, and right here in front of everyone. This would not stand. This. Would. Not. Stand. *I could take you out,* I mused, glowering at Thursday Banana once more. *I could kick the living shit out of all seven of you, right here and right now.* And in that moment, I believed it. I already had my hands clamped into talons there at my sides. I was ready to make up for a lifetime of bending to the will of the world.

Somehow, one of the groupies – I didn't catch who – must have summoned a bouncer to our alcove with the mere flicker of her eyes. The guy emerged behind us, and I turned. Oh, he was a *big* mother – tall and wide and with a head like a pumpkin sporting a crewcut.

"Is there a problem here?" he asked. And I thought: *How does he know? How can he tell a real altercation from the other kind? I mean, there are two men trying to kill each other on the floor right over there. Why doesn't he go break* that *up?*

"Nope, there's no problem, no problem," Otis said, and took Ellen by the elbow. "My *wife* and I are just going to step over here and have a conversation. You guys," and he motioned to Thursday Banana with a calming rotation of his palm, "are gonna sit and enjoy the rest of your break. And *you*, Hector, are going to stand over there," and he pointed harshly to a spot on the floor near the entrance to the catwalks leading up to the sex cages, "and not bother anybody."

But I was ready to bother somebody. I was ready for a fight. Yet I could see the desperation in Otis's face, the deep creases of concern, so I obeyed. I sauntered to the spot he had pointed to while Thursday Banana, those assholes, squeezed themselves around the table. Meanwhile, Otis stepped aside with a not-quite-reluctant Ellen to talk to her in private. I watched them as the adrenalin whipped around inside me like flames. With a hand at his chest, Otis spoke to his wife in earnest tones. At first she had her fists knotted sternly on her hips and her gaze turned away, like she was trying not to listen to him. But then he said something that caused her to look directly into his face, and she said something back. He retorted. She raised a hand and cupped her mouth. He said something else. She began to cry. Thursday Banana and the rest of the groupies let their gazes slip away awkwardly.

Through the Carrion's profuse chatter, I could catch only a garbled, truncated excerpt of my friends' exchange. I realized then how little I knew about the wedges that had driven them apart, and it was interesting to get a snapshot of them now.

"No, of course not, Otis. That was never the case. But things have changed. For the longest time now, you haven't [unintelligible], okay? So can you not realize that [unintelligible]?"

"But I haven't changed. You can't see it, Ellen, but [unintelligible] and everything I've done is so you can have that, have that life, so that you can be still close to the [unintelligible]. So the fact that I haven't picked up a guitar in two years is beside the point. I'm still the man who [unintelligible]."

"[Unintelligible]."

"[Unintelligible]."

"[Unintelligible]."

"[Unintelligible]."

"No, I know that . . . I know that, Otis."

"Well then? Is this really the life you want? I mean, God, look around you. And I wouldn't have [unintelligible] if I thought that it would mean [unintelligible]."

"You're right, no, you're right. It's just . . . It's just that . . ."

My eyes gravitated back to Thursday Banana, and I noticed that their eyes had gravitated back to Otis and Ellen. The expression on the band members' faces was pinched, worried. They were obviously not in favour of the progress my friend was making with his wife. Were they about to intervene? Were they about to rise from their bench seating and go over there to drag Ellen back to the table? I believed they were.

God, I wanted to do something. I wanted to fight. Had Otis not said to me, just as early as yesterday, *Are you prepared to throw a punch?* And I was prepared. Goddamnit, I was. Why had we come all this way, risked so much, travelled to Troy, if we weren't ready for battle? Had we not been willing to do whatever it took, rip these animals apart, to get his girl back? After all that we'd been through – including those series of calls from Alanna on our way down here, telling me what happened to poor Lesley, how those monsters had cornered her and killed her – I was jonesing for a scrap. I was ready to go!

Somehow, Otis managed to take Ellen's hand in his as she wept and wept. Her other hand was up at her face, its index finger resting under her nose. She turned and looked at the band for a moment, then back to him. Him. Her husband. Was she making a decision then? Was she really backing out of this choice she had made? I caught another sliver of the private patois of their marriage. "I never meant to poota hurt on you, little kitten . . . I never meant to poota hurt on you."

He jostled her fingers. She laughed through her tears.

I watched then as they were bumped by a group of four or five men passing by. The gaggle was headed toward the two guys trying to strangle each other on the floor. Before I knew it, they jumped upon them in a big pileup, flailing and punching and clawing at each other. The pumpkin-faced bouncer did nothing. He just stood there eyeing me suspiciously. Meanwhile, the two girls at the table behind the pileup had stopped pulling at each other's hair and were now making out, their heads turning and turning, their tongues buried deep in each other's mouths, their hands pawing over breasts. I seethed. I struggled to breathe. I began bobbing on the balls of my feet, like a prize fighter ready for the next round. The bouncer took in a deep inhale of unease as he watched me, his nostrils flaring. He knew, as I did, that I was now the most dangerous person in this club. I was ready. I was a brand-new man.

Something tugged my eyes upward, and I hurled my stare all over the catwalks and sex cages there in the high ceiling above us. In one far-off and darkened corner, I saw someone step out of the shadows and into the light. My eyes swelled and I gasped in shock. There was a familiar outline to that silhouette, a sharp blast of recognition that came from the cadence of its step. From way down here, on the distant club floor, I could have sworn that that individual looked like . . . looked like . . .

Morgana. Yes. *Yes.* At this distance, the nebulous creeper trying to sneak across those railings looked exactly like my wife. The same halo of frizzy hair, the same teardrop build, the same plucky pink mouth. A great tremor passed through me.

I watched in horror then as a crew of four bouncers went racing up the catwalk stairs behind her, screaming at her in a murderous gibber. My stomach fell out of the bottom of me. Something wasn't right. This wasn't part of the fun, had nothing to do with sex or music-fuelled moshing. It was clear, at least to me, that those bouncers racing toward Morgana were going to do her villainy. As they tore up the catwalk, she turned to them, her face blazing with panic.

I was paroxysmal. The pumpkin-faced bouncer turned briefly to see what I was staring at, and in that moment, he looked as if he might go join his workmates, to help them in their violent task. But then he turned back to me. We looked at each other with boiling hate, and I thought, *Fuck it!*

I bolted for the catwalk stairs before me. In one fluid move, the bouncer stepped into my path.

"Where do you think *you're* goi–" he began.

But I took to the air. I leaped off my feet and drove my scrawny, slacks-clad, HR manager, never-seen-a-day-of-violence-in-its-life knee right into the exposed knob of his throat. The bouncer's face exploded, first into shock, then into pain, and he keeled down and over like a sack of flour dropped on the floor.

"Hector, what are you *doing?!*" I heard Otis call out behind me.

"Jesus Christ, he's going to get himself killed!" yelled Ellen.

I mounted the steel stairs leading up to the catwalk, and they shook and rattled beneath me as I made my ascent. Two of the four bouncers now swarming Morgana and assaulting her with wild, lunging swings of their fists broke off and headed in my direction. They came racing across the catwalk and then went clopping down the steps in single file as I came clopping up. The first one reached out to seize me by the collar, but I sidestepped his grasp and then drove the butt of my head as hard as I could into his teeth. His head flew back at a ghastly angle and he went pitching sideways over the rail of the stairs. The people below screamed as he dropped through the air and came smashing through their table. The second bouncer, his face a tureen of fury, bunched up his fist and threw a punch at me. I ducked under it easily and then slammed my shoulder into his hips, the breath knocking out of him with a tremendous *whooof.* With all my strength, I backflipped him up and over me, as if I were a burly professional wrestler, and he cartwheeled onto his head and then Jack-and-Jilled his way down the stairs, landing in a moaning and motionless heap at the bottom.

Yes. Yes! I was fucking Batman up here!

I reached the top of the steps and glided over to where the other two bouncers were beating the shit out of my wife. Panting, I pivoted my shoulders and put up my dukes. Spotting my presence, the bouncers glared at me in disbelief.

The girl turned her now bloodied face up, and I noticed two things at once. One: she was not Morgana. Not Morgana at all. She only looked like Morgana – and from this close up, not even that much. Two: she wasn't a *she* at all. Plain as day, I could see where the breasts lurched out from the torn shirt, and, yes, they did look like Morgana's breasts – small and russety and with bright, candy-pink nipples. But I could also see the joggle of a penis through the herm's ripped pants. I could see the broadness of the shoulders. And the facial features, now distorted with gore and swelling, held a distinct mannishness.

What had they done? *What have you done!* I wanted to scream. *Why are you even up here? You no doubt evaded the militias guarding your entry into this town, and the bloodthirsty gangs on its streets. You came here – for what, the love of music? The allure of a live show? And maybe you passed yourself off as normal as you bar-hopped around the city, taking in the acts. Maybe you even live here. Perhaps you spend your days in a cubicle and your nights in a condo tower, just like me. And maybe you avoid the relentless advances of your fellow blomers, the temptation of their sidewalk orgies. Maybe you even avoid the occasional advance from a vip, because you're cute. You're cute. Like Morgana, you're really cute. So why risk so much to be up here, in this place? Why blow your cover for a few hot moments in a sex cage? Why have your life end in this way? Is it because you couldn't resist those urges any longer?*

It didn't matter. I thought not of myself, or even Morgana, but of my friend Alanna – poor, devastated Alanna – and everything she had been through over the last few days, everything that she had sacrificed to protect someone she loved from a violence that was so senseless and had no end. In that moment, I thought: *To hell with it. To hell with it all. I will do my part, too.*

The bouncers gave me a look that said, *Don't mess with us over this.* But I didn't care.

"Come and get it, motherfuckers!" I bellowed, and then set myself upon them.

EPILOGUE

Harpies: *The Musical!* turned out to be not half bad. The show's run time had clocked in just under six and a half hours, and with three twenty-minute intermissions, watching the performance was not the feat of endurance I had feared. Carolina, it turned out, decided to cut three or four minor sections of the play at the last minute, which meant the opening night needed to be delayed by another month as they stitched the script back together and then buffed out all the continuity issues. And *this* meant that I could come after all.

The music was fabulous, just fabulous. Those bears really knew how to write a tune. We in the audience tapped our feet and clapped along and cheered loudly at the end of each number. And yes, the onstage sex was graphic, but it was nothing beyond the public displays of fucking that we had all long been desensitized to. The best part of the play, my absolute favourite part, was that nobody laid a finger on my wife. Well, that wasn't quite true. There was one part at the end of a scene where a crow grabbed Morgana's ass, and she leaned into him playfully and made to give him a kiss. My spine stiffened at the sight of this, but then the lights cut out right before their lips could touch, and we didn't see Morgana's character again for another three scenes. In fact, I noticed that there were several vip actors who, like Morgana, did not engage in any onstage coitus. Carolina had respected their commitments to monogamy. And besides, it was just a show. A silly little entertainment. It wasn't real. It could never *be* real. What was there to be so bothered by?

When the performance finally ended, we in the audience rose off our now petrified backsides and clapped and cheered and hooted madly, sticking fingers in our mouths and releasing whistles of joy and approval into the air. The bows and curtain calls went on and on, as if they were a whole separate scene of the play. But the cast had earned it. They'd worked hard up there, giving it their all. They had regaled us with their talent and garnered our respect.

Morgana and I had agreed to meet in the theatre's lobby after the performance. It took quite a while for her to come out: she had makeup to take off, hugs and well wishes from co-stars to accept, street clothes to put back on. I was so glad I could be there. The bruises on my face and the scabby cuts across my knuckles had begun healing nicely since Otis and I had returned from Louisiana, to the point where they had raised nary an eyebrow among my fellow audience members. I feared that I had perhaps embellished in my memory what exactly happened up on that catwalk in the Carrion. I seemed to recall thinking of myself as Batman, as some sort of superhero as I moved to help that poor herm. It wasn't quite like that, I now realized. Other bouncers had come racing up the stairs and did a fairly thorough job of roughing me up. Then they kicked me and Otis out on our asses, and we sat in a heap on the curb outside the club for a while by the lineup of people waiting to get in. Eventually, thankfully, Ellen came out to join us.

The two of them said very little, curled up together in the Camry's back seat as we set off for home that very night. I didn't mind. They needed their time. And besides, the traffic getting back was nearly as bad as the traffic going down, and it was great having a third driver who could help out.

The theatre's lobby was busy. Lots of people – audience and, now, actors – milled around in engaging conversations. I wasn't sure which set of doors Morgana might emerge from, and my eyes tried to be everywhere at once. I had already rehearsed all my praiseful words to her about her success, and I would mean them. I would be *that* husband. I would be that for her.

Then she did appear. Her face was brightly scrubbed of its cakey stage makeup and her hair was pulled back in a big, nest-like bun. She looked around the lobby, her expression expectant. But before I could nab her attention, one of her co-stars broke off from the chat he'd been having, sidled up to Morgana and took her hand. I watched as they gave each other big smiles and a bigger hug, the crow practically lifting my wife right off her feet. My spine stiffened again. But after he set her down, they exchanged a few pleasantries and then he moved on, and she resumed her anxious glance around the room. There were so many people here – vips and blomers both. You could barely tell them apart.

But then she found whom she was looking for, and her face ignited into a smile. Those luscious lips of hers pulled back and up to reveal teeth as white as sugar. She came skipping joyfully through the crowd, manoeuvring around the bouquets of conversations to get at the one person, the only person, she really wanted to see.

She nearly knocked me over as she leaped into my arms.

ACKNOWLEDGEMENTS

As always, I need to thank my first readers first. My wife, Rebecca Rosenblum (to whom this book is dedicated), Gerald Arthur Moore and Patrick Hadley were all generous in their feedback on an early version of this weird little novel. Thank you.

I also owe a big thanks to my literary agent, Stephanie Sinclair, and her colleague at Transatlantic, Samantha Haywood, for welcoming me to the agency and helping to bring this manuscript into the world. Their insights and suggestions really took the story to the next level, and I am so grateful for all they did to champion this book.

A huge thank you as well to editor Paul Vermeersch, whom I've wanted to work with for many years now, and to Noelle Allen, Ashley Hisson and the rest of the Wolsak & Wynn/Buckrider team for their enthusiasm and dedication. More than ever, Canadian publishing remains a perilous trade and I really appreciate their commitment to taking risks on strange books, and to excellence in everything they do.

MARK SAMPSON is the author of five previous books: the novels *The Slip* (Dundurn Press, 2017), *Sad Peninsula* (Dundurn Press, 2014) and *Off Book* (Norwood Publishing, 2007); the short story collection *The Secrets Men Keep* (Now or Never Publishing, 2015); and the poetry collection *Weathervane* (Palimpsest Press, 2016). Mark has published many short stories and poems in literary journals across Canada, including in *The New Quarterly, The Antigonish Review, PRISM international, The Nashwaak Review, The Puritan, This magazine* and *FreeFall*. He is a frequent book reviewer for *Quill & Quire, Canadian Notes & Queries (CNQ)* and other publications. Born and raised on Prince Edward Island, he currently lives and writes in Toronto.